THE MARAUDER'S MISTRESS

(WANTON WASTRELS - 2)

TABETHA WAITE

ALSO BY TABETHA WAITE

The Piper's Paramour

Kiernan Fantasy Series

The Kingdoms of Kiernan (Kiernan – Book 1)

Collections

An Everlasting Amour (A collection of short stories)

An Everlasting Christmas Amour

An Everlasting Regency Amour

An Everlasting Regency Amour – Volume 2

The Wedding Wager

The Brazen Belles Anthology

Heyer Society (non-fiction essays)

For Patricia King who wanted to know if Constance would have her HEA. This story is for you. For Elodie Nicoli who didn't mind that I turned her into an exceptional, French modiste, and for Holly Perret who designed this AWESOME cover that I just had to have, and her tireless patience with me while I debated on the name!

CHAPTER 1

London, England
June 1832

THE LADY WALKED PURPOSEFULLY DOWN the deserted, foggy London street at night, the gas lamps providing little in the way of light. Her bootheels clicked on the cobblestones, damp courtesy of the recent summer rain. Anyone who might be looking on would see a woman wearing a dark cloak and dressed in a modest emerald gown with a fitted corset waist and the large sleeves that had suddenly begun to dominate the fashion world. A hood was placed over her strawberry-blond curls and her skin was smooth like porcelain.

But it was her eyes, a fetching, moss green that looked out at the world with a certain knowledge foreign to most of the rest, that proved she wasn't a fresh, naïve debutante, easy to manipulate.

Unfortunately, this was something that "Two-Tooth" Granelli had yet to discern.

Devin Blackmore leaned in a hidden alcove, arms crossed,

and watched from the shadows of the alley as the thief attempted to approach the woman and casually abscond with her purse by way of an "accidental" maneuver that Devin himself had performed hundreds of times. And yet, even he knew there were certain people to be steered clear of, and the mysterious woman who had just raised her parasol was one he would have merely tipped his hat to as he strode innocently on past.

He merely shook his head when Granelli withdrew a dagger, as he knew it was a mistake. The large man had more muscle than brains and a nose that had been broken at least a dozen times, if Devin had to guess. He considered intervening, but he recanted the thought as he continued to observe the exchange. With lightning-fast reflexes, the lady spun around and dodged her would-be attacker's shoddy approach. She was surprisingly well accomplished as she pointed her fashioned weapon at him. Granelli didn't stand a chance, and even Devin was impressed when a slight puff of smoke came from the end, just as Granelli clutched his thigh and fell to the ground with a howl of pain.

Instead of rushing off down the street in a fearful panic, Devin watched the woman bend down next to Granelli with a long-suffering sigh and actually offer him her pristine, white handkerchief. "Hold this over the wound. It will help cease the bleeding."

As she pressed down on the torn flesh, Granelli broke out into a sweat and moaned worse than a cheap whore. But it was her voice, soft and genteel, that made Devin take proper notice.

"You should be thankful that the ball wasn't poisoned, or you might have seen your end just now."

Devin would have laughed at the horrified look on Granelli's voice if he hadn't been so captivated by the lady. He didn't recall ever seeing her before, and although he'd just returned to London, he would have surely recalled such a stunning, lethal beauty.

"Perhaps from now on you'll think twice about assaulting a lady, as that is very poor manners. Don't you agree?"

Granelli nodded like a recalcitrant child and Devin had to snort lightly.

She rose to her feet and reached back down to offer the man some assistance. After a moment, he accepted it and favoring his bad leg, he glanced at the lady as if she was some sort of odd museum exhibit.

"Now run along home. No doubt you have a family that should be worried if you don't return soon."

Devin wasn't sure if Granelli had ever married or sired children. At least he hadn't when Devin had left London more than five years ago, but by the way he lowered his head, as if properly chastised, and turned to limp back into the darkness from whence he had appeared, perhaps some things had changed.

He glanced back toward the woman, who had lingered for a moment, either to ensure that her instructions were heeded, or make sure Granelli didn't accost anyone else, Devin wasn't sure.

With a heavy sigh that told more than she would have been likely to share, she turned to continue on her way, but Devin found that he was reluctant for her to leave. Even from the distance across the alley, he could smell the scent of her lilac floral sweetness, and he was reluctant to part with it so soon. It had been years since he'd enjoyed something so simple, and so he allowed his presence to become known.

His boots had a heavy tread as he walked out directly under the streetlamp and offered a slow clap in the silence.

～

CONSTANCE FREEWATER SPUN toward the sound of applause, not realizing that she'd had an audience. She held her parasol aimed toward the sound, poised for another attack. Although the single shot had already been spent, she had been taught, long ago, in how to use other methods to warrant off unwanted attentions. It had served her well through the years, as the good Lord only knew she'd had her share of trouble.

It was one of the reasons she'd left London, to put that sort of tumultuous past behind her, only to have it return the day she stepped foot on English soil after living abroad for the past twenty years.

Was she never to be free of a past that was littered with illicit dealings?

Any further thought dissipated as the mystery man stepped out of the shadows and into the circle of yellow light. He wore a smirk that bespoke of confidence, tousled dark hair, and an onyx gaze that shone with a wisdom that went far beyond his years. But while she thought he might be younger than her, he was most certainly a man full grown with the broad shoulders, narrow hips, and trim midsection of a man used to physical labor —or various other exercise.

Her face heated, along with other parts of her body, when she imagined him in the bedchamber. She would bet all of the coins in her reticule that he had that delicious trail of hair that slid across his taut stomach and disappeared behind the band of his trousers.

She mentally shook herself and pushed the image aside. After her last paramour died, Constance had promised herself that she would no longer be any man's mistress. But even though Madame Corressa would forever hound her every waking moment, she would not succumb to temptation again. She had returned to London to make a fresh start as a respectable woman and she intended to keep it that way. She'd even adopted the pseudonym of Mrs. Hartford to add credence to her tale.

Her current companions were Alfred Guillaume Gabriel, Count d'Orsay, his wife, and his particularly special patron, the widowed Lady Marguerite Gardiner, Countess of Blessington. The four of them were staying at the lady's house in Seamore

Place in Mayfair and was quickly becoming known as the fashionable area of town, not only because of the countess' ties to Lord Byron, but the count was being styled as the modern-day Beau Brummel. He changed his gloves at least five times a day and made sure that his coat was thrown back to reveal the extravagance of his luxurious waistcoat and perfectly styled cravats. Constance had become one of his particularly favored, inner circle of friends during his time in France, and was the main reason she had traveled back to England from Paris, otherwise she might have lived out the rest of her days in *La Ville Lumière.*

Instead, she was back in the familiar surroundings that she had tried so hard to put behind her—to forget the naïve woman she had been, the one who had relied on the attentions of a protector to find happiness. She had been alone for the past year and a half and held no regrets. While she missed Alessandro at times, and she was grateful that her Italian lover had made sure to provide for her after his passing, gifting her with enough money and jewels to allow her to live comfortably for a very long time.

But now, her attention turned back to the man standing a few feet away from her. She glanced at her parasol. "You should know that I don't need to reload to make sure you keep your distance."

The smirk never wavered. "I believe you, but rest assured, I'm not intending to accost you. I merely wished to gain the pleasure of your name."

A shiver danced up her spine at the idea of *pleasure* when associated with this man. Even though she didn't know him, something told her that he was quite skilled in that area. She slowly lowered her parasol to her side. "I'm afraid I can't assist you with that. Good evening." She turned on her heel, prepared to depart.

"Don't you want to know my name?"

Constance told herself to keep walking and ignore that deep

timbre, but she found herself pausing all the same. She glanced back over her shoulder, intrigued beyond her better judgment. But then, perhaps it was the slight inflection in his tone that didn't seem wholly British. "Why? Is it supposed to mean something to me?"

His teeth were white and even as they flashed a seductive grin. "I doubt it. I merely suspected you would want to know."

She couldn't help but laugh. "And why would that be?" She arched a brow. "Will I see your name in the scandal rags? Or perhaps the criminal section."

He stiffened slightly at the latter, the edges of his mouth turning hard. Apparently, she had struck a nerve. Interesting.

"I admit that my past hasn't always been savory." He slowly looked down the length of her frame and back up again to her face. "But then, something tells me you haven't always been the model of propriety either."

Constance knew that this conversation could easily venture into dangerous territory. He saw entirely more than she wished to convey. "That is my business, and you would do well to mind yours."

The chuckle that followed her set down was dark and smooth, like the coffee she enjoyed with her morning breakfast. He lifted a hand and ran his thumb along his lower lip. "It appears that you have a mouth on you, madam. I can think of a better use for those plump lips other than choosing to filet me."

A hot swirl of delicious desire flared to life in her abdomen. A sensation that had long lain dormant. "You, sir, are uncouth and rather than remain here and trade insults back and forth, I shall rejoin my party where I may partake of some intelligent conversation."

This time when Constance left, she didn't hesitate, even though the husky, masculine laughter followed her down the street.

∼

DEVIN LICKED HIS LIPS, as if he'd just tasted a sweet treat. He vowed right then and there that he would learn the lady's name and that she would be in his bed before the summer came to a close. But it would take time and a bit of persuasion on his part to break through that tough, untrusting exterior. Somewhere along the way she'd been hurt, but he was there to comfort her and pick up the pieces of a sour love affair, because he knew she was no simpering maiden, but a woman who knew what she wanted. And while she might not realize it yet, she wanted *him*. He could sense it in the flare of her nostrils and the flash of interest in those green eyes that she tried to hide. Oh, she would be a challenge, but that was one thing Devin had never backed down from.

"You're lurkin' about on our turf, guv'nr. I think it's time for ye t' move on."

Instead of feeling threatened, Devin turned to face the speaker with a bored expression. "After all this time, that's the best warning you've got?"

Devin waited for recognition to strike, and when it did, the guffaw was loud and full of humor. "Damn me eyes! Devin, boy, is tha' ye?"

He spread his arms wide. "In the flesh."

As he was enveloped in a manly hug with a strong pat on his back, Devin was actually glad to be back in this miserable city. While the pompous aristocrats abounded, this man who survived on the outskirts had been like a second father to Devin after his own had died and left him an orphan at the age of twelve.

Luke House had worked in Olney with Devin's father at the local tannery. It had been rather unsavory and smelly employ-ment to say the least, but it wasn't as though everyone could live in a fashionable townhouse in Mayfair. Most Englishmen had to take what positions they could just to survive. Devin remembered many nights when he'd gone to bed with a grumbling stomach, hunger gnawing at his bones to the point he would close his eyes tight and dream of a day when he could actually afford to purchase a salty slice of ham. It had taken years and a life of illegal activity, and practicing his proper speech, but it had been worth it when he had finally bit into that tender meat.

Years later, he was bound for Australia on a ship to serve out the sentence of thievery. One mistake, one betrayal, had been all it took for him to spend the next five years on that Godforsaken piece of land and toiling in the hot sun. The sweat rolled down his back even now in memory of that grueling labor.

And that wasn't even the worst part.

When Luke pulled back with a wide grin, Devin forced himself to adopt a lazy expression. It had saved him during his tenure. The bullies didn't bother a man if he pretended he didn't care.

A flicker of something like sadness, or perhaps regret, passed before Luke's eyes before he said, "How long have ye been back in London?"

"I just got back yesterday."

"And ye didn't think t' let me know until today?" Luke scolded.

Devin snorted, as the man hadn't changed a bit. While his hair was a bit more salt than pepper than before, he still had the same trim build and smooth demeanor that had won over several hearts through the decades, but nothing ever went further than a brief liaison. The neat beard that covered his jawline, which still grew in patches after twenty years was enough to forever remind his friend of everything he'd lost.

After a devastating fire had taken the lives of Luke's wife and two children in Olney, giving him the scars he tried to hide, it only masked the deeper pain that he didn't show. Only Devin had witnessed him break down one time in all of his thirty-two years, and even then, it wasn't what he might have expected. They had come across a London fire that had consumed the lives of a similar family, where the husband had been away at work, only to return to find his life in shambles.

Most men might have collapsed and wept in memory when the charred remains had been removed from the ruined structure, but it was the flat, almost ghostly… *emptiness* in Luke's eyes that Devin had found more disturbing. But then, it was probably how he had managed to become one of the most successful thieves in London. He distanced himself from his victims, while his sleight of hand was almost legendary among certain circles. Devin had learned the same skill—until the one time his arrogance and greed had nearly sent him to the noose.

It was only because of Annalise and her pleading on his behalf that he'd been spared.

"Where did ye stay last night?"

Devin blinked and returned to the conversation at hand. "At Mivart's."

Luke gave a low whistle. "Back from th' penal colony and ye're already livin' it up in high fashion. What lady did ye have t' coerce t' set ye up?" He elbowed Devin in the ribs in a teasing gesture.

He rolled his eyes. "I didn't have to do anything of the sort. I merely paid for a room at the hotel."

This time, all mirth faded from Luke's face and he narrowed his eyes. "Don't tell me ye used yer cache. That's for when ye're too old t' play th' game anymore."

"I just took a small loan for the night. Besides"—he shrugged, but his shoulders seemed stiff and unyielding—"I feel much older. The last five years weren't without their challenges."

"Aye." Luke sighed heavily. "I imagine not." He clapped him on the shoulder. "Come on. I think ye need a stiff drink. An' if not, ye know I could always use one."

Devin laughed. It was good to be home. "You should know I've never been able to turn down a good Scottish whisky."

CHAPTER 2

Constance sat at her dressing table in the guest room of Lady Blessington's house and brushed out her strawberry blond hair. In truth, it had been free of tangles for the past ten minutes, but she hadn't been able to concentrate long enough to do more than keep passing the horsehair bristles through the long, wavy tresses.

She should be furious that images of a persuasive, dark-haired man kept invading her thoughts like this. It certainly wasn't like her to be so obsessed over someone she had literally just met. But there you have it. There was just something in his demeanor that had appealed to her siren's side and Madame Corressa had awoken from her slumber and taken particular notice.

Her veins sung from the attraction that still pulsed through her blood, the desire that had lain dormant bursting to the surface with renewed life. For years, she had been some man's courtesan, had nearly perfected the art of sex, but when it came to passion—*true* passion—it was something she hadn't experienced in years, if ever.

She'd hadn't had the most auspicious beginnings. She'd lost her virginity in the back alley of an East End pub when she was fifteen. After that, her mother had vowed to send her to a madame in order to gain some profit from her newfound sexuality. Terrified, as Constance had witnessed more than one woman beaten and bloodied from an angry man's hand—including her own mother who personally entertained special "guests" of her own—Constance had fled home.

For a time, she'd lived on the streets, wearing the same rags she'd left in and begging for scraps when the hunger had become too much to bear.

Finally, without anywhere to turn and desperate for somewhere to sleep other than huddled up on the street where passing carriages had splattered her with mud and refuse, Constance had turned to the one place she had dreaded going.

Her hand shook when she'd knocked on that brothel door, the very one her mother had threatened her with. But the middle-aged woman, with her kohl-lined eyes and henna red hair, who'd answered had been warm and welcoming when she'd spied Constance on the steps. Once she'd gained a hot meal and a good night's sleep, she was informed the next day that it was time for her to earn her room and board. While Constance had been terrified to entertain her first male customer, she had managed to get through the experience relatively unscathed.

After that, she'd gained a few of the same visitors, but after weeks of the same, sweating bodies heaving over her, Constance yearned for something different. She was under no illusions that she would ever have anything more than the life of a whore, but at least she could have something other than a single room to call her own. Thus, with a sweetly innocent smile, she poured out her grievances to one of her faithful callers and finally achieved victory.

Or at least as much as she could claim.

He accepted her offer of setting her up as his mistress, and she enjoyed the independence that she had been craving at long last. He lavished her with jewels and more dresses than she could ever hope to wear. She even had a house with her own servants. She was on top of the world—until the day his wife stopped by.

Constance would never forget that day, because it was the first time she had discovered men of the *ton* enjoyed frivolous pursuits of all kinds. The woman had claimed that she was increasing and she wanted to try to make a life with her husband for the child's sake. At first, Constance was stunned, unsure of what to say. But later, when she shock had worn off, she had retched, sickened to think that she had entertained a married man.

She was sure that she would burn in hell for such an unforgiveable sin, so she had immediately cut ties with her paramour, regardless of the tears falling down his face and the pleas and gifts he offered to convince her to stay. He claimed that he loved her and even got on his knees to grovel, but she had walked out the door and didn't look back.

Knowing that she couldn't go back to the brothel and endure more of the same, Constance had set out on her own yet again. But this time she was prepared. She'd taken a few of the baubles that she'd been given and sold them for accommodations at Mivart's Hotel. She had intended to stay there long enough to come up with a plan for what to do next. She'd considered securing passage to Paris right then and there, perhaps even make a fresh start—a *respectable* start—but life had other ideas.

One day when she had returned from the park, she encountered a man who would become her next paramour. In lieu of a chance encounter in the lobby, she struck up a conversation with Sir Timothy Kingley, where she'd learned that he was a childless widower who had returned to London to bury his wife in the family crypt. They had spent most of their time in Bath, in the hopes that her continued ill health would improve, to no avail.

But it was the sadness in his gaze that eventually swayed her to consider his eventual proposal.

Until she'd met her Italian count, it had probably been the last time Constance had been truly content—at least for a time. She had enjoyed three years along the quiet, English countryside, before he was thrown from a horse and broke his neck.

A tear seeped out of the corner of her lid at the memory, as he had been so much more than a lover. He'd been a dear friend, someone who had made her laugh, and that she could enjoy late night talks with. He had been a village squire, although it was only after his death that she learned that he'd left everything to her in his will.

That was when Madame Corressa had been set free. She had turned numb to everything but doing what she did best and shied away from anything to do with love, because she found that it hurt too much to even entertain the thought. But while she searched for a new protector, she employed the funds she'd been granted and, after finding a partner who could become the face of a gaming hell, where true money could be made in London, Montfree's was born.

But that was just the start of what Madame Corressa would accomplish. Hiding behind the pseudonym, Constance became, not only one of the most desired women in London, but one of the most renowned, shrewd businesswomen in the East End. She quickly became the Queen of the Underworld. Her lovers were legendary, and her enemies were numerous. Adding extra security to Montfree's, she befriended a boxer by the name of Bull. He was a faithful confidante and loyal to a fault, but the years of trauma to his body had taken a toll. Shortly after she had sold Montfree's and split ways with her partner and decided to travel abroad, Bull had died from an apoplexy.

At twenty years of age, she'd never felt more alone.

Again, Madame Corressa had taken over and led her to where she needed to be. After leaving a trail of broken hearts from Madrid to Vienna over the intervening years, she had set her sights on Florence where she'd met Alessandro. Finding a certain enjoyment during her time with him, after his death, with enough funds to keep her well settled for the rest of her days, the happiness that had always dogged her heels but been just out of reach, had finally settled around her like a woolen blanket.

With a newfound independence, she returned to one of her favorite cities, and after declining several, gentleman's offers, Constance spent the majority of her time exploring Paris, until the night she'd attended a salon reading where she'd met her current companions.

She had been conflicted upon returning to London, as it had held nothing but heartbreak and loneliness for her through the years, but at the count's insistence that she join them, she had finally relented—only to meet an intriguing man her first night there which stirred the sensual paramour trapped inside.

"Bollocks," Constance muttered under her breath as she rose and rang for Lady Blessington's maid.

It was time to dress for the day and put the previous night's encounter behind her, because truly, what were the odds that she would see the stranger again?

A GRIN FORMED on Devin's face when he saw the lady riding toward him on the Rotten Row path. He had never chosen to partake of the sights during the fashionable hour before, but something had told him that the siren with the seductive, green eyes would be here today.

While he'd caught up with Luke the night before, he had glossed over his interaction with the lady, even though he wasn't sure why. Devin used to tell the man everything because he knew he could be trusted. Perhaps it was his time in Australia or just the past five years that had separated them that had caused his reticence to discuss everything now. But then, some of the events that had occurred on that island were best kept there. He certainly didn't wish to relive certain moments.

However, he *did* wish to make the further acquaintance of a particular woman. He would choose his moment wisely, because he didn't wish to jump out in the middle of the path and frighten her horse or have to suffer a haughty glare from the woman at her side, for he could tell she was the type who would consider someone of his ilk 'beneath' her notice. And although Devin had swived his share of society matrons, those days were behind him. For a man who'd been forced into hard labor the past five years, it made you appreciate life a bit more, and he found that there was still much he wanted to do.

Right now, he intended to find out the name of his obsession.

Keeping to the shadows of a large oak, he kept that plum velvet riding habit in his sights. When her companions decided to take a different route and she headed off alone, Devin grinned. She was almost making it too easy for him.

She paused before the bronze Statue of Achilles. Sir Richard Westmacott sculpted it from the cannons captured by Wellington's campaigns in France and dedicated it to the duke himself. Originally, the sculpted giant was completely nude with sword and shield in hand, but a fig leaf was added after society considered it to be too risqué. Devin had been twenty-two when it was unveiled and had nearly laughed at the size of the poor phallus. In his opinion, the Trojan hero's only weakness hadn't just been his heel.

But as he stood and observed the lady, he saw that instead of blushing or pretending to just glance at the chiseled male form, she quite openly studied it. But it didn't seem that she considered it with admiration or even a bit of desire in her gaze, but even so, her lips were twisted somewhat sardonically.

It wasn't until another rider paused beside her that Devin had to roll his eyes. It had been five years, but he knew the baronet quite well. In fact, he'd had several altercations with Sir Brooks Isaacson in the past and none of them had ended in the gentleman's favor. In fact, he was the bastard responsible for ensuring that Devin was sent away from England to pay off his crimes with servitude once he was spared the noose. Devin wasn't sure how he might repay *that* kindness as of yet.

He considered striding forward and interceding when the baronet attempted to gain the lady's favor, but he waited to see what she might do. Something told him that he didn't have to send the gentleman on his way, that she was more than capable of doing so. And after a brief conversation, whereas the gentleman did his best to cajole her with a wide grin, flashing white teeth that vied for equal attention from the puce shade of his waistcoat, Devin noticed that she didn't seem to fall prey to his charms as easily as other women had—those that had lived to regret it. There were likely several of Sir Brooks' bastards running about the city by now, likely engaged in the same line of work that Devin had partaken of for so long.

Nevertheless, something like pride flashed through his chest when the baronet inclined his hat briefly before he continued on his way, and Devin could tell by the stiff set of his shoulders and jawline that he hadn't been pleased with whatever the lady had said. Which just made Devin even more intrigued.

Adjusting the cuffs of his jacket, he walked out into the bright light of day.

$\sim$

"NOT PARTICULARLY ENJOYING THE VIEW?"

Constance barely refrained from sighing aloud. Thinking that the smooth, deep voice belonged to another worthless swain attempting to impress her, she glanced over at the speaker and instantly, her body felt as if it was lit from within. Heat swept over her and she gripped the reins a bit tighter, causing her borrowed mount to prance a bit nervously under her. But then, she hadn't been prepared to see the man from the previous evening striding across the lawn toward her.

While the enhanced version of the statue had failed to impress her, even after all these years when she had been present for the unveiling, there always seemed to be some man around who liked to think that they were just as monumental. While she had never met the baronet who had boldly introduced himself to her, she knew his sort and they were never without a few misdeeds to their credit.

Gentlemen on the outside but slithering snakes behind the façade.

But looking at the man standing a few feet distant, she admitted that she had trouble reading his character. Oh, she had no doubt that he was someone to watch out for, and yet, something told her that his character didn't extend to the physical. He was more of a silent weapon, a man who had honed his skills over the years and would strike only when necessary, but the power in that moment would be severe, if not deadly.

Constance resisted the shiver that wanted to travel up her spine and lifted a delicate brow. Instead of saying that the view had just turned decidedly in her favor, which is what she was thinking, she noted dryly, "I suppose you are going to tell me what a waste of good bronze this is."

He crossed his arms and shrugged. "Not at all. In truth, I would have made him twice the size, so that he could be seen above the trees."

She laughed at the absurd picture he painted. "And why, pray tell, would you do that? To offer additional boast to Wellington's brilliant achievements?"

"No. For mine."

Her lips twitched and her nose scrunched, and she suddenly seemed much younger. And flirtatious. He particularly liked this side of her—until she spoke and her tongue quickly shredded him. "Do you have a certain… issue with size?" She glanced down at his trousers and his cock stirred with interest, although his pride was rising up with fists clenched.

"Hardly," he chuckled. "Perhaps if you're lucky you'll find out sometime that when it comes to *size,* it's not something I'm concerned about."

~

CONSTANCE HAD TO TURN AWAY, lest he see the lustful lady lurking beneath the elegant exterior. If he only knew the way Madame Corressa wanted to take him up on his tempting offer… "Then I suppose I will have to take you at your word, for you have come to the wrong conclusion about me."

She turned her horse away, hoping that put an end to the conversation, but it was what he said that caused her to hesitate.

"I propose an exchange."

Constance reluctantly turned her mount around, even though she told herself to keep moving. She adopted a bored tone. "For what?"

"The man that you shot last night may lose the use of his leg. He's not very pleased about the fact."

She lifted a brow, although her heart had begun to race. "Then he should have minded his own business."

He continued as if she hadn't even spoken. "I can ensure that he doesn't cause you any trouble."

She laughed. "And what makes you think I need your protection? I obviously know my way around a weapon."

"That may be true," he agreed, although his dark eyes were nearly savage. "But I know Granelli and he has one of the top gangs in London at the moment. To be on his bad side is courting danger that you don't need, if you intend to make things better for yourself." He lifted the corner of his mouth. "Unless you don't care to make a good impression on society?"

Constance froze. She'd shot *Granelli*? She'd known of the man years ago when he was still a youngster trying to stir up a ruckus in the East End. More than once he'd have to be escorted out of

Montfree's for his drunken behavior. While liquor was common-place in any gaming hell, there were limitations when it came to annoying the other patrons. He was one of those miscreants. If he'd risen to such power in London, then she might actually have cause to worry. While most of her contacts had left the city by now, or like her former partner, Logan Montgomery, who had married and decided to rusticate in the country with a burgeoning family, she had little in the way of security if Granelli decided he wanted to make things difficult for her. She certainly wasn't about to bring such trouble to his doorstep, even though she knew Logan would help her in any way he could, he deserved the chance to live a normal life free of angst.

She withheld a sigh, because it seemed that no matter how much she tried to give up this tumultuous life, it continued to follow her. Instead of acting coy or pretending that she didn't understand what was coming, she said directly, "What do you want?"

His eyes remained direct and unchanging. "You. In return, I will be your personal attendant."

She narrowed her eyes on him. "If I didn't know better, I might think you were proposing something like blackmail. If you truly cared about my welfare, you would act as my guardian without any strings attached."

"And why would I do that," he pointed out. "When I would be dismissing the only thing that has made the blood rush through my veins since I returned to this miserable country?"

Constance blinked. She hadn't thought that he would be so forthcoming.

"The truth is," he went on smoothly, walking forward to stand at her side. He glanced around and then deftly slid his bare hand up her stocking clad leg. Her breathing hitched, but she didn't move. He glanced upward and ensnared her gaze as his palm slowly moved higher. "I want to remember something other than the torrid events of my past. I want to be between a woman's

19

thighs, but not just any woman, one who can understand the hollow emptiness that I feel on the inside."

He had reached the point where her stocking ended and there was nothing but skin on skin. Her eyes shuttered slightly, the familiar pulse pounding urgently at her core. *Touch me!* She wanted to scream the command and ride his finger until she came apart in a flurry of pleasure.

"Do you agree, my seductress?" His fingers walked up the side of her hip, but just when he would have brushed her aching center, he slipped away from her and took a step back.

Her breath left her lungs in an annoyed rush, and she glared at him. "Do I not even get the courtesy of your name?"

He grinned, a wicked promise of things to come. "You didn't care to know last night, but if your answer is yes, then I will tell you anything you want to hear."

Constance frowned, but inside, Madame Corressa was fanning herself and reclining on a settee, already half-undressed. And because she was torn about how to respond, her common sense telling her to leave him standing in the middle of the path, she found herself saying, "I need time to think about it."

"Of course." He bowed slightly. "But don't take too long, sweetheart. This is one treat that you don't want to miss out on."

With that, he turned on his heel and walked away.

CHAPTER 3

"*W*hat was that?"

Constance realized that she'd snorted aloud. *Again*. And she was fanning herself rather rapidly. However, when one's body was burning with an inner flame, it was difficult to pay much attention to anything else. It was merely the idea that the alluring stranger had referred to himself as a "treat" that she couldn't seem to shake.

"My apologies, sir." *Oh, what the devil was his name?* "I fear I was just recalling something humorous that Lady Blessington had said earlier this evening."

He laughed and didn't seem to take offense that she hadn't called him by his name, or heaven forbid, a *title*, but perhaps the rules of society had become more lenient after the death of the Prince Regent once his brother, King William IV had ascended to the throne two years prior. Already, people had responded favorably to his approachable way of thinking and the manner in which he conducted himself in a more moderate way with fewer excesses than his predecessor.

But more than likely, the reason he hadn't cared was because he was too busy staring at her chest with her low-cut bodice. It was a gown of rose pink that the countess had said set off her coloring quite admirably and would be the perfect choice to wear to the opera that evening. While Constance had never been a fan of the theatre, it was interesting to see how Drury Lane had changed. She was told that the new colonnade had been put into place on Russell Street the previous year, although even with the improvements, it had struggled to retain any permanent proprietors.

But then, the times were changing and with more modernization coming into the city, she had the feeling it wouldn't be long before the quaint streets that she had walked all those years ago would slowly fade away. It was quite disheartening to think about.

But then, certain things would always remain the same. Men like the one she was speaking with, who spoke to her breasts more than her face. She had glanced about the auditorium during intermission and found that tongues still wagged freely and gentlemen were eager to meet the new actresses backstage in the hopes of obtaining a deeper connection.

Constance nearly snorted again, but she caught herself before she did so. The count claimed that she had become cynical, that she didn't enjoy the delights that life could offer anymore, but then, she hadn't ever found much in which to celebrate. She had never yearned to become a glorified whore, and yet, that is what she had become. While Madame Corressa liked to make an appearance now and again, Constance had told herself more than once that she didn't want to just be known for her prowess in the bedchamber. Besides, beauty faded just as the walls in this theatre had and she didn't want to become just another discarded memory.

Just as she had finished that thought, a blur of movement caught her eye beyond her current companion. The figure looked decidedly familiar, and her attention was instantly piqued, while the drolling man before her perked up, as if he had finally gotten her full consideration.

Constance put a gloved hand to her throat. "If you will forgive me, I'm feeling rather parched. I think I will obtain some refreshment before the second half begins."

The man murmured something, but she was already moving away and didn't bother to respond. In truth, she was going to have a megrim if she had to listen to another word about…

"Fancy seeing you here."

Constance jumped slightly when a hand brushed her elbow, sending sparks shooting up her spine. However, she recovered quickly enough and, keeping her focus ahead, she murmured, "I suppose you are here to bedevil me further?"

"I was actually hoping to hear you moan."

She nearly missed a step, so she paused and turned her full attention on him. He was still too entirely sinful to look at, and definitely younger than she was. But then, he didn't seem to mind as he slowly lifted his hand and rubbed a thumb along his lower lip while staring straight into her soul. Or, at least, it seemed like it, for she had found the ability to function properly had deserted her. For a practiced courtesan, she should think she was above such foolish behavior, but around this man, it was as if she was an untried virgin, or some naïve debutante.

She didn't like it.

She gritted her teeth together. "I want you to stop this."

"Stop what?" he asked huskily, his tongue darting out to slowly lick his lips.

She instantly had the vision of him licking something *else* and she had to close that off immediately. "This harassment," she demanded. "I don't care to be followed like this. Besides, how am I to know you aren't the true enemy in this case, but merely wish me to believe otherwise? As far as I know you could be working for Granelli."

He chuckled, and it was so seductive that she had to bite the inside of her cheek so she might concentrate on something other than the sound. "Trust me, I have better things to do than associate with the likes of that ignorant bastard. I never worked for anyone, and I made my own rules."

She didn't doubt that, but then, the matter of his age couldn't be ignored any longer. "You hardly seem old enough to have lived such a destructive life as you claim."

He shrugged, and then lifted his arm and placed it by her head, blocking her against the wall with his rather solid form. Constance glanced around, but it turned out he had chosen quite an opportune place to conduct this little encounter, as they were in a particularly secluded alcove, quite hidden from any passersby.

"Age is only a number and one I've never been very concerned with. I've had all manner of lovers, from fresh debutantes looking for a bit of freedom, to widows who were rather generous with their offerings."

"And you think I should rejoice to be among your conquests?" she snapped. She didn't know why, but the idea that he was a libertine in his own right didn't settle well, which made her a hypocrite, she supposed, for it wasn't as though she was a saint.

"Not at all. I don't intend to conquer you." He lifted a finger and ran it softly along her exposed collarbone. Gooseflesh immediately broke out all over her skin. "I want you to conquer *me*."

Constance stared at him. In all her life, she had never had a man pursue her with such dedication, and without any sort of bauble to try to coerce her. Not that such trivial things had ever mattered to her. Granted, she enjoyed nice dresses as much as the next woman, but having a roof over her head and food in her belly to keep away that terrible gnawing hunger was more preferable.

And something told her he knew the same feeling, that they were more alike than she was willing to admit. She had never believed in the possibility of soul mates, imagining that it was too fanciful to picture a world full of people where only two were intended for one another, but as she looked into his dark eyes and saw a swirling air of mystery and torment within, she had to wonder if she'd been wrong. He might very well be her soul mate, but she doubted that love would play any sort of role in their relationship if she did agree to his terms. There was too much pain and torture there to lighten it with something so pure and infinite.

And yet, she still had to give him an answer. "Tomorrow."

He lifted a brow in question.

"I shall give you my answer then. Meet me at the Statue of Achilles at nine o'clock in the morning."

～

DEVIN WATCHED as the lady walked away from him in a delightful swish of her skirts. He imagined those hips wound around his midsection as he pumped into her hot center and he had to close his eyes against the vision, or else he would find himself running after her and collapsing on his hands and knees in a pitiful beseeching plea to put him out of his misery.

Taking his leave, so that he could give her the space that she needed to consider his offer, he left the theatre with every confidence that her answer would be yes. He wouldn't be devastated if she refused him, he would merely keep trying until she agreed. He had the art of persuasion down to a certain technique when it came to the fairer sex.

With his hands in his pockets, Devin strolled down the street, intending to return to Luke's residence. Of course, if he managed to enchant the lady, he would have to set her up in fashion. While he had the funds to do so, he'd just returned to the city and hadn't anticipated meeting anyone, especially one as lovely as *her*. Devin didn't even need to know her name to admit that he was thoroughly mesmerized by her.

As he turned a corner into an alley, Devin realized his mistake, as the shadows began to close in around him.

"Been makin' new friends, Blackmore?"

Devin stopped and considered his odds. He was sorely outnumbered five to one, and even should he end up the victor, he wouldn't look in any decent shape to woo his lady in the bright light of day. Then again, he never backed down from a fight.

With a long-suffering sigh, he crossed his arms and said, "Hallo, Granelli." He shifted his gaze to the leader, who was limping with a cane, a bandage covering his thigh. "How's the leg?"

The man spat at his feet. "Ye think ye're funny, don't ye, Blackmore?" He withdrew a severe looking metal blade. "Ye won't be laughin' when I cut out your wretched tongue."

A few malicious chuckles sounded from all around him.

"Ye could 'ave kept that woman from shootin' me, but instead, ye stood by an' did *nuthin'*." He walked forward and narrowed his eyes on Devin. "Maybe I should jus' make sure ye get sent back t' that island."

Devin stilled, all teasing gone from his demeanor. That was one place he would never joke about. He discarded his jacket and slowly began to roll up his sleeves. "I'll die first."

Granelli smiled, showing off the two, gold front teeth that he was famous for. "I think tha' can be arranged."

As he lunged for Devin, he gave a howl when his first attempt was met with a perfect uppercut to the jaw. As another one of the gang members started toward him, Granelli held up a hand. "No! 'E's mine!"

With a snarl, Granelli lifted his cane and brought it down in an arc toward Devin's head. He deftly rolled out of the way and came back with another punch to the man's kidneys that caused another grunt of pain to escape as he stumbled into the brick wall of the building.

"Are you sure you're in the right shape to do this?" he cajoled, knowing it would anger Granelli even further. But he'd long learned that men who were in a temper didn't always think clearly.

His opponent laughed. "Ye really think ye're gonna walk out o' this alley, Blackmore? An' here I thought ye were smarter tha' that."

Devin shrugged. "I've had worse challenges before. I suppose I have no choice but to take my chances now." He lifted his fists and offered a smug smirk. "Unless you're willing to concede defeat?"

Granelli didn't take the bait as Devin had hoped, but nodded toward one of his cronies, who cracked his knuckles before walking forward. Devin quickly made short work of him with a kick to the groin followed by a throat punch that had him falling to his knees and gasping for air.

The next two that came at Devin were a bit skilled. They got in a couple blows that dazed him for an instant, but since he'd defended himself the past five years against criminals worse than these, he eventually found their weakness and they were down soon enough.

After that, Granelli shouted for the last man standing and observing the spectacle wearing a hooded cloak to rush Devin. But he should have known that the miscreant wouldn't play fair and when he remained where he was and pulled out a pistol and pointed it directly at Devin's chest, he lunged for the attacker just moments before the ball ripped through his flesh.

The acidic smell of gunpowder assaulted Devin's nostrils and for a moment it was as if time itself had stopped. He stumbled to the opposite wall and put a palm to where the metal ball had lodged itself in his ribcage. His hand came back covered with blood. Either way, Devin knew that if the shot had hit just a bit higher, he would no longer have a heart to infect with hatred and angst, as it would have ceased beating entirely.

27

As it was, he glared at the man, who shoved the spent pistol in the waistband of his trousers and pushed back the hood of his cloak. The face wasn't familiar to him, but he knew that he was part of Granelli's gang, and that was enough. When he recovered, they could be assured he would come after them for this night. If he didn't, then he would ensure his ghost haunted their steps for the rest of their days and beyond.

Granelli calmly walked over, the slight limp growing more pronounced as he paused before Devin. "I suppose this makes us even."

"No," Devin corrected, blinking to keep the darkness at bay. "This makes us enemies."

Granelli tipped his hat to him. "I appreciate your return, Blackmore. I've been looking for a way to put an end this ongoing feud between Luke House and I, and I think I've just found it. I guess I should thank you for this victory, because when your mentor comes for me to take his vengeance, I'll be waiting."

With a dark laugh that proceeded his exit, Devin tried to go after him, but the blood he'd tried to keep at bay began to pour from his wound and the loss was starting to distort his vision. The last thing he remembered before he fell to the ground was that he might die—and never know the lady's name.

~

PAIN LIKE NOTHING Devin had ever felt before shot across his entire chest. In a sense, he supposed that was a good thing, because it meant that he wasn't yet dead, but at the same time, if he'd had the strength to move, he would have given a good right hook to the individual who was causing his suffering.

Even so, he offered a few choice words, but it was as if he'd swallowed a mouthful of cotton, as they only came out a pathetic mumble.

"He's trying to say something!"

He knew that voice. *Luke.* Thank God, at least he was alive.

Devin tried to open at least one of his eyes, but they refused to obey even that simple command. At least he could content himself in knowing that Granelli hadn't yet acted on his threats to see that Luke was six feet underground.

He had to warn him, but damned if he could even get his left arm to function properly. It continued to lay limply at his side where he laid on the ground. At least, he assumed he was still in that dirty alley, because he didn't remember moving.

Or *being* moved, for that matter.

"Whot is it, Dev?" Luke's baritone was urgent, almost demanding when he spoke, but then, he was probably under the impression that this was the last time they were going to speak.

Devin didn't have to be a fortune teller to realize that he was close to death, if not already on his way. Even the pain that had struck him earlier had dulled to a distant thrum. He tried to speak again, to let Luke know that he didn't have to stay here until he took his last breaths. It wasn't a pleasant experience to watch and God knows Luke had dealt with more than his fair share after burying his family back in Olney.

"It's out." The harried voice sounded distant, as if from the inside of a tunnel.

Devin thought he heard a sound of relief coming from Luke, but he was already floating back toward unconsciousness.

However, when a particularly uncomfortable sensation brought him back out of the haze, he managed to make another offering of communication, as the same harried voice commanded, "See if you can get some of this down him."

Devin's wooden lips opened, or rather, they were pried apart as some sort of liquid touched his tongue. At first, the sensation was strangely foreign, but then as some of it dribbled down his throat, it became more familiar. He tried to move his head to the side to avoid any further contact with the laudanum, but who, or *what*ever, was keeping him immobile managed to keep him still long enough for some of it to reach his stomach.

He wanted to retch, to bring the drug back up and rid himself of the taste he'd never really forgotten—and vowed that he'd never touch again. The one and only time he'd ever had laudanum had been the night Sir Isaacson had coerced him to steal something for him with the promise of a substantial reward that he'd never received and which had turned out to be a trap to send him to the noose once he'd handed the item over.

It was because of his own foolish pride that he'd sworn never to touch the vile stuff again, as it reminded him of his short stay on Norfolk Island. He would have much preferred death to the torture he'd received there, before he'd been transferred to Van Diemen's Land, which was harsh and unforgiving, but not the hell he'd previously endured.

With one last attempt to convey his wishes, Devin summoned all his energy to clamp his lips closed when more of the opium would have been poured into him. His senses were dulled enough without the possibility that he would leave this world in such a manner.

"Th' devil," Luke whispered in near awe, before he addressed the other person in the room. "Take this brown bottle away. He won't be needin' anymore o' it."

"Are you sure? The agony he must be enduring—"

"'E doesn't *want* it."

Devin finally allowed himself to relax at the firm tone, as he knew there would be no more on the matter. When he'd been a younger man, Luke had caused him to shake in his boots when he spoke like that. He had an image of the mystery man feeling very much the same, especially when a grizzled thief like Luke House was staring at him.

He would have smiled if he could.

"Can I get ye anythin', Dev?"

Devin hated to hear the helplessness in the man's voice, and although he'd struggled in vain to make himself be heard, he vowed that he would utter one word. Whether or not it made sense, he couldn't allow his friend to stand there and suffer as he was when Devin could prevent it.

And, honestly, if he did wake up, he would like to see a soft pair of moss green eyes looking at him.

Using everything that he had within him, Devin managed to croak out one pitiful word. "A...ch...illes."

Darkness consumed him.

CHAPTER 4

He's late.

Constance checked the small watch pinned on the front of her jacket and realized that it had just turned nine. So, while she had imagined that her dark stranger was running behind, she was, in fact, early to their little rendezvous.

She blew out a heavy breath and told herself she was a fool for even coming to this ridiculous statue again. She should have just gone to the coffee shop that she had recently found and sipped from a cup and smiled, knowing that she had the upper hand.

But no. Instead, she was sitting on a bench and waiting for an apparition, because while he might be real, she was quite sure that he was merely leading her on a merry chase and likely never intended to follow through with their little flirtation. Not only that, but Constance should have been smarter than to fall for his lies. But she'd allowed Madame Corressa to take the reins on this one and now she was sitting here looking completely ridiculous in her cornflower blue walking dress.

At least, that was how she felt inside. Outwardly, she supposed she looked like a lady who had chosen a lovely, London morning to venture out of doors and feed the pigeons.

She had nearly convinced herself not to stay when a horse and rider paused in front of her. "Good day, Mrs. Hartford."

Constance nearly groaned aloud when she looked up and spied the countenance of Sir Brooks Isaacson. With his slicked back, dark blond hair and blue eyes that were more shocking than striking, she hadn't particularly cared for his company the day before when he'd boldly introduced himself without a proper invitation to do so, and now it appeared that he believed that they were more than just a slight acquaintance at best.

"Sir." She inclined her head with the slightest nod, hoping that he would get the message that she wasn't in the mood for company. Instead, he must have decided it was an invitation, because he stepped down to the ground and secured his horse's reins to a nearby tree.

"Mind if I join you?" he asked pleasantly. "It's such a nice day."

"Of course," she murmured. She wanted to refuse, but if she wished to keep her newfound approval in society, then she had better tread lightly. The gentleman might be a lowly baronet, but he was still more influential than the former courtesan she was.

He adopted a relaxed pose and glanced at her with a lazy smile. She eyed him warily. "Will you be attending Lady Madsen's soiree this evening?"

"I'm not sure what our plans are yet." She wanted to ensure that he knew she was not free to move about on her own. It was already common knowledge that she joined the countess, along with the count and his wife quite frequently.

He leaned toward her slightly and lifted a light brow. "I can't convince you to run away with me for the evening?"

Constance clenched her fists in her lap, as it was all she could do not to strike out at the man. "Sir, you are too presumptuous and entirely too bold." She rose to her feet, for to remain would only anger her further. "I shall bid you good day."

Dear heavens, did she have a sign that hung around her neck proclaiming, *Former courtesan—feel free to proposition at will?*

It might have been true that she'd planned to meet another gentleman that morning for illicit purposes, but that was *her* choice. She wasn't a whore in a brothel to entertain any man that happened to come along, but apparently that was what Sir Isaacson believed. The question was if the rest of society would be expecting the same, and that certainly wasn't why she'd returned to London, to pick up where she'd left off all those years ago.

She walked steadily down the path that led to the entrance to Hyde Park, intent on hailing down a hackney and returning to Lady Blessington's residence post haste. She had imagined that if she were to meet the intriguing man this morning that they might need a carriage in order to be discreet. Now she rather wished she'd rode her mare, because at least then she could enjoy a brisk ride to cool off her frustration before she returned to the townhouse.

"'Scuse me."

Constance turned toward the male voice and stopped abruptly. She put a hand to her chest, but she was startled by the man's appearance. He wore a thick beard, but it grew oddly, in patches, and although he had a lean athletic build, she could tell by his worn, wool clothes that he wasn't a gentleman. In truth, he looked like the sort of men who would frequent her former gaming hell.

And they were generally not good news.

She ignored him and continued walking. She would have kept heading for the exit to the park, but it was what he said next that gave her pause. "Were ye supposed t' meet someone a' th' Achilles statue this mornin'?"

Constance slowly turned and pinned him with her sharp gaze. Now that she looked closer, she saw that there was something like apprehension in his expression. Suddenly, her stomach dropped into her feet, because she had the feeling she knew why he was here. Even so, she kept her tone light when she replied, "I might have been."

Relief definitely entered his expression. "Would ye be willin' t' come wit' me?" He held up his hands, palms outward. "I promise I mean ye no ill will. A... friend has been injured an' one o' th' last words 'e spoke was about ye."

Constance was hot and cold at the same time. She didn't know what to feel other than the fact she had to see the individual he was speaking of. She could feel the press of cold metal against her thigh and the small dagger she'd carried with her as long as she could remember, and it gave her a sense of comfort. If this was nothing more than a ploy to get her alone, she would have a special surprise for him.

"Lead the way, Mr....?"

"House."

She lifted a brow, sure that it was an assumed name, but since he offered no more and stalked past, she had little choice but to follow now and ask questions later.

He waved down a hackney and looked at her expectantly. She climbed inside before he joined her. He gave the driver a nondescript address that led to somewhere in Seven Dials, and she narrowed her gaze on him. "Might you offer any further information on where we're going? Or continue to keep me unaware?"

"T' my lodgings."

Well, that certainly didn't tell her anything. "Why?"

He eyed her skeptically and shot back, "Are ye goin' t' keep askin' questions, or just wait an' see?"

She snorted, having always been rather respectful of a worthy rejoinder. "I suppose I can be patient, but just so you are aware, I know my way around a pistol and will use it if necessary."

He eyed her for a moment and then nodded his head. "Aye, I imagine that's true. It's probably why Devin took a likin' to ye."

Her pulse picked up speed. "Devin?"

"Did he no' even tell ye 'is name?" This time, he snorted with a shake of his head. "No' tha' I'm surprised. It was why I'd nicknamed 'im th' Mysterious Marauder. T' this day I'm surprised 'e never wore a mask on 'is adventures."

"The Mysterious Marauder." Constance echoed, rolling the pseudonym around. It fit quite nicely on her tongue, just as she imagined he would. She quickly tamped down those sorts of thoughts and said, "What is his surname?"

"Blackmore. 'E's as close t' a son tha' I ever had." He turned to glance out the window. "An' now I'm afraid I'm goin' t' lose him after he was finally restored t' me."

Constance tried to keep her own anxiousness at bay. "What happened?" she asked evenly.

"'E was shot last night. Outside o' th' Theatre Royal."

If Constance hadn't already been sitting, she would have surely collapsed to the floor. Not only was it shocking to learn that he had been shot, but if the morose look on Mr. House's face could be believed, that would mean he would have met his nemesis shortly after he'd approached her in the auditorium.

She had the sudden urge to retch. "How bad is it?"

He sighed heavily. "Tommy was able t' get th' bullet out, but he lost a lot o' blood. 'E might die jus' from tha', an' that's if infection don't set in."

"You didn't take him to an actual *physician*?" she demanded, horrified that Devin's life might have been spared if he'd only seen an actual doctor of medicine.

Instantly, his expression darkened. "I couldn't take th' chance tha' Granelli would find 'im an' finish th' job." As the hackney slowed, House stared at her intently and withdrew a black cloth. "I'm goin' t' have t' blindfold ye."

Her lips twisted. "Don't you trust me?"

He mirrored her expression. "I'm sure ye understand tha' in my line o' work, it's important tha' I don't show all o' my cards."

"Indeed." Constance was still a bit leery, but she decided to continue this charade until its conclusion. Either he was telling the truth about this "mysterious marauder," or she would make sure he found himself with a dagger in his gullet. She waited patiently as he put the cloth around her eyes and tied it firmly in the back.

She heard the carriage creak as he departed, although he took her hand and assisted her down from the carriage while she was enveloped in darkness. The sounds of the city were quickly muffled as they made their way past a creaky door and up some rather rickety stairs. They had to walk slow and watch their footing lest she risk tumbling back down. The air also wasn't very pleasant with a mixture of foul concoctions that she didn't care to name. She wasn't surprised to find that a man like Mr. House lived in such conditions, as she recalled that John Keats had once called the Seven Dials a place 'where misery clings to misery for a little warmth, and want and disease lie down side-by-side, and groan together.'

It was certainly somewhere she had never cared to frequent before, although she hadn't been afraid to traverse the areas where refuse, rats, or fights broke out among men and women alike. Her closest friend had been a boxer, so he'd taught her how to defend herself quickly in most any situation, even when some might not believe that she could obtain the upper hand. What most people didn't realize is that fighting wasn't about strength, but agility, and in that area, she was still rather astute.

After what seemed to be a lengthy climb, they paused and Constance heard a set of keys jangle before Mr. House released her hand long enough to shove them into a lock. After pushing open a door with grating hinges, he took her hand once more and led her inside. Once the door was shut, he removed her blindfold.

She blinked as her eyes adjusted from dark to light. She glanced around to find meager furnishings—a couple chairs and a rickety table that didn't look strong enough to hold a slice of bread, let alone a full meal—and a small wood burning stove. Streaks of soot lined the wall behind it and the floor was littered in front with ash and wood splinters. At least there was a privacy screen in the corner which kept the chamber pot out of sight.

Constance had a sudden flashback to when she was young and lived in similar conditions of squalor and poverty with her mother. After she'd fled and clawed her way to the top by using her body to leave this all behind, vowing never to return, she barely withheld a shudder now, as here she stood in the midst of it once again. She pretended not to picture all of the vermin that could be inhabiting the cushions of the chairs.

Needless to say, it was definitely a far cry from the comforts she currently enjoyed in Mayfair. This entire living space wouldn't even make up the size of one of the countess' guest rooms.

"Ye'll 'ave t' pardon th' mess. I wasn't expectin' comp'ny."

She rolled her eyes at the mockery in Mr. House's tone. "And here I thought for sure you would have a kettle ready for tea," she returned in kind.

She thought she might have seen a flicker of respect in his eyes before he said stoically, "Follow me. 'E's jus' through here."

Constance walked forward and when another door was opened to reveal a bedroom that wasn't much larger than the size of a closet, it was the figure lying still as death on top that made the breath catch in her chest.

It was truly *him*. The man she had cautioned herself about was lying here, and by the sound of his labored breathing, it didn't sound as though he was long for this world.

Instantly, her fists clenched at her sides. She didn't know anything about him, his past transgressions, or what he had planned for the future, but she wouldn't allow an animal to pass into the next world in such a horrifying fashion, let alone a human.

"He can't stay here."

She turned to Mr. House to see that his arms were firmly

crossed over his chest. "There's no place else t' take 'im where Granelli couldn't go."

"I will find something better than this," she snapped. "But no more blindfolds. You're going to have to trust me."

"An' why should I do tha'?" he countered. "Th' gentry ain't done nothin' for me before."

She held her ground. "Then it's a good thing I'm not part of polite society." She brushed past him and headed for the door before she paused and turned back around. "Have him ready to be moved by dawn." Her gaze flickered back to the bedroom door. "If he makes it that long."

She shut the door on her departure.

∾

MINUTES OR HOURS PASSED—DEVIN had no perception of time when he found himself stirring once more. He tried to adjust his position, and although he managed to shift his left arm this time, the slight movement made his chest burn in searing agony. He tried to see if he was on fire, but unfortunately, his eyes still didn't want to obey the command to open.

He exhaled heavily and it must have been enough, as he could hear footsteps coming toward him. Oddly enough, that was the only sound he could hear. Whether he was still in that dingy alley, or in Seven Dials with Luke, it was never this quiet. Perhaps he'd already passed over to the other side. But then, if that was true, why did he still feel pain? Wasn't heaven supposed to rid you of that?

But then, maybe he was in hell. It wouldn't surprise him if that were so, but where were the pitiful moans and screams from torture from the condemned?

"Devin? Can you hear me?"

Now he definitely knew that he was in heaven, as that was the voice of an angel.

Although the speaker sounded oddly... familiar.

"I'm no' sure 'e's conscious."

Luke. Either he was still alive, or he'd joined him in the after-life, and he was

starting to think it was the former.

"Give him time," the angel said somewhat irritably. He would have smiled if he'd had the strength to do so. "It's been nearly a week since his accident."

Accident? That would certainly explain why he couldn't seem to get his body to function properly. But then, it all came rushing back—the interlude at the opera, the alley, Granelli...

He growled low in his throat.

"Did you hear that?" the angel whispered, almost in reverence. "Devin? If you can hear me, make another sound."

Devin decided that if he could make a noise of annoyance, then he could make one to ensure her that he was alive. At least, for the moment. After being shot in the chest, he wasn't sure what shape he was in. He could still be perilously close to death's door, but he was still on this earth.

He groaned lightly.

"Oh, thank God." Something was pressed against his lips. "Drink this." He tried to turn his head away, so she added softly, "It's just water, I promise."

He obediently opened his mouth and the cool liquid touched his tongue. He couldn't have drunk more than a thimble full, but it was enough to make him sigh in relief after he'd swallowed. He hadn't realized how parched he'd been until then. He tried to say that he wanted more, but his angel seemed to understand, and more of the wonderful drink slid down his throat.

"Is that better?" she soothed.

He attempted a slight nod and must have succeeded, because she rewarded him by placing a gentle kiss upon his forehead. He was immediately transported back in time to when he was a child in Olney, lying on a cot in a hovel of a cottage, but he vividly recalled the press of his mother's lips next to his hairline before she'd put him to bed. He couldn't have been more than two or three at the time, as she had passed away before he'd turned five, but some things in life were worth remembering.

"Get some rest now." A brief caress passed over his hair. "I bet you will feel much more revived when next you wake."

Devin was sure that a ghost of a smile touched his mouth as he drifted back off into slumber, resting much easier than he had before.

CHAPTER 5

*T*here was a lump in Constance's throat when Devin's breathing turned deep and even, proof that he had fallen back asleep. She had been particularly concerned until that point, as it was the first time he'd woken up in four days. Even when she'd gotten two of the servants from Lady Blessington's house to assist her with transporting Devin to the furnished residence she'd let at number 37 Weymouth Street in Marylebone, he hadn't even made a single noise.

Since it had three bedrooms, she'd also invited Mr. House to stay, so that Devin could see a familiar face when he woke. Until today, she'd started to wonder if that was ever going to happen. There had been several times she'd woken to check on him in the middle of the night with the fear that he would have died in his sleep, although she generally traded shifts with Mr. House. Nevertheless, she hadn't been there when Bull had slipped away and she would always regret that someone wasn't as least holding his hand when he breathed his last.

But now that Devin had made some sort of response, she was starting to think that the physician Lady Blessington had recommended she call to check on him might have been right after all.

He'd told her that he believed her "cousin" would make a full recovery, although the damage to some of the nerves in his chest might not allow him the full use of his left arm. He'd complimented the work that had been done to surgically remove the bullet, to which Luke had merely lifted his brows at her. He'd told her that Tommy, the man who had removed the lead ball, was one of the best sawbones he knew. But to Constance, a butcher wasn't the same as a true doctor of medicine.

Nevertheless, they had both been relieved to learn that no infection had set in, but he'd left instructions for a poultice should that change, as well as some laudanum that Luke had immediately waved away. "'E doesn't want it."

Constance could tell by his tone that there was no arguing with him, so she'd agreed with his decision. After four days of caring for Devin, they had slowly earned a mutual respect for the other. Luke was likely grateful that Devin was in better surroundings, while Constance was just glad that another human was there to take some of the anxiety away from his precarious situation.

She was thankful that Lady Blessington and Count d'Orsay had been so understanding of her plight. She'd had no choice but to tell them of her need to care for Devin and the circumstances surrounding his condition if they had any hope of comprehending why she had to suddenly leave the townhouse. "You must do what is right in your heart," the countess had said as Constance's trunk had been loaded into her carriage. "And it's not as if this is goodbye. We shall still see you around town, of course. I shall still expect the enjoyment of your company at social events." She'd offered a wink and added, "Rest assured, your 'cousin's' identity shall not be revealed."

"Shall I take over for a bit?" Luke offered.

Constance turned to him with a weary smile. She glanced at the watch pinned to her dress. "I would appreciate that. A warm, shower bath would be most welcome."

After she'd remained under the spray until her skin was pink, Constance left the bathing chamber and, after wrapping a robe around her, she entered her room where she donned a nightdress and sat in front of the dressing table. She had just finished brushing out her hair when there was a brisk knock at her door. Without any time to pull up the long tresses, she rushed over and pulled it open.

Luke appeared almost joyous. "He's awake."

Constance put a hand to her heart and nodded. "I'll be right there." She grabbed another wrap from her wardrobe and put her arms inside, tying it in front as she entered Devin's room down the hall.

The moment she stepped inside, she halted, because she'd expected to see Devin looking rather pale and listless, but instead, he was propped up in the four-poster, curtained bed, and although his eyes had a slight hollow appearance they were wide open.

He stared directly at her, and although she'd seen him bare-chested when the physician had attended to him, with only a bandage crossing his ribcage and covering his wound, now she couldn't help but admire his strong, muscular shoulders and broad chest with a sprinkling of dark hair. She could only imagine that as it disappeared below the covers...

Stop that! Constance chided herself, as such thoughts were highly inappropriate, considering the man had nearly died. It was a miracle that he appeared as healthy as he did.

As the minutes ticked by and they merely regarded one another from across the room, Constance knew she should say something, but the only thing she could manage to get out was, "Hallo."

He opened his mouth, but after a brief frown, he cleared his throat and tried again. "Hey." It was broken and rusty from disuse, but it was a lovely sound to hear in her opinion.

She smiled at Luke, who nodded in turn.

44

For once they were in perfect agreement.

Devin would be all right.

~

MY ANGEL.

But truly, when she smiled and something flared to life in the middle of Devin's chest, such a word didn't seem strong enough.

Goddess, sylph, dryad... nothing he could imagine could accurately describe what he was seeing. But there was one word that he wanted to say when it came to her.

Mine.

He didn't trust himself to try to speak any more, as his throat still ached with the work it had taken to say a single syllable. So, he just watched, which is something he could do all day when it came to her. She was beauty personified, exquisite.

And he still didn't know her name.

When her soft green eyes returned to him, he felt as though he'd been granted a second chance at life. Nothing else mattered but her gaze. As long as she was here, he was a new man, born again without the destruction of his past to haunt his every step, reminding him of all that he'd done wrong.

She tentatively walked over to the bedside. Standing there, with her golden hair falling over her shoulders, with just the slightest hint of strawberry woven through the strands, he was looking at perfection itself. "My name is Mrs. Constance Hartford." Her lips twitched and if he hadn't been a broken man with a hole in his chest, he would have leapt from the bed and taken her into his arms right then. "I thought it was time I introduced myself, Mr. Blackmore."

Devin! He wanted to shout it out, to hear his name cross her lips where he could actually enjoy the feeling of it ringing in his ears, instead of relying on a hazy state of memory when he didn't even know if he was alive or dead.

"You might be wondering where you are," she began, but he wanted to shake his head and tell her that the only thing he cared about was *her*. Nothing else mattered ever again. "I prevailed upon your friend, Mr. House, to bring you somewhere a bit more… comfortable, so I let a house in Marylebone." She held up a hand. "And I wouldn't worry that Granelli and his gang of miscreants will cause either of you any trouble here. Count d'Orsay has ordered personal protection for the entire household."

Devin did nothing. He just continued to stare at her, absorbing everything about her. From the slight lift of her eyebrow to the smooth skin of her face, and even the way the pulse beat at her neck—he intended to memorize it all. And when he was recovered, explore every single part. There was not one inch of her that would not know his touch, or his tongue.

When her hands suddenly fluttered at her sides, he wondered if she could see what he was thinking, the torrid thoughts that he should do his best to withhold, and yet, he didn't want to. He yearned for her to know everything.

"I'll leave ye alone t' chat a while."

Luke took his leave and Devin admitted that he'd never known his friend to be so respectful of anyone but him. This woman—*Constance*—must have made a decided impression on him for her to gain so much consideration.

Once the door was shut and they were alone together, she walked forward and sat down in a chair by the bed. He watched her, waiting for her to speak. But she could sit there all night and not have to utter a single word and he would be content.

"We've certainly had an odd acquaintance thus far, haven't we?" She laughed lightly and even though he was weak and his chest hurt like the devil, his cock stirred with interest. The damned thing certainly had a mind of its own. "One minute you're trying to coerce me into being your particular… *friend*, and the next, I'm dragging you out of a filthy boarding house

46

praying that you'll live through the night. I suppose that's what you would call irony?"

He didn't reply but gave a light snort in agreement. For two people who barely knew each other, they had definitely gone off on an oddly strange path. However, if he was confined to a bed, he would have liked for her to be there with him, and preferably *under* him, or on top, he wasn't particular.

"Needless to say," she continued. "I thought these surroundings would be more agreeable. I've invited Luke to stay here as well, as he told me what Granelli threatened. But, as I said, we have ample protection from Count d'Orsay, so you can continue to recover in peace."

Devin frowned lightly, wondering if she had some sort of understanding with the man.

"I daresay I'm curious about that expression," she murmured. "This would undoubtedly be easier if you could try to speak. Or perhaps..." She stood and walked over to a nearby desk and held up a sheet of paper and a quill. "Are you able to write?"

His lips quirked, because he knew what she was really asking – *can* you write?

Thankfully, his father had made sure that he learned his letters and how to read long ago, so he nodded his head.

With a decided smile on her face, she returned with the items, along with a pot of ink and a small, wooden writing desk that she lightly placed on his lap.

It wasn't until he picked up the quill and dipped it in the black ink that she said, "You're left-handed?"

He glanced at her, as the way she said it sounded almost anxious. He was just thankful that the feeling had returned to the previously useless limb. He scribbled on the paper. *I'm afraid it's too late to change me.*

She laughed at his statement and explained, "I apologize. It's just that I've always heard that the devil was left-handed, and I don't know if you are aware, but in Latin the word for left means sinister."

He wrote another line and turned it where she could see it. *Then I suppose you should beware.*

All teasing was suddenly gone from her expression. "I might be, if I hadn't already danced with the devil myself on occasion."

~

CONSTANCE TURNED AWAY FROM DEVIN.

Correction, *Mr. Blackmore*. She had to quit referring to him in such an intimate manner, as all of the promises that she'd made herself would be for naught if she allowed his dark, handsome looks to overrule her common sense. When he'd cautioned her to beware, he might have meant it in jest, but the truth was, she couldn't allow herself to embark on anything more than a mild flirtation. As soon as he was able to move about and get along well enough to defend himself, she would give up the lease on this place and return to Lady Blessington's. The countess had already said that the door was open anytime should she ever wish to come back, but that wouldn't be until she could send Mr. Blackmore on his way with a clear conscience.

Although she was thankful that Mr. Blackmore would survive, there was no place in her life for another liaison. She had safeguarded her heart from being broken all of these years, but she had the feeling it could easily be torn apart by this man. Already, he had some sort of invisible hold over her, because why else did she have the desire to see that he lived at all costs? With the generous stipend that she'd received from Alessandro, she didn't have any concern for the future. Leasing a townhouse in London wasn't particularly what she would call wise, but she told herself it was merely temporary, that in a couple months, at most, she would be parting ways with her guests.

She blinked as the pen was tapped against the wooden desk.

She looked back at Mr. Blackmore to see that he was watching her curiously. *What's wrong?*

"Just woolgathering," she hedged. Constance rose to her feet and realized that she needed to distance herself from him. "I'll send Mr. House back in for the evening. I have an early morning appointment that I'm expected to attend and should be getting to bed." She headed for the door, but when she opened it, she paused. Even she had to admit that she was leaving rather abruptly. To soften her departure, she looked back over her shoulder. "I'm glad you're with us once again, Mr. Blackmore."

He inclined his head in acknowledgement, and she left the room.

Mr. House hadn't gone far. He was in the hallway leaning against the wall, but he straightened when she appeared. "I gave him some paper and a pen in which to communicate until he feels able to speak again. I'm sure that by this time tomorrow he will be conversing as usual."

"Aye. I think ye're right. But then, Devin was always a strong one."

As they parted ways and Constance returned to her chamber, she leaned against the door and shut her eyes. For some odd reason, a tear slid down her cheek. She ignored it, as she had no idea why she might be feeling the need to cry. Mr. Blackmore was going to live. She had ensured that he hadn't succumbed to a vengeful man's hatred, and in spite of that, she was glad. If she had the chance to rid the world of someone like Granelli, she just might do it—if Madame Corressa was still in control of her life.

But *Constance Freewater* wanted a better life for herself. She wished to leave the sordid memories of her past behind, and although she was still a "miss," having never been married, or even engaged after almost forty years of life, she had enjoyed bed sport for many years. In such, she had adopted a faux widowed status, so that she could enjoy the freedoms that social status implied. While many would likely not believe that Mr. Blackmore was her "cousin," since she had changed her title to "Mrs." no one really cared. The only problem she might encounter were men like Sir Isaacson who imagined that she would be easy prey when it came to the bedchamber.

She gave a heavy sigh and removed her wrapper, and then climbed beneath the covers. After she blew out the lamp beside the bed, she closed her eyes and demanded sleep to claim her.

~

CONSTANCE SAT in the middle of the coffee shop the next morning and sipped the dark brew from her cup with a sigh. She'd been proud of herself for leaving the house without stopping to check in on Mr. Blackmore first. After she'd gone to bed feeling somewhat... unsettled, she had needed this time to bring her thoughts back to where they belonged.

She'd dressed in a deep orange gown around dawn and waited for the maid to add the finishing touches to her hair. She had been hesitant to hire one, but Lady Blessington said it was *necessary* to be a proper lady of society. But other than a full-time ladies' maid, as Constance had learned to dress herself quite aptly over the years, she'd hired Abigail as a house maid with a few extra duties. With the cook, a housekeeper, and two footmen in attendance, Constance decided that the need for more was unnecessary, and if she entertained a caller, it would be enough to placate those stubborn sensibilities.

But now, as the sun had fully risen and she had lingered as long as she was comfortable doing so, Constance paid for her indulgence and started walking back toward the house where she would inevitably have to see Mr. Blackmore again. Last night she'd begun to wonder if she'd made a terrible mistake, had gone back and forth with her conscience, but in the end, she'd decided that she had simply done what anyone with a caring heart might do.

At least, that was what she was trying to convince herself.

She had nearly made it to the steps of her leased home when her name was called. She turned to see Sir Isaacson jogging toward her. She offered a tight smile that she hoped appeared less grim than she was feeling.

He glanced toward the two-story brick structure and said, "I didn't know you lived in the same area." He looked back at her, his blue eyes shining as bright as his hair in the sun when he removed his hat. "I thought you were staying in Mayfair with Lady Blessington."

Constance almost groaned. "Indeed, I was, but a sick cousin needed my attention, and I didn't want to be a burden should she wish to entertain."

"I'm sure you could never be a burden to anyone, Mrs. Hartford."

He smiled in a charming manner, and she was sure that his flirtations would not be wasted on a fresh debutante, but she was sadly unmoved. "That's kind of you to say," she murmured, "But I fear my cousin needed some solitude in which to recover."

He put a hand over his heart. "I offer my sincerest wish that she is the epitome of health very soon."

"*He* is doing much better," she corrected. "And I thank you for your concern." She didn't miss the flash of disapproval in his gaze. "Now if you will excuse me?"

She started to go, but he said, "Perhaps I might call upon you both when your cousin is feeling up to guests."

Constance gritted her teeth, but she inclined her head regardless. "Of course. We should be delighted."

She picked up her skirts and nearly rushed into the house, lest he decided he wanted to delay her any longer. She didn't know what it was, but something about him quite unnerved her, and not in a way that made her afraid. It was the kind that made her yearn to see what he might look like with a black eye—where she was the one to offer it.

She made her way upstairs and saw Mr. House departing Mr. Blackmore's room, an empty tray in his hands. "Why didn't you call for one of the footmen to take that downstairs for you?"

"Th' day I can't wait o' myself is th' day I go in th' ground."

That was all he offered by way of an explanation as he took the items away. She noticed that most of it was gone, so she hoped that meant their patient had regained his appetite. If so, that would mean his strength would soon follow.

The door to his room was left slightly ajar, so she pushed it open. She had expected to see him lying in bed when she entered, but when there was movement by the window, she gasped. "What are you doing out of bed?"

His dark eyes narrowed slightly where he stood by the open curtain. He allowed it to fall back into place, and for an instant, she was struck by his silhouette. Tall and lean with narrow hips, wearing trousers and nothing else, even his bare feet looked attractive. "Why are you entertaining a man like Sir Brooks Isaacson?" he countered.

She noted that his voice was fully recovered and it was just as dark and delicious as before. However, she didn't care for his query. It sounded entirely too controlling. "He's a baronet and quite favored in society. I don't see the harm in it. Besides, I don't recall having to explain my actions to you." She lifted a brow. "Now, tell me why you are up when you should be doing everything you can to fully recuperate."

He eyed her for a moment, and then he began to slowly make his way back toward the bed. She noticed that he also held his bandage with his right arm as he did so. He might be trying to fool himself that he was doing better, but it had only been a week since he'd been injured and on the cusp of death.

He sat down on the edge of the bed. "I was feeling restless," he admitted. "I'm not used to being so... immobile."

She crossed her arms. "Should I bring you something to read?"

His mouth quirked in a half-smile. "And what sort of selection do you think you might find here? A study in philosophy or science?" He laid down and stretched his arms behind his head. "No, thank you."

She rolled her eyes. "You're rather difficult to please."

"Not really." Something in his tone made her glance at him, and the heat she saw in his gaze made her set her jaw. "I just require something a bit more... entertaining."

"You're in no shape to do much more than play cards at the moment," she snapped. "So, if you care to partner me in whist, I can do that."

He gave an exaggerated sigh. "Very well."

CHAPTER 6

*D*evin knew that he shouldn't test the lady's patience, but she was just too fun to tease. And the flash of green fire in her eyes was just too enticing to ignore. He couldn't wait for the day that same passion turned into burning desire. For *him*.

But now, he had to ignore all those lascivious thoughts in his mind, for he didn't want to push her too far and frighten her away. And honestly, his body might yearn for her, but it was also not ready for anything quite so vigorous. At the moment, he had to content himself with just watching her, and from the top of her head to the tip of her toes, he found her to be utterly mesmerizing.

He sat up as she brought the wooden lap desk over to the bed and set it beside him. In turn, she gathered a deck of cards and a whist marker that was sitting on a nearby table, and then perched on the edge of the bed.

She attempted to shuffle the deck, but he held out his hand. "Allow me."

Reluctantly, she handed them over and he immediately began to flip them around. He'd always had a certain skill when it came to manipulating the deck. He had fascinated more than one onlooker with his ability.

As he glanced at Constance, he could see that she was equally enthralled, for her eyes had widened slightly and her lips had parted. It wasn't until her dainty pink tongue appeared to lick her lips that he nearly shot the entire deck across the bed. Luckily, he managed to gain control and handed them back to her. "That should be sufficient."

She took them, as if in awe. "How did you learn to shuffle like that?"

He shrugged. "It's just something I've always done."

"I'm impressed." As she dealt out thirteen cards to each of them, she added, "I could have used someone like you at Montfree's."

"Montfree's?" he echoed curiously.

She turned her attention to the cards in her hand. "It was the gaming hell I had a half share in."

He snorted. "*You* ran a gaming hell?"

She looked at him in complete seriousness. "Yes."

"But... you're a woman."

This time, she was the one who snorted. "Don't tell me your so antiquated in your thinking that you can't imagine a woman can have a particular head for business." She cocked a brow at him. "We are good for more than spreading our legs, you know."

He offered her a tolerant look. "I didn't mean it that way. I merely meant that I was surprised that someone was willing to go into business with you. Most men are reluctant to find out that a female is better at keeping ledgers than they are."

"I certainly can't argue with that," she murmured, as the game progressed. "But luckily, I had a partner who didn't mind."

While Devin had imagined that he was quite proficient at whist, Constance made sure that he kept his mind on the game at all times, as she was quite an adept opponent. While he would never say as much to Luke, he thought she might actually be better than him. Needless to say, he wasn't surprised that she had shared ownership in a gaming hell. She could have likely tackled it on her own and done quite well for herself.

It made him wonder... "Why did you leave?"

"Hmm?" She was concentrating on the cards in her hand.

"Montfree's. Why did you give it up?"

"It was time. My partner married and I found the game I was playing had become rather tiring."

"I hope you don't feel the same about this one."

She smiled. "Not all. In fact..." She set down her cards with a flourish. "I do believe I've won."

He set down his hand and said, "Well done, Mrs. Hartford."

She wrinkled her nose. "That makes me sound dreadfully old." She gathered up their cards and handed them to him. "Shall we play again?"

As he shuffled them, he asked, "How old are you?"

"Don't you know it's impolite to ask a lady her age?"

He chuckled. "This coming from a woman who told me I was the devil for writing with my left hand."

She sniffed. "Very well. I will give you that." She eyed him warily and then admitted, "I will be turning forty years next month. On July twelfth, to be precise."

He paused in his shuffling. "You were born on the Battle of the Boyne?"

She lifted her chin. "While I can't claim anything quite so extravagant as a victory to celebrate the Protestant King William of Orange and his defeat over Catholic King James of England and Scotland, I still consider it a victory that I've made it this far in life, as most girls that had to endure the hardships I have did not make it far into adulthood."

He regarded her steadily. "I feel quite lucky to be here with you."

He saw her breath catch. As he looked into those moss green

eyes, it was as if he could see straight through into her soul, and he could tell it unnerved her.

"Would you like me to deal this time?"

She jumped slightly, and then blinked. "Of course." And then she tried to cover her sudden inattention with a slight rejoinder. "It does seem only fair since I won the last hand."

His offered a lopsided grin that many women had claimed was entirely too charming for a marauder. "You may not have the same fortune a second time."

She squared her shoulders. "I suppose we'll see."

Devin decided that it was time to play a bit more ruthless. And he didn't have to cheat to do it. At least, not with the cards in his grasp.

No, he had something a bit more underhanded in mind when it came to the alluring Mrs. Hartford.

"Mmm." He brushed a thumb along his lower lip as he looked at his cards, pretending to be engrossed in his next play. When he laid down a card, he made sure to set it down a bit too far, so that he would have to brush her hand to retrieve it. "Pardon me," he said huskily, as he set the stray card on the stack.

She cleared her throat and he thought the color rose slightly in her cheeks. "That's… um, quite all right."

Devin was starting to enjoy himself even more than before. He had to keep his smile from widening when he suddenly winced.

"What is it?" she asked, a lovely little crease forming between her brows.

"Nothing, really." He moved his shoulder and made sure to rub the muscles of his bare arm. His ploy worked for her attention was instantly drawn there.

She visibly swallowed. "Can I do anything?"

He held out his arm. "Be my guest. It just seems a little… stiff."

"Ah…" She swallowed down whatever else she'd been about to say and tentatively set down her cards, face down, and reached out to touch him. After a brief, gentle exploration that unsettled both of them, she drew away and said, "Everything seems to be perfect... ah, *in* perfect working order to me."

"Just some sore muscles from disuse then," he said and shrugged. He noticed, however, that she merely nodded her head. As she turned her attention back to her hand, he was sure that she wasn't as intent on the cards as she was before, but rather more attuned to *him*.

Needless to say, this game just got a lot more interesting.

~

WELL, this game just got a lot more interesting...

Constance wasn't oblivious to what Mr. Blackmore was doing, as she hadn't been a naïve girl for many years.

And yet...

The way he'd brushed his fingers against her hand—a burst of sensation like nothing she'd ever experienced before had shot across her skin. And his sudden attack of sore muscles? That was merely a ploy to draw her attention to his firmly toned physique, and drat if it hadn't worked marvelously.

She had to admit that he had the skill of a seasoned lover. But since those days were behind her, there was nothing he could do to change her mind, because once she returned to that path, it left the door open to men like Sir Isaacson in believing that she was fair game. It had been the same with her previous paramours and it wasn't likely to change. While times were changing and industry was starting to become further acknowledged, the oldest profession among women was still going strong.

"Are you going to make a play?"

Constance cursed her further woolgathering and quickly set down a card, praying that it was the one she'd meant to discard. The game progressed uneventfully for a time, but then, she refused to meet his gaze. She didn't want to be drawn further into his intrigue—nor tempt herself in the process.

It wasn't until she was about to finish the game with another win, that Mr. Blackmore spoke up again. "I propose a wager."

She finally lifted her gaze and the heat she saw in his dark eyes curled her toes in her slippers. "It's a little late for that, isn't it?"

He tilted his head to the side. "Are you saying that you won't humor an injured man?"

She rolled her eyes. "Very well," she replied tolerantly. "What are the stakes?"

His expression never wavered from her face. "A kiss, if I win."

Her brows lifted. "Are you sure that's wise?"

"It's just a kiss," he countered smoothly. "No harm ever came from such a tame request."

Just a kiss, indeed. In her experience, that was how it always began.

She stared at him. He certainly didn't seem too injured if he was making requests like that, even if she knew that he was. However, since she didn't think that he could possibly beat her at this point, as she had nearly won already, she agreed, "What if I win?"

He waved a hand. "Name your terms, and I will abide by them."

She thought for a moment, tapping her finger against her lips as she did so. She noticed that his gaze never wavered from the action and she resisted the urge to smile. *Two can play at this game.* "If I win, I shall insist that you don't try to rush your recovery. You certainly don't want to suffer a setback." She clasped her hands before her. "Do we have an agreement?"

His mouth quirked upward at the corner, and then he said, "We do."

Excitement coursed through Constance's veins, because in a few short minutes, she would be able to declare victory. But when she was about to crow about her winnings, he played his last trick, which was a trump card to beat anything that she had.

"How can that be—?" And then, coming to the only conclusion that she could imagine, she glared at him. "You cheated!"

He crossed his arms. "I did no such thing. I can't help it if fortune was in my favor this round."

Frustrated, Constance got to her feet, as there was no way she would believe that he hadn't won by underhanded means. She certainly wasn't going to admit that she'd been careless and hadn't paid the attention to the game that she should have.

She gathered the cards and markers and put them back where they belonged, but when she would have reached for the lap desk to put it away, he grasped her wrist, not enough to hurt, but enough that she had to remain. "I wish to claim my prize."

She shook her head. "No."

"But I won. That was the agreement—"

"The only thing you did was prove that you are a cheat and a liar, and I have had my fill of those kind of people."

Instantly, his eyes darkened, all teasing gone, and she knew she'd dared to overstep. "If that's true," he said slowly, "then I'm surprised that you allowed a man of such unsavory character into this house to stay with you." He released her. "You should have just let me die in that filthy alleyway with the rest of the rats and disease-ridden vermin of London."

Constance allowed her conscience to berate her, because truly, she had lashed out unnecessarily. And all over a kiss.

Because that was what she was truly afraid of.

She gathered herself. "Fine. You won. I will not say that I don't honor my obligations."

He snorted. "How kind of you to fulfill your duty on my behalf."

"This was all *your* idea." She tossed her head. "I was just trying to entertain a sick man so that he would stay in bed, because believe it or not, I don't want to witness your death."

He leaned his head back, exposing more of his delicious neck with a day's growth of stubble, along with his tantalizing Adam's apple. "And why should you even care one way or another, Mrs. Hartford?" he taunted softly. "You have no loyalties to me. In truth, I should think you would be glad to see my demise so that I could bother you no longer."

Constance turned away, lest he see the indecision upon her face. It was a question that she'd been asking herself this entire time and had yet to find an answer for. But to satisfy his curiosity, she shrugged a shoulder and said, "Perhaps I wish to prevail upon your good nature, so that when you are recovered you will leave me in peace."

A slow, seductive smile spread across his face. "That, sweetheart, is highly unlikely to happen, as I haven't been 'good' in quite some time." He closed his eyes, likely knowing that his next words would surely disrupt her. "And what's more, you'll be glad I'm not."

CHAPTER 7

"*I*sn't that so, Mrs. Hartford?"

Constance snapped to attention at the sound of her name, although she realized she'd missed the entire conversation that had been buzzing around her. She offered a tight smile to Sir Isaacson and didn't miss the twitch on Lady Blessington's lips. It was as if the countess knew exactly where Constance's thoughts had been wandering.

"I'm sorry. I fear I was woolgathering. Would you mind repeating the question?"

He inclined his head, but she could tell by the lines bracketing his mouth that he wasn't pleased at being ignored, however unknowingly. "I was inquiring about your ill cousin and wondered how *he* was faring. The count assures me the prognosis is good."

Constance slid her gaze to the baronet, because she didn't miss the slight inflection in his tone when he recalled that her "relation" was male. "He is doing quite well. Better every day."

In truth, she had yet to check in on Mr. Blackmore ever since their card game that had ended with him closing his eyes and relaxing in silent repose while she stood there for several minutes wondering if he was truly going to sleep when she had finally agreed to his ridiculous kiss. In the end, she'd left feeling frustrated as if she'd been the one who had been denied a prize. When she'd looked back at the bed and saw him smile—she'd shut the door soundly behind her.

But that hadn't kept her from picturing that coy little grin.

Not only was that annoying, but the man truly was sin personified. She must have not been thinking clearly at all when she'd come up with such an asinine plan as to allow him to recover under the same roof where she slept. For the past two nights since she'd left his side, she'd certainly done little of it.

"You'll be glad I'm not."

Those taunting words had haunted, not only her waking hours, but her dreams as well. A dark mist full of sensual promise would invade her sleep and she would wake up aching for male fulfillment. But instead of rushing down the hall and giving in to Madame Corressa's demands, she had just slipped her hand under the bedcovers and brought herself to completion. While it brought a temporary relief from the raging passion burning through her body, it wasn't long before she was left empty and wanting.

But whenever she thought of using another man for her needs, the fire within her quickly burned out. She wasn't that woman anymore and she couldn't believe that this man that she barely even knew affected her in such a strong way.

Unlike Sir Isaacson.

Even though she knew he would be a willing participant should she just say the word.

As the orchestra struck up a waltz, the baronet smiled at her and said, "I believe this is our dance, Mrs. Hartford."

"So it is." She inclined her head and allowed him to escort her to the floor where several other couples had taken their position.

Constance kept her chin high and a curve to her lips, as if she was enjoying every moment of attention in this man's arms.

Considering this was a moment she'd waited for several years—the approval of society and a suitor who could be a lifelong partner so that she could have some sort of respect after her alter ego, Madame Corressa, had nearly destroyed her self-worth—she found that instead of being filled with satisfaction, she was just as empty inside as she'd ever been.

Once the set was over, she struggled to maintain her composure when all she wanted to do was scream. Instead, she managed to request a moment of air from her companion and headed for the terrace.

Outside, in the warm evening, she gripped the iron railing with her pristine, white gloves. She didn't care if they became ruined. She needed something sturdy to cling to, feeling as if she was floating somewhere in the clouds and no longer tethered to the earth.

She closed her eyes against the sight of the familiar London landscape with its tendrils of smoke climbing into the heavens and gas lamps that flickered in the night and concentrated on her breathing. Alessandro had taught her much about the Indian culture and the pranayama method of how to focus to calm one's mind. She brought her hand up and held one side of her nose, and then the other, inhaling through one side and exhaling through the other. She did this for several moments until her shoulders began to slacken and her heart rate had begun to return to normal.

It wasn't until her final exhale when she opened her eyes that a deep voice murmured, "That was quite intriguing. Dare I even try to decipher what you just did?"

Constance spun toward the opposite end of the terrace where a figure stood among the shadows. But she didn't have to see his face to know who he was. Devin Blackmore. "How dare you! That was a private moment."

"Was it?"

"Yes! Why do you think I was out here alone?" She put a hand to her stomach where the butterflies she'd just calmed had begun to beat against her ribs with a renewed flurry. "It was a breathing exercise to help calm my nerves."

A snort. "I generally just have a scotch."

She lifted her chin. "I'm not a drunk. In truth, I've never really preferred spirits. I've known too many men and women who abuse the privilege."

A brief pause. "How did someone as beautiful as you become so cynical?"

She narrowed her gaze. She wasn't sure if she was being complimented or insulted, but she didn't care to hear either. "You might imagine I've had an easy life, but trust me, women have more trials to hurdle than men ever will. While some women have suffered worse than I, it has only been through my *cynicism* that I am still here today."

Another pause followed that made her grind her teeth together. Finally, he said softly, almost regrettably, "I didn't mean to intrude on your solitude. I just thought you would like to know the doctor came by to see me this evening after you left and he says I'm healing quite nicely."

Some of her frustration faded with the change in topic. She clasped her hands together before her. "I'm relieved to hear it."

He took a few steps forward, not quite into the circle of light, but close enough that she could feel the energy vibrating off of him. "You'll be rid of me before you know it."

She frowned. She couldn't help it. While his presence was unnerving, even now, the thought that he would be gone from her life was just as unsettling. Perhaps even more so. "There's no rush. Besides, if I remember correctly, isn't Granelli still a threat?" She hesitated. "That also begs the question why you're *here*. It can't be safe."

"Always looking out for me, aren't you, sweetheart?" He strode forward and this time the light from the ballroom completely illuminated him.

A small part of her lungs froze at his blatant, sexual appeal. With dark hair tousled by the light breeze, and wearing black trousers, boots, and a partly open, white cambric shirt rolled up to show off muscular forearms sprinkled with a dusting of dark hair, her throat suddenly went dry.

"I—" She was sure she had intended to say something proper, but when he stopped directly in front of her, the heat from his body was too much to comprehend.

"I wonder what I ever did to deserve you," he murmured, as he reached out and tucked one of her curls behind her ear. Shivers instantly danced down her spine. "My angel."

She swallowed, and her gaze was instantly drawn to his chiseled lips. She thought of all the times she'd lain awake at night, yearning for them upon her mouth, her skin... "I'm hardly an angel."

His head angled closer to hers. "But you are mine, aren't you?"

She opened her mouth to dispute his claim, but instead, a rush of breath left her lungs. Her eyes began to drift closed, anticipating the moment when his mouth would meet hers...

"Mrs. Hartford?" She started slightly as a rush of cold air breezed over her, just before Sir Isaacson called her name. "Are you unwell? When you didn't return to the ballroom, I grew concerned."

Constance glanced around the terrace, but there was no sign of her phantom lover. Or he would have been if the baronet hadn't chosen that untimely moment to intercede.

"I'm...yes, fine." She stammered over her own words and while her companion looked at her quizzically, all she could think of was how badly Madame Corressa wanted to burst free.

Pushing her desires aside, Constance took hold of the baronet's arm. "I believe I'm starting to get a bit chilled. Let's return to the party, shall we?"

He scanned the area around them, but eventually he was persuaded to go inside.

~

DEVIN CLENCHED his jaw so tightly that he was surprised it didn't crack as he watched Constance leave with that bastard. If she only knew what sort of man he was...

But then, he supposed she thought the same of him. Nevertheless, for a brief instant, he had believed that he would finally have a taste of those tempting lips.

"Are ye through playin' Romeo? Because we need t' get ye back t' th' house an' bandaged up 'afore yer Juliet returns an' sees tha' ye're bleedin' again."

Devin glared at Luke, where he stood at the bottom of the terrace, just a few feet from where Devin had jumped down to the ground before Sir Isaacson's arrival. But now he looked down at his shirt which held a bright red stain. "If you can shut your trap long enough, I might do that."

He started to stalk away and his friend easily fell into step beside him. "Do ye really think ye'll ever get anywhere wit' Mrs. Hartford?"

"What do you mean?" he snapped, in a foul temper for some reason. He chose to blame it on his wound. He'd never liked feeling helpless or weak and right now, he felt both.

"She's hobnobbin' wit' all them nobles." He gestured toward the townhouse they were departing.

"And?" Devin prompted, even though he should have just let the matter drop rather than engage in an argument with Luke, whom he seldom won against. The was something to be said about being older and wiser and for a man in his sixties, there was little he hadn't seen, or done.

"Either ye're wantin' t' swive 'er, which she won't allow, or ye're dreamin' o' somethin' more permanent which *you* won't allow."

Devin stiffened as he turned to face Luke. Although the man had always been like a second father to him, he wasn't about to stand there and not defend his actions. "Who says I don't want to settle down?"

Luke lifted his brows. "Can ye honestly stand there an' tell me tha' ye'd feel comfortable marryin' a woman like Mrs. Hartford when ye've spent th' last five years o' yer life as a convict?"

Devin clenched his jaw and said nothing.

Luke snorted. "Aye. That's wha' I thought. She don't need anyone th' likes o' us bringin' 'er down when she's tryin' to make a life for herself among th' gentry."

"I would think that's the lady's choice to make and not yours," Devin snapped.

He spun on his heel and intended to put an end to this conversation. Not only was it unsettling, but it was highly irritating. The thought of losing Constance to a man like Brooks was not something he would ever be easy accepting. Besides, it wasn't as if he'd been sent to that island because he'd done something as heinous as murder. He'd merely been a naïve fool to think that he had been able to trust someone like Sir Isaacson. It was only through the pleading of Devin's mistress that he'd been spared death, although later he realized he would have preferred it.

No. His fists tightened at his sides. He wasn't about to relive those dark days because they were over. The five years of hell he'd endured were done and he wasn't about to give that place even more power to disturb his dreams. He'd suffered long enough.

He'd returned to London determined to keep the past behind him, and that was when he'd stumbled upon an angel.

And he would do everything he could to hold on to that blessing for as long as he could.

His sanity demanded it.

CONSTANCE RETURNED HOME SOMETIME AFTER two in the morning. She had never been the type to request servants to wait up for her when she was capable of managing on her own. She removed the key from her reticule and inserted into the lock, latching it behind her, and then quietly made her way up the stairs and to her chamber.

She wanted to ignore Mr. Blackmore's door when she passed, intent on reaching her room without even the briefest glance, but when she caught the light glow shining underneath, she paused, but then forced herself to continue on. She told herself he'd fallen asleep and had forgotten to turn down the lamp. Either way, the idea of checking on him this late was certainly *not* a wise idea.

Constance entered her room and was glad to see that there was a small fire burning in the grate. Even though it was summer, the nights could gain a bit of a chill. But perhaps the shiver that danced up her spine now was merely the thought of her terrace visitor—and the dark, seductive mystery that had pulsed off of him, luring her into his web of pleasure with a mere glance from those dark, mysterious eyes that held more secrets than she did…

She couldn't imagine why he was there or had even taken such a huge risk when Granelli was still out there, lying in wait to finish the job he'd started. But she'd be telling untruths if she said their encounter hadn't thrilled her. If the baronet hadn't chosen such an unwelcome moment to intercede, she might have known what it was like to feel Devin's lips upon hers.

Standing in the middle of the room, Constance felt a light pressure upon her mouth and realized that she'd raised her finger to her lips. She shook her head and told herself that nothing good could come of an affair between her and Devin. She didn't *require* a lover to be happy. She could be quite content on her own and she intended to prove it to herself—to Madame Corressa.

Just the thought of her inner courtesan made some of her passion fade. For years Constance had tried to break free from the hold she'd held over her, the idea that she had to have a man to feel… *worthy*. It had been a shackle she'd fought since she was little more than a child and would likely forever resist against.

Constance kicked off her shoes and took the pins out of her hair, relieved when the heavy tresses fell down her back. She removed her gown and sleeve supports next and hung it over the back of a nearby chair. Most of her petticoats and light bustle followed, but when she was left in her stockings, chemise, and corset, she realized that while she'd never had trouble loosening the laces any other time, tonight was the exception. After several tries, she realized that something was amiss.

She walked over and picked up her hand mirror and, using the larger mirror on her dressing table as a guide, she was aggrieved to see that she had managed to get the laces tied into a knot.

What a conundrum.

With a frustrated sigh, she set her hands on her hips. She supposed she could do one of two things. She could walk down the hall to Mr. House's room and ask for his assistance, but she'd noticed that there was no light shining beneath his door, which meant he was asleep and she would hate to wake him from a sound slumber.

That meant she would have to sleep in the cursed item until her ladies' maid awoke the next morning and removed the thing. It wasn't a very pleasant thought, but the only alternative was—

Not happening.

Madame Corressa would have been more than happy to stroll down the hall and ask Mr. Blackmore for his kind assistance before they tumbled beneath the sheets, but Constance wasn't going to fall for those tempting ploys anymore. She had more will power than to—

She started at the sudden knock at her door. It wasn't loud or even brisque, just a slight inclination, but enough to cause her heart to pound ruthlessly in her chest all the same.

Grabbing her robe from the end of the bed, she shoved her

arms in the sleeves and belted it tightly across her midsection before she calmly walked over to the door and opened it slightly.

She nearly gasped when she saw Mr. Blackmore standing there. With the glow of her lamp illuminating his chiseled face, she was quite spellbound. She also didn't fail to notice that his shirt was partly open, giving her an enticing view of his chest. His midnight hair was disheveled, as if he'd just woken, or perhaps been running his hands through the thick mane.

Either way, her inner courtesan had taken particular notice and was urging her to invite him inside. Constance gripped the edge of the door tightly and remained where she was. "It's late, Mr. Blackmore. Unless it's an emergency, perhaps it might wait until morning."

His mouth quirked upward in a mocking smile. "I would imagine that two o'clock counts as morning, don't you?"

He easily pushed the door out of her shocked grasp and made his way inside. Once the initial intrusion had worn off, she said, "I didn't give you leave to enter my chamber and you certainly don't have the right to barge in here like this."

He quirked a brow at her and strolled about the room as if she hadn't just spoken. She was about to utter a demand that he leave, when he paused by the mantel and picked up a trinket she kept there. "Interesting," he murmured. "I never took you for a collector of nautical items."

"It's a Burghley Nef."

His brows drew together. "A what?"

She reluctantly walked over to where he stood holding the gilt ship. "It's a salt cellar. It's normally placed on the dining table to mark the place of an honored guest."

"Then why don't you put it there?"

She swallowed. "It was a gift from a special friend, so I suppose I treasured the memory more than the original meaning. Besides," she shrugged. "It's not as if I plan to entertain a lot of dignitaries or royalty."

"You never know." He gently set the ship back in its original location, allowing his thumb to linger slightly before he pulled away and glanced at her. "You do seem to be getting on rather well with Sir Isaacson."

She crossed her arms, feeling as though an inquest was coming. "Oh, you noticed that, did you? I suspect you have an opinion regarding the baronet."

He shrugged. "Why would I?" His dark eyes became intent on her. "But I would caution you against getting involved with someone of the upper classes."

"Ah." Constance smiled. "If that's the case, I'm afraid you're a bit late for that. I've had my share of well-to-do companions over the years. I understand the game they play."

He lifted a brow. "Do you?"

"Indeed." She turned away, as the only thing she'd found threatening in several years was her body's response to *him*. "It may vary from time to time, but it seldom alters." Once she felt she was a safe distance, she spun her gaze back to him and added, "Society, especially London society, is full of liars and ne'er-do-wells and while I would like to say it's none of your business who I associate with, I can tell you that when it comes to remaining in England, that is not necessarily a personal goal of mine. I merely joined Count D'Orsay, his wife, and the baroness because it suited me."

His gaze never wavered and Constance wondered what he was thinking. But then, maybe it was best that she didn't know. "I wonder," he uttered softly, "Considering London is a place you seem to dislike, because you don't even speak of England with much fondness, I wonder why you truly *did* return."

To prove that there is more to me than the ability to spread my legs.

The words nearly escaped her before she caught herself. What was it about this man that, not only made her want to lose sense of reason, but her entire sense of privacy? Never had she allowed anyone to have that much power over her. The moment the door had shut behind her at her mother's house, she had made a personal promise to herself and had yet to veer from it.

The very thought of her first home, if it could even be called that, as it was so overrun with vermin and male visitors that it was little more than a brothel of its own, was the one place she had always avoided. And yet, even though it gave her cold chills with the thought of returning there, she knew she had to go there eventually, just to lay those old ghosts to rest. However, she wasn't sure she could make the journey without sour memories rearing their ugly head. She couldn't even say if her mother was still alive after all these years, but if she was and Constance stood face to face with her again, she couldn't say how she would react.

She might even allow Madame Corressa to retaliate, as she was ruthless and the reason Constance was trying so hard to be free of her. She could end up like her mother, a ruined shell of a woman, unless she ignored Madame Corressa and her urgings.

She wrapped her arms around herself and lifted her chin slightly, finally answering his query. "Let's just say I have my reasons." She headed for the door and opened it fully. She stared into the hallway. "Now I shall bid you good evening, Mr. Blackmore."

There was a slight hesitation where her heart threatened to jump out of her chest, it was pounding so hard, but she heard the sound of his slow footsteps approaching. But when she waited for him to pass through her line of vision and depart, he paused so close that she could feel the heat emanating from him. "I have just one more question, Mrs. Hartford."

"Oh?" A tremor passed over her skin and she could feel a slight trickle of perspiration trailing down her spine. "And what is that?"

"Do you intend to sleep in your corset all night?"

CHAPTER 8

*C*onstance froze. "What are you talking about?"

His eyes slowly traveled down her front and then back up to her face. "When you turned away from me earlier, I could see that you had a considerable knot in your laces."

Her mouth fell open. "How could you possibly—?"

He offered a lopsided grin. "With the light from the fire, and that thin fabric, it wasn't hard to decipher that there was a mess of strings underneath." He lifted a brow. "Or am I mistaken?"

Constance shifted her stance. "Well, no, you're not, but—"

"Then turn around." He lifted his hand and used his finger to spin in a circle. "And allow me to assist."

She backed up a step. "I don't think so."

He laughed. "Don't tell me you'd prefer to sleep in that contraption." He shook his head. "I never understood the appeal that women have when it comes to wearing such horrid articles of clothing."

"It isn't as if we have much choice," she snapped. "It's the style that is expected of our sex."

"And here I was under the impression that you didn't conform to the rules of everyone else."

She snorted. "I don't when it comes to making my own decisions, but fashion is another matter entirely. I would be laughed out of the London ballrooms for donning men's clothing."

"I beg to differ."

She stared at him. "Pardon?"

"Haven't you ever heard of a metamorphosis ball? I understand they were quite popular in Russia and that Catherine the Great held several of these parties."

Constance blinked. "What does that have to do with my attire?"

He shrugged. "Merely that, if you chose to do so, you could enjoy the same sort of freedom by convincing your benefactor, Lady Blessington, to host such an event, so that you can eschew such torture devices for at least one evening."

She couldn't help but laugh, the idea was so absurd. "You seem to forget two, very important keys to your suggestion. First of all, Catherine the Great lived more than fifty years ago and second, England society is hardly comparable to that of Russia. I can't imagine such a ball would draw much interest, let alone approval."

His lips twitched, and although he didn't move from his position by the door, she was affected just as much as if he'd reached out and brushed his hand along her cheek. "I bet if you suggest it, your count would be rather impressed." His eyes darkened. "And wouldn't it be a thrill to be able to slide your hand up *my* skirts?"

Constance hadn't blushed in as long as she could remember, but she could feel her face flaming now. "What gives you the impression that I would even consider that?"

"Because you want to have all the power and I'm the man willing to give it to you."

She swallowed heavily, although she tried to keep her tone light. "And you would dare to don a powdered wig and a corset just for me?"

"If I thought it would gain that kiss from you, then yes, I most certainly would."

~

DEVIN KNEW he was playing with fire, threatening to push Constance too far and eventually away from him, but he loved it when her green eyes shone with that inner passion. He yearned to explore it, because something told him that while she might have had her share of lovers in the past, she had never truly reached the full pinnacle of pleasure.

And honestly, the idea of their roles being reversed, where he pretended to be the coquette while she took control, was nothing short of intriguing.

"You're mad."

"For you," he added. His gaze swept her form again, pleased when her face flooded with color once again. Damn, but she was beautiful.

The moment she'd answered the door, his cock had responded instantly to her charm. With those strawberry-blond locks reaching her lower back and curling enticingly near her buttocks, he had imagined that hair covering him in all its glory as he thrust wildly inside of her until they were both completely sated.

"Don't be nonsensical," she scolded, but he didn't hear much conviction in her tone. She turned her back on him and moved her hair out of the way. "Fine," she added stiffly. "If you insist on staying until you've acted as my ladies' maid, then be my guest. I would be more comfortable with it removed."

Devin moved toward her, until the scent of her skin began to tantalize his nostrils. He smiled when a light wave of lilac wafted to his brain. It was as if the sweet flower clung to her.

"You'll need to remove your robe."

"Oh. Yes."

He watched as her hands shook slightly as she removed the item from her shoulders and tossed it aside. He hoped that it wasn't because she was afraid of him. If that were the case, he couldn't abide it. But if it were due to something else…

He resisted the urge to bury his nose against her neck and run his fingers along her bare arms, memorizing every inch of her with his hands, until she was permanently imprinted on his brain. He barely refrained from doing so and concentrated on working to free the knot in her corset ties.

As the seconds ticked past and he struggled with the laces, he could hear her breathing start to turn more shallow than before. The idea that she was as affected by him as much as he was by her was tempting his resolve. It would be so easy to turn her around in his arms and hold her against his chest—heartbeat to heartbeat.

"Are you nearly finished?" she asked in a decidedly ragged voice.

"Almost," Devin returned just as rough.

When the last knot had been freed and the laces were loose enough so she could easily remove the garment, he found that he was reluctant to go. Instead, he dared to reach out a finger and lightly run it along the nape of her neck.

She jerked. "What are you doing?"

"Relax," he murmured, as he dared to take the same finger and run it up the graceful column of her neck, and then adding the rest of his fingers, he gently trailed them along the side of her jaw. Her breathing hitched and a gasp escaped her and he knew then that she wasn't wanting him to hurry because she couldn't stand his touch, but because she *wanted* it.

His cock pulsed with that knowledge and it caused him to grow bolder. With the back of his knuckles trailing down the side of her neck, he then made a path along her exposed collarbone and down the side of her arm, just barely brushing the side of her breast.

She moaned, and her body became lax as she leaned more heavily on him, the corset completely forgotten. He wound his arm around her midsection and brought her backward until she was flush against his front. Without a single word between them, he used his other hand to trail down the other side of her body until it reached the top of her thigh. There he paused, in an unspoken request. In return, her legs moved restlessly, so he took that as a sign to continue.

He slowly took the cotton material of her chemise and lifted it up until the center of her femininity was revealed. The sight of those red-gold curls at the apex nearly sent him to his knees. It was either touch her or expire right then.

He held her close as he watched his fingers creep steadily closer until his index finger swiped up the center of her crease. His cock was hard as granite when he found she was hot and wet, more than eager for his attentions. If that wasn't proof enough, she inhaled sharply and thrust her hips, trying to get closer to him.

He rewarded her by finding the bud within her folds and pressing his finger against it. Her legs trembled as he began a swift rhythm, but when she neared her peak, he would pause. Over and over again he teased and tormented her until she uttered a single word, *"Devin."*

With sweat breaking out on his forehead, and his cock pulsing with urgency, he continued his pleasurable assault on her body until her back arched. Her bountiful breasts nearly spilled out of their confines as her head lolled against his shoulder. Her eyes were closed, the color high on her cheeks even in the dim lantern light, as the orgasm swept over her.

～

BURSTS of light split through the darkness of her lust-filled haze until her lungs had seized and her body was replete. The pleasure continued, wave after glorious wave, until there was nothing left behind but a perfect... contentment. In the past few days, everything that Constance had tried to do to ease the discomfort of her desire paled in comparison to the exquisite ecstasy that he had just uncovered. In her experience, not one of her lovers had caused her to feel such a powerful, earth-shattering experience, but him.

Only Devin.

But now that it was over, with her head still spinning slightly, Constance attempted to find some way to make sense of why she'd allowed this to happen. She supposed Madame Corressa had struck again, and yet, she couldn't find the shame necessary to regret what had transpired.

She slowly stepped out of Devin's embrace, because thinking of him as formally as Mr. Blackmore was quite ridiculous at this point, and turned to face him. She could tell by the hard look on his face and the way his fists were clenched at his sides that he was doing his best to control himself. While she might resist inviting him to her bed, there was something she could do to relieve his discomfort. It was the least she could do after what he'd made her feel.

She dropped to her knees.

"What are you doing?" he said huskily.

She said nothing, merely began unbuttoning his trousers. When her hand brushed against his hardness, he hissed through his teeth. "Constance..."

She wasn't sure if he was pleading with her, or trying to urge her to stop, but once he was free and his girth was jutting proudly in front of her, she leaned forward to lick the large tip, gripping his firm buttocks, and he said nothing further.

Opening her mouth wide to accommodate him, she took his entire length and slowly began to slide him in and out. He made some sort of guttural, incoherent noise, but when she felt his hand gripping a handful of her hair, not hard enough to cause her pain, but enough to let her know he was willing to continue, she popped him out long enough to lick her lips enticingly, and then she began to suck. Each pass she made became faster and faster, until his entire body tightened.

His cock jerked, and she eagerly took in all of his pleasure. She swallowed everything that he had to give, and when he stumbled back a step in order to grasp the back of her dressing table chair, she glanced up at him with a look that she knew held more than a little feminine satisfaction. She ran a finger along the side of her mouth as she rose to her feet.

However, it wasn't until she saw the slight red stain on his shirt that she gasped in alarm. "You're bleeding!"

He shook his head, looking as dazed as she'd been earlier. "I don't care."

"Well, I do," she scolded lightly. She walked over to her washstand and wet a cloth. Once she'd wrung it out, she returned to his side. He had yet to tuck his member away and she was surprised to find that it had yet to soften. Most of her lovers, after they had found their pleasure, were generally lax and ready for bed.

When she would have reached out with the rag, he grasped her wrist. His dark eyes were bright, almost fevered. "I don't believe we're finished."

"Yes," she returned firmly. "We are. In truth, I should have never let it get this far, but maybe now our desires will be sated and we can act as sensible adults henceforth."

He laughed. "If you think for one minute that I will ignore what has happened tonight, you are sadly mistaken." He reached out and cupped her cheek and damn if Madame Corressa didn't stretch with renewed anticipation.

She slapped the courtesan back down. "I fear that's the way it has to be."

He frowned. "Why?"

"Because I don't wish to embark on another senseless love

affair," she snapped. Growing irritated with herself more than with him. "I've had my fill of those."

"What makes you think that's what this is?"

This time it was her turn to laugh. "How can you believe it might be anything else?"

He waved a hand. "What about what we just shared? I don't know about you, but I've never experienced anything like it and I'm sure I've been more prolific than you have."

"I don't doubt it," she murmured, suddenly jealous over all the other women who had been blessed to know this man. And the knowledge that she could never do the same. "But I'm standing my ground on this matter. Sex leads to too many entanglements."

"There are ways around intercourse, as you just saw, and if that's the only way I can have you, I'll feast on you every single night."

A shot of pure lust slammed into her core and she gasped. "Don't say things like that."

"You don't want to hear the truth?" he challenged.

She closed her eyes briefly for patience and said, "Just let me tend to your wound and then perhaps we can both get some sleep."

He lowered his mouth until it was a hair's breadth away from hers. He licked his lips and she could almost feel the sensation on her own. "What if I want to hear you screaming my name all night?"

She looked into his eyes. "No."

His focus dropped to her mouth. "I never did get the kiss you owed me."

"That's not a good idea. Your wound—"

"I'm fine." He took the rag from her grasp and wound her arms around his neck. "Kiss me, Constance."

The sound of her name on his lips was so dark and wonderful and seductive that she nearly gave in to the taunting request. However, she dug down deep and found her will. She removed her arms and stepped a considerable distance away. "Perhaps it would be best if you left and saw after your own injuries."

"But what if I want you to take care of me?"

She walked away from him, saying over her shoulder. "I must decline." She stood in front of the window on the other side of the room, both to put as much distance between them as possible, but also to keep watch of him in the reflection.

After a moment's hesitation, he tucked himself away and buttoned up his trousers. "Someday, you will ask for that kiss, but for now, I'll take my leave of you."

Ignoring the rag she'd offered, he walked out of her room and softly shut the door behind him.

It wasn't until he was gone that Constance's legs began to give way. She stumbled to the bed where she collapsed onto the soft mattress. She thought she did good in acting as though she was unaffected, when her body had flamed anew. She wanted to chase him down the hall and beg him to take her, against the wall if there was nowhere else. Madame Corressa urged her to do just that, but again, she ignored that voice inside of her head.

Instead, she stood up long enough to turn down the covers, and while it wouldn't be nearly as wonderful as the touch of Devin's hand, she brought herself to completion a second time that night, imagining herself with him the entire time.

CHAPTER 9

*D*evin returned to his room in a sour mood. He removed his trousers and took himself in hand almost roughly, as if by doing so, it would remove the wondrous interlude with Constance. When he found his release, it was her mouth he felt on his cock, the tips of her breasts he saw stuck out in hard points as she'd soaked his fingers with her desire.

When it was over, he sat heavily on the bed and winced when his wound pulled uncomfortably in his side. With a curse, he got up and changed the dressing. While the injury still looked red and angry, jagged flesh around the area where it had been sewn together, at least it was free of infection. But then, he wondered if it wouldn't be better if he was unconscious again, as while he was awake and aware of his surroundings, all he could think of was the woman who laid that glorious head down a few doors away.

Once his bandage had been changed and he'd gotten in bed, he threw one arm over his head and crooked one leg out of the sheets as he stared at the ceiling. With two orgasms, he thought his cock would be satisfied enough to allow him to rest, but it was his mind that refused to abate.

He wondered if Constance might take his suggestion for a

metamorphosis ball seriously. It would give him the perfect excuse to spirit her away to some secret room where he could remove *her* trousers and pleasure her with his mouth.

He nearly groaned aloud at the vision, because tonight she'd almost brought him to his knees with her beauty. But while Constance was an angel to look at on the outside, it was her inner goddess that shined through the brightest. For some reason, she was holding herself back from the joy they could find together, as if she had some sort of penance that she had to atone for.

What she didn't know, is that it couldn't be further from the truth. She had saved him from a dark death, had chased the grim reaper away with her determination and kindness to a stranger, while he had done nothing but cause her to be wary of his intentions. He understood she was still hesitant to trust in him when it was obvious that she didn't fully trust any man.

His brows drew together, because if he knew who it was that had hurt her, he might be inclined to pay the scoundrel a call. He sighed heavily. Unfortunately, such actions would only prove that he was a ne'er-do-well that hadn't changed. And he had. He had made that choice when he'd been freed from that terrible island and made the vow when he'd spied a delicate female take charge as if she'd been born into the role of a gentleman.

Constance was a woman like no other of his acquaintance and he would be a fool to push her too far too quickly and lose her entirely. Luke might think that a lady of her ilk could never truly engage in the attentions of a man like him, but Devin intended to prove him wrong, as well as convince her otherwise.

If life had taught him nothing else, he'd learned patience. When days had been as bleak as he'd ever known them to be and he'd looked at the stars and prayed for the peace of death, waking in the morning to be disappointed when it hadn't come, he realized now that it was because he had been spared for a higher purpose. All of his past transgressions had led to this one woman and he wasn't about to squander this chance at happiness when he had endured so much pain to get here.

He closed his eyes with that single thought and found the blessed relief of sleep.

～

CONSTANCE FOUND that she had trouble meeting Luke's eyes across the breakfast table the next morning. It was absurd. Even if she had chosen to embark on a torrid affair with Devin, it wasn't as though she was a child, nor was it anyone else's business but their own.

However, perhaps the reason she couldn't seem to look at him directly was because of the smirk that seemed to be permanently curved upon his lips. Unable to take any more of it, and with the absence of Devin, she set down her teacup a bit too hard. While it didn't break, it did make a decidedly loud clatter in the otherwise, silent room. "Is there something on your mind, Mr. House?"

He casually leaned back in his chair. "Why would ye think tha'?" The smirk remained.

She glared at him. "Because of the way you're smiling this morning. Has something amusing taken place that I'm unaware?"

He shrugged. "I couldn't rightly say." When Constance was sure her teeth couldn't be more on edge, he rubbed his chin and added, "I guess it could be tha' I might 'ave gotten up last night t' check o' Devin an' 'eard 'im in yer room."

"Yes, well." She sat up straighter and said primly, "He was assisting me with my corset. There was a knot that I couldn't get loose."

"Is tha' what it was?" The smug expression turned into a full-blown grin.

She frowned. "It's certainly not what you think."

He held up his hands. "There's no need t' get so defensive. I didn't say a word."

Constance sighed and pushed the rest of her half-eaten meal away. "If you'll excuse me," she said irritably. "I should be going. I have an appointment this morning."

He offered her a mock salute. "I'll take care o' our patient."

She barely refrained from rolling her eyes. Devin was hardly a child that needed continual observation, and yet, the threat from Granelli was still very real and the idea that someone *was* there who cared about his welfare was rather comforting. She just hoped he corroborated her story and wasn't the type to chat about his peccadilloes with the older man.

As she headed for her room to gather her things to depart, she paused by Devin's closed door. Instead of walking past, she decided to knock on the hard wood and make sure he had the same understanding.

When there was a muffled sound to enter, she walked inside and abruptly stopped short. Her mouth instantly gaped open when she saw him standing on a ladder, leaning quite precariously in her opinion, against one of the posters holding up the maroon, bed canopy. She set her hands on her hips. "*What* do you think you're doing? And where did you get *that*?"

He was dressed in buff trousers and a white shirt rolled up to his elbows and glanced at her with an infuriating grin. "Taking a lady's advice."

"I told you to stay in this room and *rest*, not do…" She waved a hand with a huff of breath. "Whatever it is that caused you to climb up on that rickety thing!"

He lifted a brow. "You mean this?" He moved up and down slightly, and she was quite sure her heart ceased beating entirely. "It may not be the prettiest item made out of wood, but it's quite sound, I assure you."

She wasn't satisfied. "I demand that you get down at once!"

He ignored her and turned back to his task. "Calm down. I'm nearly finished."

Her frown deepened. "Just what exactly are you working on?"

"I'm sewing this loose piece of canopy back together," he mumbled, as if he had something between his teeth.

As she drew closer to him, she looked up and saw that he had just bit through a piece of thread. "There." He patted the fabric. "All done."

She blinked. "You can sew?"

He flashed her one of those heart-melting smiles. "And here I thought you would be impressed by my handiwork instead." He turned back to inspect his stitches one last time. "My mother taught me before she passed. After all these years, I suppose her teachings sort of stuck. I might have even been able to close up my own injury if I hadn't lost so much blood."

"Oh, dear." The very image nearly made Constance ill. She waved her hand at him now. "Well, now that you're finished, please climb down from there."

He gave an exaggerated sigh. "Very well."

"And promise me that you won't do anything so dangerous when it could slow your recovery even further," she added firmly.

"Yes, ma'am," he murmured, but there was a decided hint of mockery in his tone.

Constance intended to give him a proper scolding when he reached the safety of the floor, but when he was nearly there, he started to teeter on one of the rungs. She instantly rushed to his side. "You're going to fall!"

"I'm perfectly—"

But his words were cut off when he tilted to the side. Constance uttered a shriek just as he fell directly on top of her—pinning her neatly to the bed.

Her eyes fluttered, because she wasn't entirely sure what had just happened, but now that the danger had passed and she couldn't feel anything but a firm male body pressed intimately against hers, she found it particularly difficult to breathe.

"It looks like you were right," Devin said huskily, as he propped himself on his elbows and peered down at her.

For a moment, she couldn't make her mind function properly. "I… what?" After this morning when she hadn't been sure how she might approach him again, now the previous night's interlude came flooding back into her brain and Madame Corressa was screaming at her to finish what they'd started.

"The ladder," he reminded her with a hint of a smile, as if he too, knew the turn of her thoughts. "It turned out to be quite dangerous. I'm lucky that you were there to catch me."

"Don't be ridiculous," she chided, although her words lacked the necessary conviction. "Now that you have been aptly *rescued*, perhaps you might get off of me?"

"I'm not sure I can do that," he murmured.

She inhaled calmly through her nose. "And why not?"

His brows drew together, as if in concern, but she saw those dark eyes dancing with amusement. "I seem to be feeling a bit lightheaded. It could cause further injury if I were to move too quickly."

She glared at him, his excuses finally catching up to her foggy brain. "I hope you're having fun with this."

He grinned fully now, flashing his even, white teeth at her. "Quite."

She pushed against his hard chest, but he remained where he was. "*Move*," she demanded.

"You're no fun," he grumbled under his breath.

But just as he rolled to the side, the door opened and while Constance expected to see Luke's smug face in the doorway, when she glanced over, the older man was there, but there was also another, unexpected guest.

And when Sir Isaacson glanced from her to Devin, he didn't look very happy at all.

~

All merriment vanished as Devin faced the newcomer. The moment his eyes clashed with the baronet, Devin's fists clenched at his sides. He had yet to forgive the man for sending him to hell. He would have preferred the noose to the place he'd called home the past five years.

He stood by stiffly as Constance scrambled off of the bed. She smoothed her skirts and patted her hair and Devin wanted to snort. Why she might care about how she looked for this man, he wouldn't ever understand.

"Sir Isaacson. I wasn't expecting you to call."

"Yes," he murmured. "I can see that." His focus hadn't yet wavered from Devin's face.

He barely resisted the urge to smile back.

"A... allow me to present my... cousin." Constance stammered, as she waved a hand to encompass Devin.

His lips curved upward. "I understand you've been recuperating." He lifted a brow. "Although it seems you are in rather good health to me."

Devin smiled with a devil-may-care demeanor, knowing that his words would cut the deepest. "That's because I have a particularly lovely caretaker looking after me."

"Indeed." The word was clipped, and Devin knew his barb had hit the mark.

"I assume you've already met my... uncle?" Devin didn't think Brooks had even caught the question in her introduction. "Mr. House."

"Aye. That'd be me," Luke muttered, catching on to the game and reluctantly being a part of it.

"Sir." The baronet barely inclined his head as he acknowledged Luke.

The slight caused Devin's fists to curl even tighter. Brooks might hold an honorary title, but that didn't give him the right to act as though Luke was beneath him. Speech and manners didn't make a man. In the colonies, especially Van Diemen's Land, backgrounds didn't matter. There, they were all equal. There was no class differences. They were all the same—criminals.

"I thought I would surprise you by popping by to check on your… cousin." Sir Isaacson hesitated over the familial connection as he addressed Constance, as if it stuck in his throat. "And to escort you to Lady Hartley's."

"I didn't realize you were attending a ladies' salon. Curious about the latest *on dits?*" she murmured almost flirtatiously.

When Devin frowned, he noticed that Brooks stood a bit taller. "I confess that I was also wishing to see you as well. Perhaps have a chance to talk?"

"Of course. Just let me get my wrap?" She glanced toward Devin, and then excused herself.

When Luke followed shortly thereafter, leaving Brooks and Devin alone, he crossed his arms, ready for the inquest that would surely follow.

As suspected, the baronet wasted no time in demanding, "What are you playing at, Blackmore? Honestly, I'm surprised to see you back in England. I thought the men in the colonies might have taken care of you by now," he smirked.

It was all Devin could do not to let his fists fly and connect with the man's jaw. It was only because of his respect for Constance and her desire to mingle with this world that he refrained, because while Brooks could be utterly ruthless, he still managed to carry a lot of influence in society.

"You would have liked that, wouldn't you? So I wouldn't return and make you wonder if I might enact my revenge on you for being a filthy betraying coward." Devin smiled evenly, placing his barbs exactly where he wanted them to land.

The baronet's jaw clenched with unconcealed fury. "It really is too bad your whore had to plead for your life, letting you escape the hangman's noose." His eyes flashed maliciously and his voice fell an octave. "Unfortunately, the lady wasn't so lucky in escaping me."

Devin stilled. He hadn't thought of the repercussions that might have befallen the charming widow after he'd been sent away. Annalise Coventry, Countess of Tyne, had been very well liked in the *ton*, because of her fashionable salon gatherings. It was only during an attempt to engage her reticule had she met Devin. He had failed to take off with her purse, although he hadn't wanted to steal from this particular lady, because whenever he'd seen her walking along the park paths early in the morning, her expression was always particularly sad.

It was Luke who had encouraged him to make her his mark because he knew of her wealth. It was the older man's job to scout their victims and Devin's to remove them of certain articles. But on that day, he'd wanted to get caught. If nothing else, just to talk to the lady and find out what always caused such a forlorn look.

Surprisingly, she wasn't mad when she caught him, but invited him to sit with her on a nearby bench instead. "Do you know why I walk this path every morning?"

Devin still remembered, with vivid clarity, how she had looked that day. It was a chilly November morning and her breath had fogged before her. She wore a blue velvet cloak that matched the shade of her sapphire eyes and turned her fading, blond hair even more golden. As a man of twenty-five, he'd been rather smitten. Although she wasn't still in the blush of youth, at over forty years of age, he thought she was the most beautiful woman he'd ever laid eyes upon.

Since he had remained silent, she continued, a ghost of a smile on her full lips. "It was my husband's favorite time of day. He would come here and ride every day that the weather would allow." She looked down at her lap with a heavy sigh. "I regret that we were never blessed with children during our union, but alas, it was not meant to be. But I had always been able to deal with the fact I would never be a mother, so long as he was by my side. He's been gone these past three months and I daresay I mourn his loss as acutely now, as I did the moment he took his last breath."

"Death is difficult," Devin had uttered, not sure what else he could say, other than he'd never even considered a future that included a wife and children of his own.

She'd turned to him then, and then after a brief pause, she fished into her reticule and pulled out a guinea. She brought forth his palm and placed it there, closing his fingers around the coin. "Thank you for listening to a sorrowful woman for a time. Perhaps if you meet me here tomorrow, I shall give you another gift."

For weeks, that had been Devin's new routine. Before he set out to relieve the wealthy of London from their precious gemstones and riches, he would go to Hyde Park and linger near the bench where he knew Annalise would soon arrive. Other than the first time when he wondered if she would actually arrive and did, they had started to gain a strangely unconventional friendship.

But one day that all changed.

He could tell Annalise was feeling more melancholy than usual, and that was when she'd confided in him. "I miss his warmth next to me, his arms around me in comfort. I know I must sound terribly silly, as most marriages within society aren't a love match, but for me, he was all I ever wanted or needed."

She had closed her eyes and it was the solitary tear falling down her cheek that clenched Devin's heart. Without conscious thought, he set his hand beneath her chin and leaned forward, kissing her softly on the lips.

Her lids had fluttered open with a gasp and she had merely stared at him, before she made the most heartfelt request, "Again."

This time he exuded a bit more pressure when he'd kissed her and she lifted her hands, clutching at his shoulders. When she pulled back, her breathing was as unsteady as his. "Would you be... averse to coming back to the townhouse with me?"

That day had been the most tender moment of Devin's entire life. He would never forget the care and understanding that had coursed through him as they had made love for the first time. When it was over, Annalise had cried. Not because he had hurt her in any way, but merely because he knew her heart was breaking over her loneliness, and perhaps a bit of betrayal toward her buried husband.

Instead of meeting at the park, it became a silent agreement that he would meet her every morning in her bed, as opposed to the cold, hard bench. For the next several months, their relationship escalated into something deeper than friendship, but not love. Her heart was forever lost, and while she put on a brave face for society, Devin knew the darkest depths of her soul that she kept hidden from view. That is what he did his best to wipe away with his visits, and hopefully, bring the smile back to her face.

Life seemed to be going as well as it could for a common thief, but then Devin had made the mistake of crossing paths with Sir Isaacson. With the promise of a life free of crime, he'd coerced Devin into trying to retrieve something personal that had been stolen from him. In truth, it had merely been a ploy to remove Devin from his way so he would have a clear path to Annalise and her money without any impediments.

Devin could still see the torment in the lady's eyes as he'd been taken away. He realized then that he'd broken her heart a second time and the guilt that had swamped him had nearly brought him to his knees. It was then he vowed never to steal again. If nothing else could honor her memory, perhaps it could be that.

While his life had been spared from the hangman five years ago, he could see the truth in Brooks' eyes that she hadn't been as fortunate.

"What happened." It wasn't a question, because he knew there was no use looking for her—other than in a cemetery.

"I fear it was a nasty spill down the stairs." Sir Isaacson shook his head regrettably, although the smirk on his face told Devin all he needed to know. Annalisa's death had been no accident. "I was surprised when she agreed to my suit in the first place, considering her strong, personal attachment to you, but then later I found out why, which was the reason for her untimely fall." His lips curved maliciously. "I wasn't about to raise another man's bastard."

It was as if the other man punched Devin in the gut, as the pain that followed was pure anguish.

Devin didn't reply, but something must have shown on his face, because Brooks added, "Oh, yes. She was carrying your child, didn't you know? You really should have been more careful." He leaned closer, his nose inches from Devin's. "And it seems as though history shall repeat itself once again. Dear Mrs. Hartford is quite well-to-do, I understand. She will make a lovely replacement, as it is past time that I married again."

Devin knew not to engage, as it would only cause Brooks to feel as though he'd won, but he couldn't resist saying, "I'll see you in hell first."

The sideways smile that followed was pure malevolence. "We shall see. I put you away once before, Blackmore, and although I failed to send you to the noose, I shall not fail a second time. I suggest you remain on your guard, for what good it will do."

The baronet sauntered out of the room and Devin released a slow exhale, although his gaze never left his enemy's back. Not only did he have a personal score to settle with the baronet for his betrayal and those five years in hell, but now he had another motivation—vengeance for Annalise.

CHAPTER 10

Constance was in her sitting room penning a letter when there was a knock at her door. She set down her quill and walked over to greet the visitor.

Her heart began thumping against her ribs when she saw Devin standing on the other side, but it was like that every time she saw him, which was why she did her best to avoid him, if at all possible.

In fact, she hadn't seen him since Sir Isaacson had caught them in a rather uncompromising position. Thankfully, he'd saved her from having to stumble through an explanation as to why Devin had been lying in his bed on top of her, fully clothed or not. Instead, they had enjoyed a nice ride to Lady Hartley's salon, whereas he'd taken his leave with a particularly chivalrous kiss upon her gloved hand. She'd never known the baronet to be quite so charming, but perhaps her mind had been clouded by men of Devin Blackmore's ilk for too long, that she didn't notice a gentleman of stature when he was right in front of her.

She clutched the doorframe as she addressed Devin. "Yes?"

His hands were shoved in his pockets, a considerable frown upon his brow. "I thought we might take a walk."

She realized then that something must be weighing heavily on his mind, as he generally had some sort of seductive comment or look upon his face. In truth, he appeared rather torn over something. "Of course. Just let me grab a shawl."

They walked down the steps of the townhouse and began a slow, but steady progression along the row of shops and houses lining the street. Various people and carriages passed, but they were ignored as Devin and Constance strode in silence. She was waiting for him to speak, while he was likely gathering his thoughts.

He stopped abruptly and faced her. "I know you don't care for my council, and I have no right to give it, but you are making a mistake by encouraging Sir Isaacson."

She lifted a brow. "Am I?"

"Yes," he retorted firmly.

"I see." She rolled his warning around her mind for a moment and then inclined her head. "In that respect, I will be cautious around the baronet, but only if you can give me a reason why, other than your apparent dislike for men of his standing."

His jaw clenched several times before he finally said, "I don't trust him."

She waited, but nothing further was forthcoming. "That's it? That vague warning is all you can say?"

"Yes."

"Then I'm afraid that's not a good enough reason." She shrugged and started walking again, saying over her shoulder, "If you expect me to trust you, then you need to do the same for me and tell me why you feel this way."

She gasped when she found herself moved into an alley beside two buildings. Instantly, the bright sunshine that they had been enjoying turned dismal and intruding, but when Devin trapped her against the brick with his hard body, her breathing hitched with something other than alarm.

"What are you doing?" She hated how breathless her voice

sounded.

"If you won't listen to reason, then perhaps I can get you to listen to this." His mouth descended on hers in a passionate entreaty.

Constance groaned when his hand found her breast. He flattened his palm against her corset and rubbed enticingly. A flood of warmth rushed to her core, where she pulsed with arousal. When he thrust his hips forward and rubbed against her, she had to bite her lip to keep from groaning a second time. "You're not playing fair," she panted.

He moved slightly and she closed her eyes briefly, the flames within burning even higher. "When it comes to Sir Brooks Isaacson, I don't."

"What... do you have against... him? Really?" She flattened her palms against the rough brick behind her, hoping that the harsh surface would keep her brain functioning properly.

"I have several reasons to dislike him." He bent down and nibbled the sensitive skin behind her ear. "But you don't need to hear all the torrid details. Can't you just take me at my word?"

She laughed lightly. "This, coming from a confirmed thief who just served a five-year sentence in Australia?"

He stilled. "Who told you?"

She blinked, some of her ardor cooling somewhat by his tone. "Luke. But I didn't think it was a secret. Perhaps he thought I needed to understand who I was shielding under my roof before I brought you there."

He stared at her hard, those dark eyes chips of obsidian in the dim alley. "So, you believe a criminal like me can't possibly be a good judge of character, is that it? Or you just can't believe me because I'm a commoner instead of someone who holds a title?"

Frustrated by this game of cat and mouse, she put her hands against his chest and shoved, but he remained steadfast. "If you're going to be like this, then you can just release me."

His gaze softened once more. "How would you like me to be,

Constance?" he murmured, and she felt the cool air of her upper leg being bared, followed by the teasing dance of his fingers along the top edge of her stockings. "I can be anything you want."

He swiped a finger along her nether regions and her hips bucked, the memory of his hands upon her flooding back with a vengeance. "Stop teasing me and let me go."

"Never," he whispered in her ear, before he bent down and disappeared beneath her skirts.

At the first swipe of his tongue, her legs nearly buckled, but he had grasped her hips and held her upright with his strong hands. Keeping her in place, he continued to pleasure her with his mouth while she began to see stars dance before her eyes. Everything around them faded, even the fact that they were in a deserted alley where anyone might come upon them, but Constance was so focused on Devin and the pleasure he was giving her, the pleasure she suddenly craved, that she didn't care about anything else at the moment.

When she crested, she leaned her head back against the wall and rolled her hips with the convulsions that continued for several minutes. It was difficult to stay silent when she wanted to scream his name aloud, but she managed to do little more than whimper. When it was over, he reappeared before her line of vision and steadied her when she would have swayed on her feet.

With her breathing still erratic, she stared at him through hooded eyes. "Why are you doing this to me?" It was both a benediction and a desperate plea.

His eyes were bright when they lit on her face. "Because, I have to save you, and if seduction is the only way to do that, then you can be assured I'll be a devoted admirer."

~

CONSTANCE OPENED and shut her fan countless times where she sat in Lady Blessington's drawing room later that afternoon. She couldn't seem to ignore Devin's final warning to her before he'd escorted her back to the townhouse. Although, it wasn't as though she could truly consider his attentions as a *warning*.

That was only how her heart saw it.

"I know that look."

Constance slid her gaze to Marguerite before she forced herself to set down her fan and pick up her teacup. She had been invited over for this intimate chat, and right away the countess had picked up the signal that something was wrong. Blast the woman for seeing more than Constance wanted to reveal.

Nevertheless, she tried to attempt ignorance as she murmured, "And what is that?"

"You have a new lover, don't you?" Lady Blessington looked her up and down, and Constance wondered if she might be wearing a sign that proclaimed her current, lust filled status.

"Actually, no," Constance returned evenly. And while it might not be perfectly true, as she had yet to lay with Devin, she remained firm on that vow that she never would. But after today and the way he'd managed to coerce her into something so shocking, and in broad daylight in an alley next to a busy street, she wondered if that personal promise might soon be broken.

"But *something* has occurred. There's no disguising that look of satisfaction on a woman's face," Marguerite noted, but then she gave a little moue of disappointment. "It's your choice to keep things secret with your 'cousin,' of course, but I thought we were friends who shared a confidence. Tsk, tsk, Mrs. Hartford."

Instead of getting into an argument that might cause Lady Blessington to withdraw her friendship, Constance changed the subject. "Have you ever heard of a metamorphosis ball?"

Her companion laughed. "What a change in topic! But you do know how to divert my attention." She thought a moment. "Do you mean the gender bending events held by Empress Elizabeth of Russia, and her niece-in-law, Catherine the Great? Naturally, everyone has heard about them."

"Do you think you might be persuaded to host one?" Constance asked.

"Here?" At first the lady seemed reticent as she glanced about the expanse of the parlor, which wasn't entirely modest in furnishings or riches by any means, but then she slowly appeared to warm to the idea. Constance could almost see the wheels beginning to churn inside her mind. "It would definitely be the most talked about event of the season and would certainly get me noticed among the circles of the upper echelon," she mulled aloud. "But do you think William might disapprove of his subjects coming to such a scandalous affair? He doesn't appear to be as brash as Prinny was, although I could definitely picture his predecessor coming to the ball dressed in an extravagant gown."

Constance had known Prinny when she'd previously been in London and it was true he had been prone to certain, outlandish behavior. In truth, he quite reveled in it. "While William might be happily married to Princess Adelaide now," Constance noted. "He kept an Irish actress, Mrs. Jordan, as his mistress for a number of years. Together they had ten illegitimate children, so perhaps we are underestimating his ability to enjoy a good-natured affair."

"Hmm. I suppose you're right. I will definitely give it some thought." The lady lifted a brow. "If I address it as a masquerade as well, that might offer a bit of mystery and anonymity to those that might be hesitant to attend. Should we request that the recipients come dressed in Georgian attire to honor the original balls held in Russia?"

Constance instantly imagined Devin standing along the sidelines in a silver sack back dress with a white feathered mask, while she wore a black waistcoat, jacket and breeches with white stockings and buckled shoes. Their eyes would meet from across the crowded room and they would slowly move toward each other, and then slip away to a quiet, secluded room... "Oh, most definitely," she returned in a breathless whisper.

Marguerite clasped her hands together. "I do believe that you have convinced me! I daresay the count and his wife will be over-joyed to see some of these stuffy English dandies turned on their heads."

Again, Constance thought of Devin and how she wouldn't mind if he was horizontal. On a bed. On top of her. "I daresay I'm rather eager about the prospect too."

"What prospect is that?" As the Count walked in and Marguerite began to gush about the upcoming ball, practically speaking as though it was her idea, Constance just let her enjoy the moment. She would be hosting it, after all.

When the countess finished speaking, D'Orsay murmured, "It sounds intriguing. I shall visit the modiste this afternoon and begin looking for just the right fabric."

"No doubt you will be the belle of the ball," Lady Blessington cooed with unconcealed admiration.

Taking that as her cue to depart, Constance bade them both a fond farewell and promised to meet them later that evening to attend Almack's. While Constance had heard that the assembly rooms had started to decline in recent years, the excitement of gaining one of those rare vouchers was still very much alive. In order to achieve entry, one had to impress the reining patronesses whose approval could make or break a hopeful young lady in society. Because of this, Constance was still delighted to have the chance to attend. If nothing else, it would give her a glimpse of everything she had always been denied as a courtesan. But as the Countess of Blessington and Count D'Orsay's personal guest, her entrée was properly secured.

A smile had graced her face as Constance left Mayfair, but as the hired hackney deposited her in front of her current residence, for some reason her spirits started to falter. She had been excited to tell Devin that the countess had agreed to the metamorphosis ball, but then she realized that wasn't what bothered her the most. It was that she was starting to enjoy this little acquaintance a bit too much. It was as if she was already his mistress and this was the home she *shared* with him, as opposed to where she was merely allowing him to stay while he recovered from his injuries.

Constance stopped on the front step and put a hand on the railing to gain some sense of equilibrium. She could *not* go down this destructive path again. Madame Corressa was quickly starting to take control and Constance was allowing it to happen. Desire was once again charging ahead and another section of her soul was being chipped away. If she ever had any hope of recovering anything that she had allowed passion to destroy, then she had to resist the urge to succumb, no matter how much she was tempted by Devin and his wicked charms.

Standing up straight, Constance walked through the front door and climbed the stairs to her chamber. It had been a rather warm, summer day and with the trickle of perspiration trailing down her spine, she was anxious to take a long, soaking bath.

After her maid had assisted her with her clothes, Constance realized how grateful she was for the pump that had been built into the basement, so she didn't have to employ a trail of footmen just to heat water and make several trips upstairs before the tub was finally filled. While she enjoyed the shower bath most of the time, right now she felt the need to relax before that evening's events.

With her hair hanging down her back, Constance sank into the lilac scented water and slowly exhaled as she submerged her body beneath the water, the edge lapping just over the tops of her breasts. The steam quickly made her sleepy and she had difficulty keeping her eyes open. Giving in to the urge to take just a short repose, she leaned her head back against the lip of the tub.

She wasn't sure what woke her, or if she had actually dozed off, but there was no mistaking Devin and his coy expression as he leaned against the wall in front of her and appeared to enjoy the view. His thumb was slowly moving across his lower lip and his eyes were so dark that the pupils nearly eclipsed all the color.

She gasped and reached for something to throw at him. She found the soap and threw the bar at him, which he easily evaded. "Get out of here! Don't you understand *privacy?*"

"Generally, yes."

When he didn't move, she threw her hands up in the air. "Then why don't you practice some of it and leave me in peace?"

He seemed distracted and that was when she realized that, in her frustration, she'd sat up, gaining him a perfect view of the tips of her breasts. She huffed and reached for the nearby linen that had been left out. She stood up and wrapped it around her, tucking it securely under her arm as she stepped out onto the floor.

She would have marched into her bedchamber and slammed the door, but Devin suddenly blinked, as if coming out of some sort of trance. "We have a problem."

"Indeed, we do," she returned sourly. "You can't make a habit of entering my rooms unannounced and *uninvited—*"

He shook his head. "Luke went out earlier this afternoon and hasn't returned yet."

That put a brief halt to her tirade. Over the past few weeks, she'd quite come to respect Mr. House, even if his record as a thief might not normally have recommended his good character, she had never felt threatened by him. "How long has it been?" she asked.

"Almost three hours." Devin said evenly. "He's normally not gone this long."

"Where did he go?" Although she hadn't expected Luke and Devin to remain in the house like prisoners, Granelli and his gang were still out there prowling the streets. While they were staying in a better neighborhood than any of Granelli's men might be expected to inhabit, that didn't mean Luke hadn't been coerced away to somewhere more nefarious.

Or that his gang hadn't decided to keep an eye on their movements.

"He mentioned something about seeing an old friend."

When nothing else was forthcoming, she blinked. "That's it? You didn't question who or where?"

He shrugged. "I understand that it's important for women to know everything, but I have never asked Luke details before. He is allowed to have a personal life beyond me."

"Even when it might be dangerous now?" she gritted out.

Devin lifted a brow but didn't reply as she headed for her bedchamber where she began to go through her things. As she was tossing undergarments on to the bed and riffling through her wardrobe, Devin asked, "What are you doing?"

"Isn't it obvious?" She snorted. "I'm getting dressed and going to look for Mr. House."

"You can't do that."

"Can't I?" she retorted over her shoulder. "You might be reticent to search for him, but I'm not a coward who intends to sit around and do nothing when—"

Her upper arm was grasped roughly, but it wasn't until she looked up into those dark eyes that she gasped, not in fear, although they were flashing with fire. "You're not going *anywhere*," he growled.

"Oh? And who's going to stop me?" she taunted.

"Luke will return."

"If you believe that," she countered, "why did you seem to think there was an issue with his absence?"

His nostrils flared. "Maybe it was just an excuse to see you in all your naked glory, sweetheart."

She glared at him. "That's not funny. Luke's disappearance might very well be serious and you're making a jest like that?"

He sobered instantly. "Luke was like the second father I never had. Being forced to sit here and wait for him to return is not something I prefer to do, but it's the only option we have at the moment."

CHAPTER 11

In all good conscience, Constance couldn't leave the house, considering Luke was missing, so she sent around her regrets to Lady Blessington. As much as she wanted to see the inside of Almack's, it would have to wait for another time.

Dinner came and went, and although the cook had been kind enough to bring them both a tray where they had retired to the parlor, the food had gone untouched. Time seemed to move at a snail's pace as they waited for Luke to return. Thus far, the only sound was the ticking of the mantel clock with the occasional chime to proclaim the passing of another torturous hour.

Devin stood by the fire and stared into the small flames, while Constance paced back and forth in front of the window, anxiously checking on any noise she heard.

She finally sank down onto the settee and rested her elbows on her knees, covering her face with her hands. Tears threatened, but she did her best to keep them at bay. Turning into a watering pot wouldn't do anything but make her eyes puffy and red. It certainly wouldn't help to bring Luke home any faster.

She could just imagine Bow Street knocking on her door with

news of a body found floating in the Thames that needed to be identified…

Needless to say, she felt sick at the very thought.

"Here."

Constance glanced up to see that Devin was holding a brandy out to her. When she looked at him quizzically, he shrugged.

"You look as though you could use it."

She took the glass gratefully and took a sizeable swallow, even though it had been many years since she'd drank such strong spirits. But when her nerves were stretched this thin, it went far to calm her. "Thank you," she said sincerely as he sat down across from her, his own glass dangling from his fingertips.

"I hate this," she admitted.

"I don't particularly care for it," he murmured, taking a sip of his drink.

Constance considered doing something to occupy their thoughts, like playing cards, but she wasn't sure she could concentrate enough to follow through on a proper hand. Not only that, but she couldn't be assured that Devin wouldn't make another ridiculous wager where she had to forfeit a kiss if she lost.

Even though she had yet to actually admit to following through on her loss. But she didn't care to think of that now.

"Tell me about your life," she said, hoping that some conversation might put her mind at ease.

His dark eyes were assessing. "What do you want to know?"

She shrugged. "Anything you wish to share. Just… talk."

After a brief pause, he said, "I hope you don't expect me to paint a fairytale. Most everything I did was in excess. Nothing that could be found in London was off limits." His gaze was intense. "And no one."

Constance swallowed. Instantly, her mind was whirling with the implication of his words. It sounded as though he had been very wicked, indeed.

Something dark and not completely unwelcome swirled in the lowest regions of her body. She downed the rest of her drink and set the glass aside, deciding that it was the alcohol that had caused this sudden change in her body. It surely wasn't because he had just revealed what a scandalous libertine he had been. She would truly have to be deprived to think that such a torrid confession was *appealing*.

"Why did you get caught?" she asked, hoping to move the subject to safer ground.

"I was arrogant, and foolish." His eyes sparked with a delicious inner depth. "When I realized my mistake, that I had been set up, it was too late."

"So, the Mysterious Marauder wasn't quite so untouchable," she murmured.

He lifted a brow. "I see Luke has been telling tales. Trust me, I wasn't the dashing hero that you might imagine. I earned that alias because of how easily I was able to remove valuables from my targets."

She tilted her head to the side. "You were that good?"

His mouth slowly curved upward. "I was."

Constance wasn't sure if it was the brandy that made her bold and sit up straighter, but nevertheless, she offered a challenge. "I want to see this Mysterious Marauder in action for myself." She reached up and touched the choker that she wore around her neck. It was made of pearls with a black cameo in the center. "Can you take this from me?"

He lifted a brow, clearly unimpressed. "Yes."

"I can see some of your arrogance hasn't worn off completely." She continued stroking her necklace. "So, what do you say? I want to see if you are worthy of your nickname." Her lips twitched. "Unless, of course, you think you've lost your touch…"

He rose to his feet. "I'm more than happy to demonstrate my talents for the lady," he said huskily, and something told

Constance that he was no longer talking about his ability as a thief. "Stand up."

"Very well." She got up. "Now what?"

"Go to the mantel." She did as he instructed and saw that he had moved over to the entrance to the parlor. "Now walk toward me and act natural as if we were strangers passing each other on the street."

"Now?" she asked.

"Whenever you're ready."

Constance took a deep breath, feeling suddenly flushed. She never recalled being so out of sorts after a dram of brandy before, but perhaps it had been longer than she'd imagined that she'd enjoyed a drink. Nevertheless, she set her shoulders back, and doing her best imitation of a woman casually walking down the street, she steadily grew closer to Devin, who remained where he was.

When she was almost directly in front of him, she wondered if he was even taking this little *tete-a-tete* seriously. But just when she was about to speak, he reached out and pulled her into his arms. His mouth slammed down on hers and for a moment, she was so stunned that she didn't respond. But as his mouth began to tease and coax hers, the heat that had been threatening turned into a consuming inferno.

She temporarily forgot their little game, as her arms found their way around his neck and she kissed him back with the full abandonment of her senses. Her mind was swimming, intoxicated with his manly scent and the feel of his hard body pressed intimately against hers.

It wasn't until he pulled back with a smug grin that she realized distraction had been his plan all along. He held up her cameo by a single finger. "How was that, Mrs. Hartford?" he whispered.

She cleared her throat and held out her hand for her necklace, which he placed in her palm. "Well done, Mr. Blackmore."

Discomfited, she turned away from him and attempted to reattach the necklace, but for some reason, her fingers were shaking and refused to cooperate with such a simple command.

"Allow me."

The voice drifted across her ear with the slightest breath and she shivered. When his hands lightly brushed her neck, she had to bite her lip to keep from leaning back into his warm embrace.

With the cameo back in place, Devin gently turned her back around. "Would you like another demonstration? Perhaps on the settee? We can act as though you are relaxing in the park."

He glanced toward the green velvet object in question and Constance followed his glance. Her pulse fluttered, but she walked over and sat down. As she resumed her earlier position, her heart was pounding beneath her ribs, anticipation climbing along every nerve ending.

"Are you ready?" he asked softly, as he sat down beside her.

She nodded, and without taking her eyes off of him, she watched as he looked straight ahead. When he finally turned his gaze back to her, she licked her lips, because while this was supposed to be an experiment in his prowess, something told her he was proving a different sort of expertise altogether.

"Do you have the time?"

It took Constance a moment for his words to enter her lust-filled brain, but when they did, she blinked. "What?"

He smirked and repeated the question. "Do you have the time?"

She could feel her cheeks heat. "I'm sorry, I don't."

He casually laid his arm against the back of the settee. "It's not as if time matters when in the company of such a lovely woman."

She lifted a brow. *Surely he didn't think he impressed any woman with such a ridiculous compliment.* She wrinkled her nose distastefully. "You can't expect me to believe something so asinine—"

"Would get me what I want?"

Constance turned to him and was shocked to see that her

necklace, once again, dangled from his fingertips. Instinctively, she touched the area where the cameo would have sat. He truly was a master at his craft. "How...?"

He set the jewelry on a side table. "It's what I did to survive, so I had to be skilled if I wanted to eat and have a roof over my head."

"I admit that was impressive."

"No." He lifted his hand and gently cupped her cheek. "You are the one who is impressive, Constance." His gaze dropped to her lips. "You made it very hard to concentrate on what I was supposed to be doing, when all I wanted to do was this."

Constance moaned slightly when his mouth descended, eager for his kiss. As she focused on the sensation of his lips moving across hers, his tongue flicking in and out of her mouth in a teasing manner that mimicked a very similar, seductive movement of another kind, she wasn't prepared for the shock of his thumb brushing across her nipple. Streaks of scorching hot need shot to every part of her body, from the tips of her toes to the ends of her fingertips, and finally settling in her lower abdomen.

"Devin..." His name was a plea, a benediction on her lips, as he began to trail a path of fire along her exposed collarbone. She told herself that this interlude wasn't going to go as far as it had previously, that she would tell him to stop, but just... not yet. It felt too good and she wasn't quite ready for him to pull away from her.

A slight breeze drifted over her left leg and she knew that he was slowly inching his way to where she burned for him the most.

She held her breath, waiting for the moment when he would touch her...

A door shut somewhere in the house, and although Constance was drifting in a haze, Devin was apparently aware of the disruption. He released her with a muttered curse and shot to his feet, pacing hastily toward the mantel—just as Luke walked inside the room.

It took Constance a moment to gather herself, but once she did, shame washed over her. Here she was supposed to be so concerned over Mr. House, and yet, it hadn't taken more than Devin to kiss her before she'd completely forgotten the older man was still missing.

She stood and smoothed down her skirts, careful to hide her shaking hands within the folds of the fabric. "Mr. House. There you are. I daresay we've both been worried sick about you." She waved a hand toward Devin as if it wasn't obvious who she was referring to.

Luke glanced from her to Devin, who had turned around to face the occupants in the room, although the former wisely remained silent. "Blasted thief. I should 'ave known that 'e wouldn't do what I asked." He exhaled heavily, and then explained. "I told th' lad t' bring a message lettin' ye know that I was goin' t' be late gettin' back."

"Fleeced by a fellow swindler?" Devin noted. "I can't help but appreciate the irony in that."

"Aye." Luke nodded. "It was one o' Maria's boys, so I thought 'e might 'ave followed through considerin' I gave 'im a shillin'." He regarded Constance in all sincerity. "I'm sorry my...errand took...ah...longer than expected."

Constance couldn't be upset with him, especially since his face was practically scarlet and he was doing his best to explain his tardiness with a bit of decorum. "There's no harm done, Mr. House. It's not as if you are a prisoner here. You are free to come and go as you please. But, if you will excuse me, now that I am assured of your wellbeing, I believe I will retire for the evening." She didn't look at Devin as she left.

In truth, she wasn't sure she could meet his gaze without risking a silent invitation to meet her later so that they might finish what they'd started.

~

DEVIN WATCHED Constance walk away with passion still simmering in his veins. If only she would have looked back at him.

Just a slight glance…

But—nothing.

"Do ye mind tellin' me wha' tha' was all about?"

Devin finally turned his attention to Luke. "I don't know what you mean," he hedged.

The older man eyed him tolerantly, although he sat down in a chair by the fireplace where he picked up a book from a nearby table. Devin frowned, as he'd never known the man to read, let alone feign interest in anything remotely resembling a treatise on science. "I told ye t' leave Mrs. Hartford alone."

Devin clenched his jaw. "I believe she's quite capable of taking care of herself, *and* making her own decisions," he added for good measure.

Luke tossed the book aside and crossed his arms. His hard stare was direct and as bold as the beard on his face. "Have ye forgotten Granelli is still a threat? Do ye really want t' drag 'er down into th' mire?"

"I'm not doing any such thing," Devin snapped.

"Then wha' did I walk in on between th' two o' ye jus' now?" Luke countered. "I may be older than ye, but I can still sense tension in th' air an' it was so thick ye could 'ave cut it with a knife."

Devin said nothing, because if there was one person on this earth he couldn't lie to, it was Luke House. He'd known him far too long to withhold the truth, but at the same time, he didn't feel as if he needed to offer a full confession. Let him come to his own conclusions.

Luke frowned and then got back to his feet so he could be on more of an equal level with Devin. Standing before him, he said,

"Ye're jus' as stubborn as ever, ain't ye?" He shook his head. "Jus' know that I won't stand by an' allow ye t' take advantage o' our lovely hostess. Ye'd do well t' remember that If'n if it wasn't for 'er, ye'd already be six feet under, and for tha' alone I owe 'er my loyalty."

Devin snorted. "And you don't feel the same about me any longer?"

Luke stepped even closer, until they were eye-to-eye. "I've known ye since ye were a wee lad in short pants, an' I don't 'ave t' tell ye tha' ye are th' son I never got t' 'ave. What I'm worried about is yer history wit' th' fairer sex. Constance is worth more than a quick tup, so if ye can't keep it in yer trousers, then maybe we should pack up our things an' move on now."

Devin lifted a brow. "That seems rather hypocritical considering you were late returning because of a female *friend*."

"Aye, I was," Luke admitted. "But tha' was a mutual affair an' she knows nothin' permanent will ever come from it. Wha' do ye think ye can offer Constance? She 'as a chance t' make a fresh start, somethin' tha' th' two o' us have only dreamed about." He paused and finally shook his head. "Do ye really think ye can take tha' from her jus' because ye fancy 'er? If ye truly care about 'er, when all this business is over wit' Granelli, ye ought t' let yer angel go, no' tie 'er back down t' a world full of criminals and pickpockets."

Those damning words hung in the air long after Luke departed. While Devin wanted to be selfish enough to keep Constance at his side forever, Luke had made a valid point. Constance had told him that her life had been difficult, and even though Devin didn't know the particulars, he had a good idea of what kind of life she'd lived.

She had only returned to London now in the hope of making a better life for herself, and yet, Devin had pulled her back into the same lifestyle she had tried to escape. He knew that was why she kept holding part of herself back, even though there was a powerful attraction between them. He hadn't wanted to open his eyes to the truth before, he'd merely wanted to hold on to his angel, but Luke had forced him to see it all more clearly.

While it might be like shoving a knife into his chest, Devin vowed that he would release Constance once Granelli was no longer a concern, because he finally admitted that she deserved someone better than him.

CHAPTER 12

The next morning, after a bit of tossing and turning, Constance woke up with a new resolve in place.

After Luke had gone missing the previous night, she realized that it could have been so much worse. While it had merely been a case of miscommunication, next time, they might not be so lucky. Granelli was still a threat, perhaps to all of them and not just Devin, and with his own gang at his disposal, she decided that it was time she sought out her own reinforcements.

No matter how long she had fought to put all of the former nastiness of her past behind her, it seemed that London was determined to draw her back into its evil clutches. To go on unproperly armed was only courting further trouble.

Thus, an eerie calm had settled over her. Madame Corressa had been silent for far too long, but it was time for her to dust herself off and get to work.

Setting out under the pretense of going to see the countess as usual, Constance directed the hackney to another destination.

As the carriage deposited her in front of the gaming hell in the East End, she stood a moment and observed the brick exterior. It had been exactly one thousand, eight hundred and forty-two days since Constance had stood at the threshold of Mont-free's. It was the day she had bidden her old life goodbye in London and embarked on a new adventure abroad.

She walked up to the plain, unassuming door and felt a slight tug at her heart. This moment was bittersweet in more ways than one. She had devoted her life to this place for so many years, even though the protectors she'd had were quite generous in their offerings. Well, most of them, at least. As with many of Grimm's fairy tales, she had always considered her past as resembling that of "The Frog Prince." She'd endured several toads along the way, but had yet to encounter the fictional, handsome prince.

The image of Devin flashed in her mind's eye and she quickly pushed it aside. The Mysterious Marauder was certainly no hero and she was starting to think that she would never be anything more than a courtesan, some man's mistress that he might parade about on his arm until the fine lines on her face began to deepen, whereas she would be cast aside in favor of a new mistress.

She ignored a shiver and raised her hand to knock on the hard wood.

Constance didn't have to wait long before the door was opened and a familiar face appeared. "Hallo, Brutus. It's been a while."

The former pugilist threw back his head with a rowdy burst of laughter. Before Constance knew what was happening, he'd opened the door and had both of his arms around her, crushing her in a bear hug.

She laughed at his apparent enthusiasm, but only when he set her back on her feet and glanced behind her to ask, "Where's tha' devil ye ran off wit'?" did her throat truly close up.

"I'm afraid that Bull is no longer with us," she said somberly.

"Bugger." Brutus' expression turned decidedly downtrodden, but he recovered quickly enough. "I know ye was there for 'im until th' end."

She nodded her head. "I was." She would never forget the

memory of his large hand in hers as long as she lived, nor the bright light in his eyes. After he'd died, she had never felt more helpless in her life, and there had been plenty of times she had wondered where her next meal might come from.

Pushing all of the unfortunate memories aside, she asked, "Is Mr. Plainview in?"

"Aye. He's in th' office. I'd take ye there, but I figure ye know th' way."

"That I do," she concurred. It had been where she'd signed over her share of the gaming hell, with only a slight hesitation as she'd done so.

As she took her leave of Brutus, she walked past the tables where cards, dice, and various other implements of personal damnation were laid out to tempt the downtrodden hoping to turn luck in their favor. Of course, very few ever succeeded.

A twinge of conscious struck Constance, as she had never considered the ramifications of what it meant for those people who had walked away after they had lost everything they had. Granted, she wasn't the one who had held the door open for them, they had entered her establishment of their own free will, but neither had she paid much heed to the regulars—until they were no longer there. By then, it was too late to offer any sort of advice or aid.

She had slept at night merely because she'd told herself this was a business and to keep it running and her own head above water, she had to distance herself from every patron that stepped foot inside. However, that didn't mean she hadn't hated witnessing the destruction when she knew they were headed in that direction.

Climbing the steps to the second floor, she made her way down the hall to a closed door. Not only had she trod these boards beneath her feet countless times in business, it had also been her safe haven, the place where she could go and be alone when the pressures of her second occupation became a bit too much to bear. Not until her partner-in-crime, the other half of Montfree's, had left his separate set of rooms to embark on a journey of love, and who was now happily married with a growing family, did she realize how lonely she had actually been.

Taking a deep breath, as she had known this path was going to be difficult to traverse, but necessary, she lifted her hand and rapped on the closed door. The brusque command to enter was given, and she walked inside to see a desk that was surprisingly clear of clutter and bookshelves carefully in order. The man with the light brown hair had yet to glance up, busy scribbling something down in a ledger.

She lifted a brow. "This place was never as neat when I sat in that chair. You must divulge your secret in case I decide to offer you some competition."

His head instantly shot up, and his hazel eyes warmed slightly as they lit on her. Constance had always thought Mr. Drennan Plainview was anything *but* plain, because even though five years separated them, she could tell that he had kept his physique. With his shirt rolled up past his forearms, she could see the corded strength was still there, as well as those broad shoulders. When he stood up, his waist was still trim, his hips narrow. But while he bestowed a welcoming smile on her as he came around the side of the desk, he sadly didn't make her heart flutter like Devin Blackmore did.

But then, she doubted that he felt anything toward her but a fond acquaintance either, as she was quite sure that he preferred the company of his own sex.

"Well, aren't you a sight for sore eyes?" He embraced her in a friendly manner, pulling back to look her over. She instantly wondered what he saw. She knew not too much had changed since they had last been in the same proximity but looking at one's reflection every day compared to the span of several years could wrought many changes. However, he merely grinned broadly. "Still as lovely as ever with that magnificent strawberry-blond hair." He lifted a brow. "And I'm quite sure just as deadly in her business dealings."

You have no idea. Over the years, Constance had learned how to deal with problems, with lethal force, if necessary. She hadn't wanted to resort to such foul means, but if it meant her life, she wasn't going down without a fight. "Still quite the flattering rogue, I see." She slid him a saucy glance and walked over to sit down in the chair in front of the desk.

"Ah. So, this isn't a personal call," he murmured as he resumed his own seat. He sat back in the leather chair and crossed his arms over his chest. "I admit that my pride is a bit wounded."

She rolled her eyes. "I have no doubt you find enough bed sport to entertain you."

He shrugged. "On occasion," he returned evenly. "But then, you were the one that got away." He put a hand over his heart. "This shall forever be yours."

This time she had to laugh. "You really should be on the stage. I know the only person you truly adore is yourself and the money you make off of Montfree's."

"I was going over the ledgers just this morning, and I admit it has been a good investment since you sold it to me." He leaned forward. "My question is, are you here to try to take it back from me?"

She leaned forward as well. "Not at all. I'm here for something even better."

"And what is that?" he asked, his tone intrigued.

Her smile was slow and steady. "Information. And I know you're the man who can get it for me."

❦

SINCE CONSTANCE HAD RELUCTANTLY MISSED the outing to Almack's in her concern for Luke, she'd promised Lady Blessington that she would join her for a musicale that evening. So, she'd returned home earlier than usual to prepare for the event.

However, it wasn't until she was passing the library, that she heard a slight groan coming from inside. Every nerve ending went on alert as she slowly crept to the slightly ajar door.

And that was when she made the mistake of looking inside.

Her blood began to bubble and boil in her veins, as her gaze immediately flashed to Devin, who stood in the middle of the room with nothing on but a pair of trousers. His torso was bare, and she noted that he no longer required a bandage for his wound. Perspiration coated his broad chest. Muscles stood out in stark contrast on his arms as he lifted himself up off of the floor with his hands, while his entire body was suspended above him.

She watched, transfixed, as he slowly lowered himself until his head was almost touching the hard wood then pushed back up until he was straight once more. He did several various exercises like this, and then he allowed his legs to touch the floor before he jumped up and grasped the top of one of the wooden bookcases, where he proceeded to lift himself up and down.

His methods were so methodical and precise that Constance didn't even realize she was holding her breath until it came out in a rush when his feet touched the floor once again. He turned in her direction and she realized that he must have heard her. Instead of running away, since he'd already caught sight of her staring quite brazenly at him, she pushed open the door a bit further and acted as though it was perfectly normal to spy on one's house guest.

He offered her a curt nod and an equally cool, "Good day," before he returned his attention to the settee.

For a moment, she was surprised. Until now he'd always said something in an attempt to scandalize her. Or at the very least, he would offer her a heated glance.

But—nothing.

Curious, not only about what sort of act he was performing,

but about his sudden change in demeanor toward her, she asked, "What are you doing?"

He paused in what he was about to do and walked over to a nearby table. Picking up a book, he gently tossed it to her. She caught it rather awkwardly, and then turned it over to read the title, "*Treatise on Gymnasticks*' by Friedrich Ludwig Jahn."

She glanced up again and saw that Devin was using the settee to hold himself up. His legs were straight behind him as he used the arm of the loveseat to carry his weight with the strength of his forearms.

And what fine appendages they were...

"Do you perform such... stunts often?" she wondered somewhat breathlessly.

After a brief pause, he lowered himself to his feet and finally paused to face her directly. She was both relieved and unnerved by his sudden regard, as the fire in his eyes was still carefully banked while the slight sheen of sweat that covered his body was particularly... distracting to her peace of mind. "I've only taken it up recently. I found that book and decided to utilize what was around me, since I don't have a false horse at my disposal." He shrugged. "And I thought it would assist in the healing process by making me stronger."

He rolled his shoulders and her mouth went dry. Her gaze was abruptly drawn to every single movement. He truly was the most well-built man she'd ever met. But as he reached over and grabbed his discarded shirt that had gone unnoticed before now, she nearly regretted it, as covering such a virile form was surely a criminal act.

Thankfully, he didn't button the front right away, but kept it partially open as he walked over to her. Bringing his arm up, he leaned it against the wall so that she could gain an even better view of his chiseled torso. If it wasn't for the slightly pink, puckered scar there that reminded her of what Granelli had done to him, he would almost be perfect. Even that light smattering of dark hair on his chest that turned into an enticing trail that disappeared just beneath his trousers was enticing in the extreme.

"Did you need anything else?" he murmured.

"I...er..." *Blast!* She couldn't think properly when he was this close and so... undressed.

"If you recall anything, you know where to find me. I should wash up before lunch is served." His gaze swept over her face and then he pushed off of the wall. Constance stiffened, both eager and reluctant for him to come near, however, he moved past her. At the doorway, he offered her a slight wink. "By the way, you employed a wonderful cook."

～

DEVIN CLIMBED the stairs to his chamber, but it wasn't until he was safely ensconced inside that he allowed his frustration to escape. He clenched his fists and barely resisted the urge to pound his head against the hard oak of the bed post.

How was he going to survive days, let alone the possibility of *weeks*, under the same roof with his angel without touching her soft skin and kissing those delightful lips?

How could he not pleasure her until she was moaning his name?

He knew what Luke would say, of course. That he should just go and visit a brothel to satisfy his needs, but that was only a temporary release. What Devin felt for Constance went far deeper than anything he might find in the arms of a willing whore. There were very few women who possessed the red-gold hair that Constance had, nor did they carry themselves with the confidence of a woman who had seen the world and understood how it worked. She was a treasure, the pearl in the oyster, and the brightest star in the heavens.

And just as unattainable.

Devin tore off his shirt and tossed it carelessly on a chair as he walked over to the washstand in the corner of the room. He gathered some of the cool water and splashed some on his face, hoping that it would cool his ardor, though he doubted it would. However, what Luke had said last night had been quite effective. He might desire Constance to the point of distraction and with a threat to his own sanity, but he truly *did* care about her enough not to put her future in jeopardy through associating with him.

She deserved a man who could protect her from men like Granelli, who could afford to spirit her away to Paris and ensure she was dressed in the best fashions that money could buy.

She needed someone like Sir Isaacson, but Devin would rot in hell before he allowed Brooks anywhere near her. He would not lose his angel to that demon. Annalise had already suffered that fate, but where he had failed with her, he would ensure that Constance didn't meet the same end.

He paused for a moment to think about his former mistress. He hadn't allowed himself a moment to grieve for her loss, not wishing Brooks to have any more satisfaction at his expense. It was bad enough that Devin had allowed him to steal five years of his life away in Van Diemen's Land.

But it wouldn't happen again.

No matter what might occur between Devin and Constance, Brooks would never catch him off guard again. He was made a fool of once, but there wouldn't be a chance for a second opportunity.

If the baronet attempted to send him back to hell, this time, he would be ready.

CHAPTER 13

"*A*h. The loveliest woman in London has arrived."

Constance had to steel herself to turn and acknowledge Sir Isaacson. She'd been fretful of this meeting ever since she'd been caught with Devin in a rather compromising position in his bed. Since she hadn't heard from the baronet since then, she wondered if perhaps his regard had waned. While she wouldn't have cared if it had, as they had nothing but a friendly acquaintance between them, she worried that he might have spread some unnecessary gossip about her "cousin."

However, as she offered him a polite greeting in return, she was relieved to see that the smile he bestowed on her wasn't condescending, nor arrogant. In truth, his striking blue eyes were welcoming, as if nothing untoward had occurred in the slightest.

"Sir Isaacson. What a pleasure to see you again."

He bowed over her hand and kissed the back of her gloved knuckles. "As if I would miss an opportunity to be in your kind presence." He lifted a sandy-colored brow. "I understand this evening's performance shall be quite memorable."

"Indeed?" Constance hadn't yet had the opportunity to check out the musicale program, but the countess had gushed about the performers all the way there as they'd rode in her carriage. She had told her that the viscountess's eldest daughter had quite an impressive voice. "I daresay I'm even more intrigued."

"I hope that you will allow me to escort you to a seat, and perhaps join you?" He held out his arm to her in a silent entreaty.

She glanced at Marguerite, who waved her away with her fan. "Have fun, my dear. The count shall entertain me if I grow bored this evening."

She offered a slight smirk and Constance inclined her head before accepting the baronet's arm graciously. "In that case, I should like that very much, Sir Isaacson."

As they took their seats, he asked, "Is Lady D'Orsay not attending this evening?"

"I heard she was under the weather," Constance said noncommittally, hoping that he wouldn't ask her to elaborate. While she had often wondered about Marguerite and Alfred's rather close, personal association, she didn't wish to add to the rumor mill when it was always anxious to churn.

"I do hope it isn't serious," he returned, although he left it at that.

As the performers began to take their position at the front of the room where a section had been set aside as a makeshift stage, the baronet leaned over and whispered in her ear, "I trust your cousin is faring well."

Constance felt her pulse flutter at the mention of Devin. She wasn't inclined to speak of him, so she said coolly, "Yes. Quite."

"I'm relieved to hear it. Perhaps this means you will be making more public appearances? Or at least, that I will be able to steal you away more often."

She turned to look at him, the slicked back hair and smooth, clean-shaven face that was likely the work of a valet, and she couldn't help but compare him to Devin and the jawline that was struck with a constant hint of stubble.

But more importantly, Constance wondered if Sir Isaacson's

sudden, outward charm wasn't just a way to give her a false sense of security so that he might expose her current situation for the lie he likely knew it was. She decided that he would be worth watching closely, and since she had learned long ago to keep her potential enemies near, she merely smiled and said, "I shall count upon it."

A short time later, after Constance applauded all the performers thus far, the musicale paused to offer the guests some refreshments. As the baronet escorted her to get some punch, he asked her who her favorite was. "I have to agree that the countess was right, and the viscountess's daughter had a lovely soprano." She accepted the cup he offered and took a light sip.

"She is very talented," he concurred. "Although I have to wonder..."

"Yes?" she prompted, although she feared what was coming.

He regarded her steadily. "What sort of talents you might possess."

And there it is. Constance stiffened slightly. Now it all made sense. He had played the part of a gentleman all evening just so he could find a way to indulge her in a proposition. And there was no doubt it was coming. His expression told her that, because she had seen it countless times before. She drank her punch, but the flavor had dulled considerably. "I fear it's nothing terribly exciting, I assure you."

"There's no need to be modest with me, Mrs. Hartford," he returned softly, and then he dared to reach out and run his finger along her upper arm. "Perhaps I should ask your cousin his opinion?"

Her eyes sparked with warning. "That is uncalled for."

"Then surely a small demonstration wouldn't be amiss?" His lips curled upward slightly. "Maybe we can discuss it somewhere more private tomorrow morning."

Constance did her best not to let her revulsion toward his touch show. Although she couldn't keep the impatience out of her voice. She knew she had to agree to this little liaison if she wanted him to keep his silence. Perhaps by tomorrow she would figure out a way to dissuade his attentions. "What time," she said flatly.

"Ten. I'll pick you up in my carriage."

"Very well." She set aside the rest of her drink. "If you will excuse me, I believe that I shall forgo the rest of the entertainment. I fear the punch isn't agreeing with me."

She didn't give him a chance to reply as she went to find the countess, praying that she didn't actually cast up her accounts knowing what tomorrow would bring.

~

CONSTANCE WAS thankful that Lady Blessington didn't ask many questions about her departure, nor argue when she said she would take a hackney back to the townhouse.

When she arrived back at 37 Weymouth Street, she walked in the front door and leaned against the solid strength of the door. Tears stung her eyes, but she ignored them. She had hoped that after Alessandro had died she would finally be free from a man's empty flattery and even more shallow affections, but it seemed that Madame Corressa was not only alive and well but thriving.

"I didn't expect you back this soon."

Constance gasped at the sound of the masculine voice in the darkness. Devin was silhouetted in the doorway of the parlor, but he slowly walked toward her. "I didn't realize you thought it necessary to wait up for me," she countered coolly. "I'm quite capable of looking after myself."

She knew she was being unkind, but after her encounter with Sir Isaacson, she wasn't in the mood to accommodate anyone. Not only was she feeling frustrated and somewhat vulnerable, the sight of Devin's dark, sultry looks and his casual attire, only unnerved her further.

However, it wasn't until he drew closer that she noted he was wearing a dark frown. "You're crying," he said softly.

She instinctively reached up and wiped the moisture from her cheeks. She hadn't realized she'd allowed such a terrible weakness. It wasn't often that she gave in to her emotions, but perhaps the fact that she wasn't a woman in the blush of youth any longer had allowed the tears to fall. "It's nothing," she muttered.

Attempting to leave, she closed her eyes when he caught her arm in a light grasp. It was firm, but not enough to hurt. "Don't lie to me. Something happened tonight to upset you. Tell me what it was."

His tone allowed no argument, but what could she say? That the baronet intended to coerce her into a more intimate situation? As usual, when she tried to scramble for something to say that sounded plausible, her mind was a blank slate. In the end, she gave a heavy sigh. "I don't want to talk about it."

She waited, expecting him to force her to talk. Instead, he held out a sealed missive. "This arrived while you were out, which is why I was up."

Constance nodded, swallowing over the guilt that wanted to swamp her. It wasn't until she broke the seal and read the brief message inside that some of her edginess eased. "It appears that Granelli has taken his leave from London for a brief time, so that is one less problem to contend with at the moment. At least, until you finish recuperating."

"And how do you know this information comes from a worthy source?"

"I spoke with a trusted confidante yesterday," she explained, grateful to turn her mind to something other than the baronet and his upcoming ultimatum. "Not much escapes Mr. Plainview when it comes to the word on the street."

"Mr. Plainview?"

"Drennen Plainview to be precise. He runs Montfree's now, so I knew he would be my best chance for information. It's one of the few places in London that I feel comfortable going without the threat of causing a scandal or a knife in my back."

"And Mr. Plainview offered his assistance to you after five years abroad with no strings attached?"

Constance's eyes narrowed. "I'm not sure I like your tone, *Mr. Blackmore*," she snapped. Her strained patience was abruptly coming to an end. "I hope you aren't trying to imply something unsavory."

He shrugged, but his dark eyes were silently assessing. "In my experience, nothing is seldom free."

"And I don't take well to being accused of doing things that aren't true."

She would have left him standing in the middle of the foyer then, except his voice carried after her. "And yet, you pay a visit to a notorious gaming hell on your own."

Constance slowly turned back around to face him. She strode forward without any hesitation and glared at him. "You seem to forget that I used to *work* there. As a woman, I've done business with more cutthroats and criminals in London than you can even begin to imagine. They knew not to cross me or else they would pay the consequences with their lives. Be cautious that you don't become my enemy."

Since she was within reach, he lifted his arm and touched a lock of her hair. "If I could gain access to all of you, then I will gladly be anything you want."

While Constance had been struggling with her attraction to Devin, after tonight, it wasn't difficult to spin out of his hold. "Don't be nonsensical." She made it to the bottom of the stairs a safe distance away, and only then did she turn back around. "You should know that I won't be around much the next few weeks. I took your advice about a metamorphosis ball and Lady Blessington has agreed to host it, so I will be spending most of my time assisting with the preparations."

With that, she stalked off to her chamber.

~

DEVIN WAS ENSNARED in the throes of a nightmare.

He wasn't sure why his mind had decided to distress him tonight, whether it was the sour way he'd parted with Constance, or the haunting remnants of a life he feared would claim him once more.

Whatever the reason, it had been weeks since he'd suffered the torments of his early days in the colonies, but as he thrashed about on the bed he was transported back in time...

In his subconscious, he was shoved roughly onto the ship carrying transports for the long haul down the Atlantic. His heavy, iron chains bit into the skin of his wrists and ankles, quickly rubbing them raw, as they clanged with his every step across the rough wooden deck.

He was led down a narrow set of steps into a hold that resembled that of a slave ship and forced to sit on a wooden bench next to men who looked at him as though it might be a guess who would actually arrive to their destination alive.

On that ship is where the first battles officially took place. The food rations were few and Devin went to sleep many times with his stomach gnawing with hunger, and that was when he wasn't keeping one eye open with the threat he might be murdered. And it happened often. Either the victim was suffocated or stabbed with a rogue splinter that had become a makeshift knife, as the panic for survival was all too real.

Those that died didn't even have a proper burial. As a criminal already sentenced to die somewhere other than England, their bodies were wrapped up in a section of tarp and shoved over the side of the rail for the inhabitants of the sea to feast upon.

After the first few, Devin stopped trying to keep count, because what did it matter? He would either make it to the colonies alive, or he would perish soon after he got there.

It was inevitable.

Even though he might have been resourceful at picking pockets, it meant nothing the moment he'd arrived on Norfolk Island. In truth, he wished he'd died on that ship, as it would have spared him the horrors that would come…

"Devin! Wake up!"

The voice sounded like that of his angel, but that was impossible. She had never visited him in this hell.

As hands reached for him, he lashed out, caught in between the realm of reality and fantasy. "Shh. It's all right. You're safe here. No one can hurt you."

Not until a slight whiff of lilac surrounded him, followed by the touch of a cool, feminine hand on his forehead, did the horrific images slowly fade and Devin's eyes popped open. He was still wary at first, expecting to see the enemy standing above him, but it was Constance's face staring at him through the torment.

Devin blinked, confused. "Where am I?" he asked hoarsely.

From her position beside him on the bed, his angel spoke again. "You're safe with me. In London," she added, as if for good measure.

Earlier that evening her eyes had held censure, but when those green orbs looked at him now, he saw something far worse —empathy. "I don't want to know what happened to you in those colonies, but I've seen the scars on your back, and then the sound you made just now…" She paused, as if collecting herself. "I've never heard anything like it. It was like an animal in pain—" She shook her head. "I couldn't just stand by and let you suffer alone."

Devin shoved aside the covers and got up on the opposite side of the bed, feeling equal parts foolish and embarrassed that, he'd not only allowed the criminals of his past to return, but that Constance had found him in such a harsh state. Since he slept naked, the trousers he'd discarded were in easy reach, so he hastily slipped them on. As he fastened them, he tried to ignore the way his hands trembled.

Keeping his back to her, he shoved a hand through his hair with a harsh exhale. "I'm sorry to have disturbed you. I'm fine now, so you can go back to bed."

The bed rustled, her footsteps making a whisper of a sound as she moved toward him. "You don't seem fine to me," she said softly.

He closed his eyes, as her breath caressed his shoulder and made him yearn to take her in his arms and pleasure her until she was screaming his name. But he knew that was not what she wanted. Or, at least, it wasn't what she would *acknowledge*. He set his hands on his hips. "It's not wise to taunt me right now."

"That's not what I'm trying to do," she whispered. As she placed a light touch upon his arm, he hissed between his teeth.

"Isn't it?" he growled. He spun around and captured her hands in his. He backed her up against the wall and lifted her arms above her head, pinning her there with his body. His cock was hard, but his emotions were tumultuous as he ground his hips boldly against hers. He wanted to bury himself inside of her, to forget the memories that still swirled around him like a nightmare that he knew would never truly end. "The only thing I want right now isn't something you're willing to give." He released her as abruptly as he'd caught her in his grasp and stalked over to the other side of the room. "Now, I'm not telling you again. *Leave.*"

CHAPTER 14

Constance's throat had been tight when she'd dared to open the door to Devin's room. He'd left his lamp turned down low, which didn't offer much light, but what she saw was enough that it made her stomach clench.

He was lying in bed, but the sheets were a tangled mess about his bare legs, his chest rising and falling with every deep breath that he took. His brow was furrowed and a glistening sheen of sweat covered his body, plastering his dark hair against his forehead.

Her chest had ached as she slowly moved forward, because she knew a desperate cry for help when she heard it. And she hadn't been lying when she said that she'd saw his scars. It had been difficult not to do so when the doctor had examined his wound from Granelli. But she'd wisely not mentioned anything to Luke when those crisscrossed white scars had been revealed. However, her heart had shattered just imagining what he'd gone through.

She also knew it was the invisible cuts that hurt the deepest.

In that instant, Constance made a decision, and there was no going back. "I'm not leaving you like this."

His back stiffened, and he pivoted to face her. He opened his mouth to speak, but she was already undoing the back laces of her blue satin dress that she'd worn to the musicale.

He hadn't been the only one who'd had trouble sleeping that night. In between her upcoming confrontation with the baronet the next morning and the regrettable way she'd acted toward Devin when he had treated her with nothing but respect, her conscience had been gnawing at her for the past couple hours. She'd actually dared to imbibe a bit of brandy to ease some of her anxiety.

Now, as her gaze traveled the length of Devin's strong frame, she brought to mind something even more effective than alcohol when it came to calming a nervous countenance. And if she was going to be forced to entertain Sir Isaacson upon the morrow, then Madame Corressa might as well enjoy one magical night with Devin.

Devin's dark eyes followed every move she made, his nostrils flaring slightly as her gown slid to the floor in a puddle of material, as if inhaling her scent, her very essence from across the room. She allowed her petticoats to follow suit, and once she removed her slippers, she stepped out of the pile. Attired in her corset, chemise, and stockings, she recalled a night not so long ago when he'd touched her so intimately. This time, she wasn't going to tell him to stop.

But when she would have started on the laces of her corset, he uttered a command. "Stop." It was gravely and low, but she heard it all the same.

Constance slowly lowered her arms to her sides.

And waited.

Devin crossed the room and stood before her. He reached out a trembling hand and cupped her breast through the confines of her corset. "You're so damned beautiful," he whispered.

Constance exhaled in a rush and her eyes threatened to close from just that simple touch, but she refrained. She didn't want to miss anything. She wanted to enjoy every moment together, as it would likely be the first *and* last time.

She reached forward and rubbed her hand along his thick, impressive length. She made a noise that sounded suspiciously like a purr in the back of her throat, remembering the girth of his manhood in her mouth, and then the taste as he found his release. "I want this, Devin." She didn't break eye contact with him. "I want *you*."

The muscles of his neck bunched, evidence that he enjoyed her touch, but when the fire would have sizzled in his gaze, he said evenly, "I don't want you to have any regrets."

She reached behind her back and loosened her corset. As it sagged and fell away, leaving only her stockings and thin chemise behind, clearly showing off her tight, pink nipples, she whispered, "Does this set your mind at ease?"

His mouth descended and he captured her mouth in a kiss so intoxicating it was more potent than the finest opium. His hands grabbed her hips and bunched the fabric in his grasp until the hem was within reach, then he left her lips long enough so he could lift the material and toss it aside. He paused, appearing to take in every inch of her nudity. "I was wrong." He swallowed heavily. "You're not an angel. You're so exquisite that I can't even put your beauty into words."

And then she was in his arms again, while his hands roamed over her curves, leaving no spot untouched.

Constance was panting with desire as he got on his knees and used his teeth to remove her stockings. But it wasn't until he licked his way back up the side of her leg that her arousal turned from delicious to almost painful. He was teasing and tormenting her everywhere—but he had yet to reach the one place she most wanted his touch, his tongue, his *cock*…

She vaguely realized that he had lifted her and she was being carried. Not until he gently placed her on the bed, did he slip off his trousers and finally dip his head down to pleasure her. With the first swipe of his tongue, she was lost to the sensation, and it wasn't long before she was pulsing, crying out as wave after wave of her orgasm crashed over her.

She was still delirious with her release as he crawled back up her body, but instead of giving her what she most craved, he tormented her even more until she was tossing her head from side to side, begging him to fill her and ease this ache.

He lifted her legs until they were resting on his shoulders and then he positioned himself at her entrance. "Is this what you crave?"

"God, yes," she panted, as she reached forward and stroked him. "Please, Devin…" A slight bead of moisture formed at the tip of his cock and she licked her lips in anticipation. Instead, with a groan, he began to ease into her, inch by torturous inch, until she became dizzy from the sensation.

Once he was fully inside of her, his pelvis began an exquisite rhythm, rocking against her buttocks, slowly retreating until only the tip of his cock remained, and then sliding back into her slick passage until they were as close as two bodies could be. Over and over again, he kept this teasing pace until Constance was holding her breath and clutching the sheets on either side of her, the hair that had been pinned up in a neat chignon tumbling about her shoulders in disheveled chaos.

It wasn't until he withdrew that she moaned in displeasure. However, when he abruptly reversed their positions where she was holding herself up on her hands and knees while he was standing behind her, her blood begin to boil even faster. She flushed, knowing what was coming and eager for the result as he entered her again. His pace was ruthless, his thrusts faster and more aggressive than before. But it wasn't until he grabbed her hips in a possessive manner, the feeling of his fingers biting into her flesh, that Constance began to quiver around his cock, her second orgasm even more powerful than the first.

As many lovers as she'd taken in the past, this was a feeling like nothing she'd ever felt before—the perfect release of her soul. It was as if she'd actually left earth and soared somewhere among the heavens.

With a low, guttural groan, he left her body and spilled himself on the sheets.

Constance collapsed onto the bed, unable to support her weight any longer, although a slight smile graced her face as she closed her eyes. She didn't even have the strength to open them again when the bed dipped slightly. As Devin gathered her against him, she sighed in contentment. "My love," he whispered, as he swept aside a lock of hair from her face and tucked it behind her ear.

It was the endearment that brought her out of her current trance and back to harsh reality. She was sure that he hadn't meant it in the literal sense, but it was still a dangerous emotion that she had eschewed for many years, ever since the death of her beloved squire that had stolen her heart over the love of his deceased wife. Even then, she wasn't sure if it was love, or just sympathy she'd felt for him when he'd cried on her shoulder over the loss.

Ever since she had carried the guise of Madame Corressa, she had been cautious about who she allowed into her bed, determined that it would be solely about a physical union and nothing else. She'd always held back from giving in to more, because she knew how devastating it could be.

As she opened her eyes and turned to look at Devin, her heart twisted in her chest, for she knew it could be so easy to give him everything—her body, her heart, her very soul—but then all that she had been trying to accomplish would be for naught. Not only that, but he didn't seem inclined to send her on her way. Before, once her lovers had enjoyed their pleasure, they'd bidden her good evening with a light kiss on her forehead for a job well done. The way Devin was looking at her, it was as if she truly was the angel that he believed.

It couldn't be further from the truth.

She glanced away and got up. "I should be getting back to my room." She donned her chemise and gathered the rest of her things.

She held her breath as he followed her and trailed a light finger down her arm. "Can't I persuade you to stay the night here?"

She regarded him steadily. She didn't want to hurt him any further than he'd already suffered in his dreams, but she couldn't remain and pretend that this was anything more than what it was. Someday soon her lease would be up on this townhouse and she and Devin would part ways. Their situation was only temporary.

One night. That was all she had allowed, and it must never be repeated—for both of their sakes.

"I don't want the servants to gossip and have it injure Lady Blessington after she's been so kind. I'm sure you understand." She turned to him and attempted a smile, but she was sure it came out as brittle as it felt.

His hand fell away, his dark eyes unreadable. "As you wish. Good night, Constance."

"Pleasant dreams." She hated how detached and empty that simple comment sounded, but there was nothing she could do but walk out the door.

~

CONSTANCE REMAINED in her room as long as possible the next morning. She didn't like to admit that she was avoiding Devin, but that was what she was doing. She'd even requested a breakfast tray as opposed to going downstairs and seeing the disappointment on Devin's face, or worse yet, the cool detachment in the light of day.

Nor could she withstand the knowing gleam in Luke's eye,

because it wasn't as if she would be able to hide the tension that would likely be between her and Devin—as well as the pleased flush that seemed to be permanently imprinted on her face that morning every time she looked in the mirror. She looked like a woman well loved.

And she still had to face Sir Isaacson.

Constance took a restoring breath and headed downstairs at three quarters after nine attired in a cheery, peach day dress that she hoped could account for the additional color on her face. She entered the parlor and exhaled when she found it to be empty. The baronet would be arriving soon and she wanted to ensure that she had full control of her facilities when he did.

However, when she spied the book sitting innocuously on an end table, heat instantly suffused her, as she recognized it as the one Devin had been reading when he'd been performing those delicious exercises in the library. Just bringing that day to mind likely added to the rosiness of her color, so she hastily averted her eyes.

"Constance?"

She turned at the sound of Luke's voice. They had dispensed with the formalities long ago. "Yes?" She steeled herself for whatever he might say.

"Tha' baronet is 'ere for ye."

Her brow lifted at the resentful tone in his voice. "Something tells me you don't care for Sir Isaacson." She didn't add that she was inclined to believe the same.

"I can't say tha' I do."

Constance was curious now. "Do you mind explaining why?"

His eyes narrowed and his beard twitched, as if he was considering what he should reveal. "I guess it wouldn't 'urt t' warn ye about 'is character."

Every instinct went on alert. "Have you two met before?" she asked.

"Only in passin'," he admitted. "When 'e tried t' 'ang Devin as a thief."

"What did you say?" she breathed.

"Th' baronet promised Devin a large payday if'n 'e did a job for 'im, then deceived 'im when 'e got what 'e wanted." Luke's expression hardened. "It was only due t' Devin's mistress at th' time, who was a countess, tha' 'e was spared an' sent t' Australia instead."

Constance stilled. She had no idea the baronet and Devin had a history. Why had Devin never said anything? Surely he would have thought that to be pertinent information considering the baronet was a current acquaintance in her life.

"I appreciate that you confided in me," she told Luke. "Rest assured, I will ensure that your caution is not in vain."

∾

CONSTANCE WAS CLIMBING into the baronet's carriage when she glanced down the sidewalk and saw Devin striding back toward the townhouse. He looked up and caught her gaze just as she shut the door behind her. After what Luke had just told her, she didn't think it was a good idea for her to linger and allow Devin a chance to tangle with Sir Isaacson.

The gentleman in question tapped on the roof of the carriage and they set off at an easy gait. "Good morning, Mrs. Hartford."

One problem at a time, Constance told herself as she regarded the slick-backed blond hair and piercing, blue eyes of the baronet, who eyed her as though she was a peach, ripe for the plucking. Now she wished she'd worn puce.

But at least now she was under no illusions as to why they were having this chat. "I assume I'm not here to talk about what pleasant weather we've been having lately?"

He smiled. "You are very astute. Which is why I was drawn to you upon your arrival in London."

Constance remained silent, as she wasn't about to tell him she knew this city like the back of her hand—including the sections that weren't that savory.

He reached out and took her hand, rubbing his thumb along her knuckles. "Since I have the feeling you appreciate directness, I was hoping that we might turn our association into something a bit more... exclusive."

She eyed him tolerantly. Luke's warning was still swimming around in her mind, as well as Devin's kiss upon her lips. "What exactly did you have in mind?"

"Oh, come now, *Mrs.* Hartford." She didn't miss the emphasis he put on her title. "There's no need to be coy with me. I know who you really are."

Her heart began to pound. "And who is that?"

He leaned forward and whispered in her ear. "There aren't many people who would forget a lovely face like yours, my dear, but even fewer still who could ignore the talents of Madame Corressa that were bandied about White's." He leaned back slightly in order to gauge her expression, but she kept it perfectly neutral. "There were many who thought you might be the death of old Huntington."

Constance fought to withhold a wince at the familiar name. Lord Huntington was one of the reasons she'd ended her association with English aristocracy and London in general. He had been entirely too tenacious for her tastes, although he showered her with countless gifts. While she had vowed never to entertain a married man again, his wife had enjoyed her share of lovers during their marriage, so Constance had pushed aside her moral compass in favor of the funds needed to keep Montfree's afloat, as it wasn't easy running a successful business. It was only that way with a lot of hard work and dedication. And money.

Constance considered lying, but then realized it would be no use. It appeared that the milk was already spilled at this point. "That's the problem with gentleman's clubs," she murmured.

"There is entirely too much vilifying of women. If any of you had known the old codger at all, you would know that he didn't last long enough in the bed chamber for his health to ever be a concern."

Surprise flashed in the baronet's eyes before he threw his head back and laughed. "You are an intriguing woman, Madame Corressa." She cringed at the use of her pseudonym, because she knew he wouldn't treat her as anything more than a glorified whore now. But perhaps she deserved it for a life filled with drudgery and sin.

Her companion sobered. "I guarantee you wouldn't have that problem with me." She resisted the urge to snort, as every man always liked to brag about his own worth. Even Devin, but in his case, it was actually warranted. "Does this mean you will consider my proposal?"

"As much as I would be honored to be the recipient of such a request," she said. "I fear I must decline it."

He lifted a brow. "Dare I ask why?" He flashed her a grin. "I've heard that I'm quite handsome."

This time she was the one to lean forward. "I don't have fault with your appearance, Sir Isaacson, but rather the way you treated my cousin. Family is very important to me and I don't like them to be disparaged."

"Family, is it?" he noted quietly. "Tell me, what sort of games do you and your cousin play when the sun goes down? Perhaps if you give me a demonstration, I will ensure that he lives to see a new day."

He grabbed her roughly by the back of the head and attempted to shove her face into his lap where there was a decided bulge in his trousers. Constance acted swiftly and had the point of the dagger against that area before she was even halfway down. He carefully released her.

She glared at him. "Shame on you, Sir Isaacson. You are not

comporting yourself in a very gentlemanly behavior. I'm disappointed. Now, instruct your driver to take me back home."

He knocked on the roof of the carriage, and she could feel the shift as it turned around. "Good boy."

His eyes immediately sparked. "You'll regret this, Madame Corressa, I promise you. I'll ruin your precious reputation and expose it for the façade it truly is."

"You can try," she smiled, and dared to dig the point against his trousers even further. While he wasn't excited anymore, his weak, flaccid cock was still there. "Tell me, do you even know how to use this properly?" she asked. No doubt she was making a mistake by goading him, but when faced with men of his ilk, she couldn't resist questioning their lack of manhood. "I bet you can't even make it hard when you need it to be."

His eyes glittered. "Maybe you'll find out someday," he warned.

"Not likely," she countered. "For you see—" She twisted the knife just briefly, but it was enough for him to suck in his breath. "—You aren't the first man I've had to dissuade." She smiled sweetly. "Or dispose of. So, you might be careful who you threaten in the future, because I promise that if you follow through on your threats, I will follow through on mine." With that, she ensured that a drop of blood seeped through his buff trousers before she removed her blade and tucked it back out of sight. "Just remember that I always have a blade at the ready."

They glared at one another across the expanse of the carriage until it rolled to a stop. "This is where I leave you, Sir Isaacson, and I would suggest that you heed my council if you wish to keep all of your…" She dropped her gaze to his trousers. "Appendages fully intact."

She opened the door, but just as she was about to step down to the ground, he ground out behind her, "Indeed, madam, as you should heed my words. You aren't the only one without proper resources."

Constance shut the door and walked up the steps of the town-house as the carriage rolled away. She was even more discom-fited now than she had been the night before when she'd left the musicale, but at least she knew the storm was coming. Which meant it was time for Madame Corressa to put together her own reinforcements. First, she needed to confide in Devin and Luke, so that they were aware to be on the alert, and then she intended to visit the countess, and likely pay another call to Montfree's to speak to Mr. Plainview, as well as engage the help of Brutus. Former pugilists were faithful to their own, and she knew she could count on him because of Bull.

However, the moment she walked inside, it was as if a spark of repetition struck her. Once again, she had to face Devin when her thoughts were scattered. The moment she saw him at the entrance to the parlor, she recalled what Luke had told her about Devin's past with the baronet. It made her even more determined to see Sir Isaacson pay for what he'd done—and ensure that his threats didn't come to fruition, so he couldn't hurt anyone else again.

Before she could say anything, Devin looked at her flatly. "You were out with Sir Isaacson again." His tone was cool and detached.

She sighed heavily, because she knew that he was drawing the wrong conclusion. "Yes, I was, but—"

"I've heard the baronet could be alluring." He crossed his arms and leaned against the doorframe. "But I thought you were smarter than to fall for his charms."

She frowned. "If you would only let me explain—"

"I don't think that's necessary," he murmured, his dark eyes flashing fiercely. "I think I can see where things stand at this point."

"Is that so?" This time, Constance crossed her arms. "Then how about you enlighten me."

"You realized that a thief isn't good enough for you, so you are determined to seek out the attentions of the first man with any sort of title, whether or not you've been warned of his character, just so you can seduce your way into society." He lifted a brow. "How close am I?"

At first, Constance couldn't speak. She had thought that no one could make her feel as cheap and worthless as Sir Isaacson just had, but Devin's harsh accusation cut more deeply than anything she'd ever felt before. And she had absorbed her fair share of insults through the years.

With frustration, anger, and even a bit of shame spurring her on, Constance stalked over to Devin and allowed her hand to fly of its own accord. When her palm connected with his cheek, his head whipped to the side, but his stance didn't alter.

She didn't even wait to gauge his reaction but spun on her heel and slammed the door on her departure.

CHAPTER 15

*D*evin tested his jaw. For a slap, the recoil had been quite impressive.

"Ye bloody jealous fool."

He glanced over to see Luke shaking his head. The older man had been in the library, but by the look of disappointment on his face, it was apparent he'd been privy to the recent exchange.

"If she wasn't payin' for this residence, I wouldn't blame 'er if she didn't even come back after wha' ye said t' 'er." He frowned darkly. "I've never known ye t' be a cruel man, so I can only assume ye're no' thinkin' clearly, but if ye don't want t' lose a woman like tha', then ye best think o' a way t' earn 'er forgiveness."

Seeing as how his opinion had been expressed, Luke headed back the way he'd come, leaving Devin standing alone.

And he realized that was how he would end up if he allowed his emotions to overrule his common sense. *He* was the one who had set out to seduce Constance, and yet he'd accused her of some sort of offense when he hadn't even bothered to listen to her explanation. It didn't help matters that Sir Isaacson was his hated enemy, the man who had destroyed his life, and who had blatantly admitted to murdering Annalise. However, that didn't mean Devin hadn't been in the wrong. He'd lashed out without thinking of the consequences, or how it might have hurt Constance.

After last night, he'd believed that something could evolve between them, but he might have just wiped all of that away with a few harsh words that were impossible to take back.

He shoved a hand through his hair and stared at the floor, considering the best way to fix this mistake, and praying that his actions didn't cause her to run to the baronet just to spite him.

Suddenly, the solution hit him. While it might not completely repair the rift he'd shoved between them, at least it would prove to Constance that he wanted to earn her forgiveness.

He headed off in search of Luke and found him back in the library, sitting in a chair by the fire and staring absently into a glass of brandy. Not until he explained his plan to the older man did Luke stare at him as if he'd lost his mind.

But then, he shrugged. "God moves in mysterious ways, and I admit that I would like to see it."

"Good." Devin clapped him on the shoulder. "Because you get to come with me and pick out the material for the dress."

Luke groaned, but he got to his feet, nonetheless. "I 'ave th' feelin' ye're goin' t' be a hideous woman."

❧

SEVERAL DAYS PASSED before Constance actually allowed herself time to think about Devin. She arose each day with the dawn and returned well after supper when she was sure they wouldn't encounter one another. The countess had remarked that she was spending so much time at her townhouse that perhaps she should just move back in, whereas Constance had remained silent and said nothing in return.

But what could she say?

It wasn't as though she could unburden herself upon the lady, who had enjoyed more than her fair share of peccadillos after her husband's death. In fact, Constance was quite sure that her friendship with Count d'Orsay went beyond a chat in the parlor and might well extend to that of his wife as well, although Constance had never asked, as it wasn't her concern.

Lady Blessington, however, seemed particularly curious about Constance and her love life. But since she wasn't willing to share what she couldn't quite explain, except for the fact she had been hurt by her argument with Devin, she was generally successful in diverting the lady's attention by turning the subject back around to the upcoming metamorphosis ball. Invitations had been sent out to all the higher echelons of society and most had already accepted, quite eagerly as it would seem.

She had also attended several ladies' salons with Lady Blessington, where the majority of the women in attendance spoke of little else. They were quite excited about the prospect of dressing in trousers and buckle shoes from the golden age of Marie Antoinette, before the Revolution had absconded with her head. But mainly, they tittered over women's fashions of the day and how marvelous it would be to see their husbands in a sack back dress and tall, powdered wigs.

"I've already chosen the material for the marquess," one lady mentioned. "A lovely puce to go with my grandmother's amethysts. He shall be the belle of the ball, I'm quite sure!"

A round of laughter erupted as another woman chimed in. "The duke is trying to act as though he detests the idea, but I've nearly convinced him that orange is his color! I'm sure he will look ripe for the plucking with his red hair!"

Constance enjoyed the merriment around her, although her thoughts began to drift as she sipped from her tea and listened to more ladies extol their husband's 'virtues.' She was struck by the vision of Devin's dark eyes flashing as he donned a gown of silver embroidered satin with a row of bows trailing down his front.

But it was the seductive scene that followed that tantalized her the most. She clearly saw the moment when her hand trailed up the inside of his muscular thigh and she grasped the hard manhood between his legs. She flushed just thinking of disappearing beneath *his* skirts...

Such wicked musings were her constant companion, and even though she was still angry at him, each night she still burned with fiery desire for him. It was why she didn't return home until she could be assured that exhaustion would finally overcome her, because she couldn't allow herself to give in to the passionate hunger that tested her resolve. Although she had allowed certain aspects of Madame Corressa's personality to reappear, Constance refused to lose everything to her.

Again.

Thus, she concentrated all of her energy on ensuring that this ball was a success for the countess. If it was, her position within the upper echelon would be further ensured. Even if Sir Isaacson was successful in bringing Constance down, at least her friends would be spared from his maliciousness.

As Constance rode beside the countess in her open landau, enjoying the warm summer day as they made their way to the tailors to be fitted for their masculine attire for the ball, she briefly lifted her face to the warmth of the sun. She wasn't one of those ladies who had ever worried with gaining a freckle or two on her skin. In truth, Alessandro had claimed she looked rather appealing with a bit of color. She had always found the bright rays went far to soothe a melancholy spirit.

"Isn't that your cousin?"

Constance turned to where Marguerite had indicated and her heart skipped a beat when she saw Devin walking along the street with Luke. She frowned, as she couldn't imagine why they might be on Bond Street—

But then she noticed the box he held from a popular ladies' establishment.

The furrow between her brows deepened. "Why would he go there?"

Constance hadn't realized she'd spoken aloud until Lady Blessington leaned across and said dryly, "Perhaps he had some shopping to do?"

Her lips twisted. "At the modiste?" Instantly, her stomach dropped to her feet, as she imagined him buying something for a new love interest. But even then, she had to wonder where he'd gotten the funds for such an extravagant purchase. Constance only went to Madame Elodie's when she was looking to buy something extra special, and it was nearly impossible to make an appointment for an exclusive fitting, as most of them were already reserved for the elite class and members of the royal household.

"Constance?"

She whipped her head around to her companion. "Yes?"

"My, you really are quite besotted with your house guest, aren't you?"

She instantly flushed, her face warming considerably, although she waved a hand. "Don't be ridiculous."

"Ridiculous, is it?" the lady murmured knowingly. "I was speaking to you for five minutes and I'm quite certain you didn't hear a word I said."

Other than being contrite that her attention had wandered to such a degree, Constance was annoyed that she'd allowed Devin the power over her to ignore everything else around her. But him.

"I'm terribly sorry, Marguerite." She reached out and took the lady's hand in hers. "I daresay you have my full consideration now."

The countess rolled her eyes, although she said, "I was just pondering what color I should make my waistcoat. Do you have anything in mind?"

Constance could feel her lips twitch. "I'm quite fond of puce."

The laughter that followed caused more than one head to turn in their direction. She threaded her arm through Constance's. "Oh, you wicked girl! It's why I adore you so."

~

THAT NIGHT, Constance left the countess earlier than usual. She told herself it wasn't because she intended to confront Devin about his trip to Madame Elodie's, that she shouldn't care in the slightest what he did with his time, and yet, as she walked in the front door of the town house they currently shared, the first thing she did was seek him out—considering he was even there.

When the parlor and the library came up empty, she walked up the stairs and saw a light shining from beneath his closed chamber door. She closed her eyes and exhaled a slow breath. She did *not* want to have this discussion in his room, as it was entirely too intimate, especially considering what had happened in there the last time she'd entered his domain.

Somehow, she found the will to straighten her shoulders and glare at the door as if it was her nemesis and boldly knocked on the oak.

She waited.

And waited.

Annoyance began to bubble in her veins. How dare he *ignore* her?

With a huff, she pushed open the door, expecting to see that smug look where he reclined in bed. But it was empty. A quick glance around the room showed the same.

She stilled. Was he even here at all, or had his new paramour been so pleased with her expensive gift that she'd invited him to stay the night?

She was about to spin around and find Luke and demand what was going on, when she heard a splash coming from the closed door of the water closet.

Immediately, her mind conjured up all sorts of images of Devin's naked body, rivulets of water coursing over the hard planes of his chest and the rugged contours of his stomach and legs. Her throat went dry as she imagined joining him in the tub, the slick contrast of their skin causing the water to steam with their passion...

Constance knew she needed to move, that she *had* to leave now, before he emerged from that room, but she was rooted to the spot. Her legs wouldn't obey even that simple command.

She listened as the water sloshed even louder—and then stilled.

Moments later, the door opened and Constance instantly looked away. She finally broke out of her trance and spun toward the exit of his room.

"Leaving so soon?"

Her hand was on the doorknob, but then his dry comment made her pause. *Blast!* When she'd owned Montfree's she'd dealt with men even more handsome than Devin and infinitely more dangerous, and yet, for some unknown reason, she was only discomfited by *this* one.

She clenched her fist and dared herself to turn around and face him, praying that he was properly dressed.

He wasn't.

Her mind went blank as her gaze took in every glorious inch of his strong, muscular body. And she meant *every* inch. His cock was strutting boldly out in front of him, pulsing with energy, although it was his crossed arms and his piercing, dark gaze that held her captive.

"Why are you here, Constance?" It was a softly spoken query, but one that held a decided edge.

She wanted to play the coquette, to play with his emotions as she was accustomed to doing in the past, but even Madame Corressa had quietly shut the door on this interlude. "I saw you today. On Bond Street," she blurted out.

He lifted a lazy brow. "And?"

She gritted her teeth. "What were you doing there?"

He lifted his hand and slowly rubbed the backs of his fingers along his jaw. "Hmm. You expect me to explain myself when I asked the same of you with Sir Isaacson and didn't get the same regard?"

"You didn't give me a chance!" she cried, and then caught herself from saying more. She never lost her composure, and yet, Devin managed to bring out all of the emotions she'd buried deep inside.

"So then, tell me now," he challenged.

Constance opened her mouth, but nothing emerged but a sound of frustration. She lifted her chin, intent on gaining control of herself, as she didn't like this feeling of utter helplessness. It hadn't been in her nature since she was fifteen and the choice of her future had been taken from her with a brief, carnal interlude in a dingy, dirty alleyway. She'd been naïve back then, imagining that what she'd just done wouldn't irrevocably change her entire life, that her mother, who enjoyed the same copulation, would welcome her into the fold, rather than cast her out into the land of the wolves. Since then, she hadn't allowed herself to fully trust in anyone.

For her own security, she couldn't start now.

"It doesn't matter," she returned evenly. "I merely stopped by to tell you that if you choose to engage in any liaisons, then you will have to leave this house. I will not abide rumors to run rampant about my 'cousin' and his nocturnal activities."

Instead of being remorseful, or perhaps confess to any misdeeds, his gaze heated as it locked with hers. "If I didn't know better, I would think you were jealous."

She laughed. "My, but you are arrogant! As if I would care one way or another what you did with who—"

She broke off when his hand lowered and he wrapped his palm around his thick girth. He began to move it up and down the length while keeping his focus entirely on her. "So, I suppose it wouldn't bother you if I pleasured myself in front of you?"

Her breathing deepened, but she said, "Not at all."

His jaw tightened as his pace quickened. She was fixated on his shaft and the shining bead of moisture that appeared at the tip. She wanted to fall to her knees and lick it away, and then take him fully into her mouth until he released himself inside of her, where she could swallow all that he was willing to give her.

The impulse to act was so strong that Constance had to let her nails bite into the tender flesh of her palms as he continued to stroke.

A sheen of perspiration broke out on his forehead and his chest rose and fell as he grew closer to an orgasm. He stared at her the entire time, until he threw his head back as the spurts of his ejaculation burst forth.

It was the most erotic thing that Constance had ever witnessed.

Her lower body thrummed with the urgent need of her own release, but she wasn't about to perform in front of him. She wouldn't give him the satisfaction of doing so.

As he grabbed a nearby cloth and began to clean himself, he said, "I would have preferred to have your mouth there."

"I'm sure you would," she said woodenly. Dear God, she had to get out of here, or the sight of his moderately hard cock would drive her insane. She didn't even care about an answer to her question now. In truth, she'd nearly forgotten why she was even there.

She headed back for the door, but before she could open it, Devin had a hand there, holding it in place.

"Let me go." Her voice was breathless and she detested that he could hear it.

"Not until I see your pleasure."

She shook her head. "That won't happen."

He rubbed his newly erect member against her backside, and

even through her gown and petticoats, she could still feel it. She couldn't hold back a moan. "Damn you," she whispered.

"I was damned long ago, my angel. It's you who is giving me a second chance to live." He grabbed her skirts and started to pull them up. He kissed the side of her neck. "It's only fair, Constance. I love to see you when you're in the throes of rapture and since I know you won't let me take you to my bed tonight, I have to content myself with this."

Constance was trembling with need, her hips yearning to roll with release.

"Please. I'll get on my knees if I must…"

It was the soft plea that made her hand drift lower.

"That's it. Touch yourself, my angel."

She closed her eyes and allowed her fingers to delve where she yearned for Devin the most. He held her dress as she started a familiar rhythm that she knew would carry her over the edge of oblivion.

It didn't take more than a few deft strokes before she was moaning. Her head lolled back against Devin's shoulder and he wrapped his free arm around her midsection to keep her upright, as already her legs threatened to give way. The pressure built and rose until finally, it crested and her body convulsed.

"Yes, that's it," Devin crooned in her ear. "You're magnificent, Constance."

Although seeking her own pleasure wasn't a foreign sensation, Constance had never known her heart to beat so fast and hard before. It threatened to burst out of her chest.

But then, she had never been cradled in the arms of a man like Devin before.

A man that she could easily love.

CHAPTER 16

*D*evin's cock was as hard as before, because he had just beheld something miraculous. The sight of Constance bringing herself to the heights of ecstasy was more arousing than if she'd had her lovely lips wrapped around his member.

As Constance began to breathe normally, Devin reluctantly released her and stepped back. He donned a pair of trousers before he tried to coerce her into doing something more, something she would resent him for.

After days without hardly even seeing her beautiful face, no doubt this hadn't been her plan when she'd dared to enter his chamber that evening. He knew her well enough to know she wouldn't be very pleased if she succumbed to her base desires when she wasn't the one initiating the affair. As a former courtesan she likely wasn't used to trusting people, especially men. He knew the moment he'd stood in the shadows and watched her defend herself against a cretin like Granelli that it wouldn't be easy to win her affections, but beneath that hard exterior, inside still beat the tender, emotional heart of a woman. It had been injured and abused over the years, but he vowed that he would be the one to mend it back together. If nothing else, he owed his unending devotion to her for saving his life. She may not have been the one to stitch his wound, but it was the faithful care she'd shown him that he'd managed to survive.

Granted, he'd made a mistake in earning her regard when he'd cast out that accusation regarding her acquaintance with Sir Isaacson, but he intended to atone for his sins. Already, the gown he'd procured for the metamorphosis ball sat in the back of his wardrobe, along with the personal invitation that Lady Blessington had sent along. He'd been surprised when a messenger had arrived from the countess while Constance had been out. He was confident that Constance hadn't told the lady of their relationship, and yet, he had the feeling she had guessed it all the same, and that she was accepting his suit on her behalf.

It gave him hope that there was someone he might be able to appeal to if Constance remained determined to push him away.

"This wasn't supposed to happen."

Her quiet words shot through Devin's heart because they told him she was already regretting what they had done. Or rather, what they *hadn't* done, as other than holding her when she'd let herself go, he hadn't touched her. He decided to remind her of that fact. "There's nothing to regret, because nothing happened."

She turned to him and the moisture he saw in her haunting, green eyes cut him even deeper. "Don't you see that I can't control myself around you?"

"Is that so terrible?" He kept his tone gentle and empathetic.

She didn't even hesitate. "Yes. Because not only are you younger than me, but our past history is too complicated to build anything more than a brief affair, and I promised myself that I wouldn't become a fallen woman again." She pressed a fist against her chest, directly over her heart. "I can't be your mistress, or any other man's."

He considered what she was saying. "So, you'll live the rest of your life alone?"

"Yes." She spoke hastily, and then a slight furrow formed

between her brows. "No." She put a hand to her forehead. "I don't know. See? I can't even think properly around you."

"I think the problem is you're thinking *too* much."

She sobered. "It's what has kept me alive. I have to consider the next prospect ahead if I want to ensure I have a roof over my head and a decent meal."

"Didn't your last protector ensure that you didn't have to worry about that any longer?" he pointed out. "You can still be independent without losing yourself in the process, Constance."

"But that's the problem," she said. "I've pretended to be someone else for so long, that I don't really even know who *I* am."

"There's time to figure that out." He swallowed thickly and dared to add, "Together."

~

CONSTANCE HELD the tears at bay, but just barely. She yearned to throw herself into Devin's arms and agree to everything that he was promising her. While it wasn't anything more than his friendship, it was still too dangerous to traverse that path. She'd been let down too many times in the past to rely on anyone but herself. Even Bull, the most loyal companion that she had ever had, knew her limits and didn't dare to cross those boundaries.

But the man standing before her didn't see those invisible lines. She wasn't even sure he would heed them if they were drawn out before him.

"I'm not seeing anyone else."

Her glance flicked back to him.

"The only woman I want is you."

Her chest ached and she knew she had to leave or else crumble before him, and she wasn't ready for that. In truth, she might never be able to completely break down the wall she'd built around herself. "I'm relieved to hear I don't have to worry about more unnecessary gossip." *Or competition.*

This time when she moved to go, he didn't stop her, and for that, she was grateful. At least he knew when she needed some time to herself to reflect.

Entering her chamber, Constance paused in the middle of the room, and then she made a decision and walked toward her desk. She sat down and picked up her quill, opened the pot of ink and withdrew a blank sheet of vellum.

For several minutes, the pen remained poised above the paper. She wasn't even sure how to start this sort of inquiry, or even if she was prepared to do so, although she knew it needed to be done. If not, then she truly couldn't move on with the rest of her life.

Not until she knew if her mother was still alive or not.

While she could likely pay a visit to the former residence that they had shared all those years ago, she wanted to know what had happened to her mother before she traversed that dreaded path into the past. She was resilient about many things, but going back to that place, to where her life had changed irrevocably, wasn't something she was particularly thrilled about doing.

Taking a restorative breath, Constance finally allowed the dreaded words to form. Each one of them cut straight through her soul, but she forced herself to continue until a brief paragraph had taken shape.

Before she could stop herself and rip the missive into shreds, she quickly folded it and sealed it with a dollop of wax. Even then, she stared at it for countless minutes, wondering what the reply would be from the investigator. He had come highly recommended by Mr. Plainview, although she hadn't bothered to tell Devin that. He would likely only jump to the wrong conclusions, just as he had with Sir Isaacson.

With a weary sigh, she set the letter on her dressing table where it would sit until morning.

That would give her enough time to reconsider her actions if she chose to do so.

THE COUNTESS of Blessington looked about her ballroom and clapped her hands together in delight. "This will be a masquerade like no other. One that will be spoken of for years to come." She slid a sly glance to Constance. "And it's all due to you, my dear Mrs. Hartford. You have solidified my position in English society by this fete. It's all anyone can talk about."

Count d'Orsay was by the lady's side in a striking yellow waistcoat with green embroidery. "Indeed. I daresay it will be perfectly splendid, even if it will likely take me all that afternoon to powder my face."

Constance couldn't help but snort, knowing the man's penchant for flamboyancy. "That may be, but I bet your costume will be envied by all."

"On that, my dear, you may rest assured." He grinned coyly. "I do have the best reputation when it comes to my fine threads." He bowed deeply to both of them. "Until Saturday evening, my fellow conspirators."

Dipping into a pair of impressive curtsies, the countess and Constance bade him farewell. The latter walked over and threaded her arm through Constance's. "Do you have a partner for the evening's festivities? I daresay it won't be Sir Isaacson. After what you told me about him, I wish I hadn't sent him an invitation. Perhaps he'll cry off at the last minute and spare us all."

While Constance had focused most of her time on the preparation for the metamorphosis ball, the few events that she had attended where the baronet was present, their interactions had been strained and brief, his expression promising her that retribution would come, and that he hadn't forgotten the way she'd insulted him in his own carriage. "One can only hope," Constance murmured, although something told her that he would, indeed, make an appearance. She just prayed he wouldn't make a scene in front of Lady Blessington. "As far as an escort, I will be attending alone, but it's not as if my reputation is in any danger. I will be a gentleman, after all, not some helpless female in need of protection." She offered a wink that made the countess laugh gaily.

"I have no doubt that you'll make a smashing success as a male." The lady lifted a brow and her eyes grew mischievous. "I am anxious to see what you look like in a pair of trousers."

Constance grinned. "Then I shall ensure that I walk directly ahead of you so that you can enjoy your fill."

Lady Blessington's lips twitched. "You are a true diamond in the rough, Mrs. Hartford. I have the feeling all heads will be turned in your direction. I shall have my work cut out for me, I'm sure of it." She opened her fan and steered them out the terrace doors. There, they took a short walk through the gardens.

The lady was quite proud of her flowers, so she was eager to point the new recruits out to Constance. "And my new gardener has been a Godsend." She wagged her fingers as they passed a man bent over a fresh area of dirt where he had just planted a lavender bush.

He turned his head and Constance was struck with a frisson of alarm. She had never lain eyes on the man before, but the way he glanced past his employer and looked directly at her, it just didn't set well. "What did you say his name was?"

The countess put a finger to her lips and thought for a moment. "John? Jacob?" She waved a hand. "You know, I can't really recall. Why do you ask?"

Constance smiled stiffly. "I thought he might have looked familiar," she returned vaguely, as she couldn't very well mention that she was merely being paranoid, that the sixth sense she'd always relied upon was knocking firmly upon her conscience.

To ease her mind, she decided that she would pay a visit to Montfree's to find out if her instinct was still as faithful as it had always been.

However, when she arrived at the gaming hell later that afternoon, Brutus wasn't at his usual post at the front door. When a strange man with a dark expression and hard eyes faced her on the front step with arms crossed, she asked about the former pugilist's whereabouts.

"'E's not 'ere."

His tone was clipped and considering he didn't move aside Constance took that as a hint she wasn't welcome to enter the establishment. Instantly, the fine hairs on the back of her neck prickled in caution. "I can see that. What I'd like to know is why. He's not one to slack his duties."

He shrugged carelessly. "Can't say."

Constance sighed inwardly. *So, it's to be the hard way...*

She removed the pistol that she'd concealed in her skirts and pointed the barrel straight at his chest. His eyes bulged and he slowly lifted his arms in surrender. "Now, let's try this again," she enunciated clearly. "Besides, don't you think it's rather impolite to leave a lady standing outside?"

He quickly bobbed his head and as he backed up, she kicked the door shut behind her with her boot. She glanced around quickly, to see if there were any other brutes that she had to concern herself with, but all was quiet. And during the day, with a popular establishment like Montfree's to be without a single customer—needless to say, it didn't add up.

She tilted her head to the side and stared at him unflinchingly. "You will find I'm not easily dissuaded when I want something."

Again, he nodded, and she could actually see his arms trembling. It was always so easy to decipher the brawny men who were actually cowards beneath all their gruff. "Now, tell me. *Where* is Brutus?"

"'E is...indisposed."

Constance didn't like the sound of that. "Here?" She could almost see the wheels turning in his mind, still weighing his options about whether he should come clean or not. She gave an annoyed sigh and cocked the hammer back. "I'm not asking again—"

He pointed toward the ceiling. "Granelli's got 'im. Upstairs wit' th' owner. In th' office."

"Ah. So, my good friend has returned to London," Constance murmured. "How many more men does he have with him?"

Again, there was a moment of hesitation, to which she stepped closer. He closed his eyes in fright. "Th-three. There's three."

Constance prayed he was telling the truth. Nevertheless, he had served his purpose. "I do appreciate your assistance. But since I can't have you sounding the alarm…" She replaced the hammer on the pistol and turned it around, using the butt of the weapon to strike him in the temple, just like Bull had shown her all those years ago.

He collapsed in a heap at her feet.

Constance stepped over him and kept the pistol steady in her grip. She also withdrew the dagger from beneath her skirts. She'd told Devin that she was never unprepared, and she'd meant it. Too many times this slight blade had been the saving grace between life and death in this city.

It might be the same now.

Since Constance knew Montfree's like the back of her hand, she knew where each step creaked. She kept her back to the wall and snuck up the stairs. She paused just outside the closed office door, grateful to see that there wasn't anyone outside, although it nearly made her snort to see it empty. For someone who was leading one of the most notorious gangs in London at the moment, Granelli didn't know much about fortifying one's keep.

Muffled voices came from inside, and now and again Constance could hear a grunt of pain. She gritted her teeth, as she had no doubt they were abusing Mr. Plainview. Because of her.

She closed her eyes for a moment, as it seemed that circle of hell would never end. She had already lost count of how many times she'd brought danger to her front door. Afterward, Bull had helped her clean up the mess, but it wasn't without a twinge of guilt for putting him in that position to begin with. But as far as the assailants went, it wasn't as if they would be sorely missed. In truth, the earth was better without their presence lingering to further contaminate it.

Constance opened her eyes and allowed Madame Corressa to rise up. She took hold of the door handle and boldly pushed it open. She walked inside with her gun cocked once more and her knife concealed from view, and offered Granelli a wide grin. "Hallo, boys."

CHAPTER 17

"*A*re you sure it was one of Granelli's men?" Devin asked with a frown. They were headed toward the gaming hell where Luke had claimed he'd recognized one of the gang members. Considering it was Montfree's, the establishment that Constance used to run, he didn't think it was a coincidence.

They'd hired a hackney to drop them off about a block away and then chose to walk the rest of the way, ensuring that they blended in with the rest of the crowd meandering about that afternoon.

"I never forget a face an' I'm tellin' ye it was 'im."

Devin's fists clenched. He knew that Constance believed the owner of the club to be a trusted confidante, but he wasn't so sure of that. Most men were adept at lying and they played both sides of the game and sold out to whoever held the better profit. At this point, Constance didn't stand to gain much from a partnership, while Granelli and his men could set up quite a nice money exchange.

He hated the fact that Constance had been forced to lead such a life. She should have been brought up with the finest things money could buy, draped in luxury like a spoiled debutante.

Instead, she had survived the only way many other women did—by offering their bodies up for sale.

It sickened him.

He wished he would have found some way to find Constance first, as he would have done everything in his power to lift her up out of the mire of this detestable city and treat her like the queen she deserved.

He knew she still didn't trust him, nor her responses to him, believing that nothing good could actually come from their time together, but it was his job to ensure that he followed through on his promises and not break them like so many of her former paramours.

Devin snapped out of his musings as they stopped before the gaming hell and Luke knocked on the door. They waited for a time, and then he tried again.

Nothing.

Devin's focus was fixated on the door as he strode forward and pushed it open. It did so without issue. However, it was the large, male body that lay motionless on the floor, a dark bruise along the side of his temple that caused the blood to congeal in his veins.

"Whot th' devil," Luke breathed.

"Indeed," Devin returned. He looked around at the space littered with empty chairs and tables free of any inhabitants and added, "Something's not right here."

"Aye," the older man agreed. "Should we investigate?"

Devin's glance caught something small and shiny on the floor. He walked over and picked it up, holding the item in his palm.

It was a lead ball.

The kind that one would tamp down into the barrel of a pistol.

His mind began spinning, but before he could come up with a direct conclusion, there was a crash above them.

He looked at Luke and together they sprinted toward the stairs.

$$\sim$$

FOUR PAIRS of eyes stared at Constance as she entered Mr. Plainview's office.

Well, three and a half pairs, at least. One of Drennan's eyes was so swelled it was practically shut. She was angry about that fact, but she was careful not to allow her expression to change. It was important not to let your enemies know how they could further hurt you by injuring someone you cared for. And while Mr. Plainview was an acquaintance at best, she didn't wish to see him beaten further.

Her gaze took in each of the ruffians directly, two of which were holding a listless Mr. Plainview by either arm, while the other stood on the other side of the room. But it was the beefy man standing with a cane and the crooked nose that her eyes finally lit upon.

With a smug expression, she said, "Mr. Granelli, I presume?" She gestured toward his cane. "How's the leg doing? I daresay I should have poisoned the ball." She shrugged. "Information I shall remember for next time."

The shock of seeing her had worn off and his lip pulled back from his few remaining teeth in a snarl. "Fate must be smilin' o' me." He patted Mr. Plainview's shoulder. "I was just havin' a word wit' my friend 'ere about yer whereabouts." He waved a hand before him. "And 'ere ye are. I'd call tha' divine providence, wouldn't ye?" His knuckles turned white where they clenched his cane. "An' I wouldn't get so 'igh an' mighty about shootin' me. I owe ye for tha'."

She smiled tolerantly. "I'm sure you would think so, but from my perspective, I see someone who tried to murder one of my good friends." Her eyes narrowed. "I don't take too kindly to that."

He paused for a moment and then said, "Ye ain't talkin' about tha' worthless Blackmore, are ye?" He snorted. "Th' bastard should 'ave been in th' ground long ago." He eyed her with something akin to disgust. "But I see 'e's got ye right where 'e wants ye."

"If he has me anywhere, it's only because I allow it," Constance countered. "I'm not a stranger to London's East End, nor it's dealings." Keeping her pistol firmly aimed at him, while making sure to keep his men in her peripheral vision, she asked, "The question now is, what do you want?"

"Ye haven't figured tha' out by now?" He glared at her with so much spite that Constance would have shivered if she hadn't been stronger than she was. "I want ye six feet under for makin' me lame."

"Oh, come now," she cajoled sweetly. "There's no need to make such a fuss over such a slight wound considering you nearly killed Mr. Blackmore. Surely we can come to some sort of understanding."

He spit at the floor near her feet. "Ye 'ave my terms. An' since I know tha' Blackmore survived, I'll make sure 'e gets 'is due when I'm done wit' ye."

She shrugged. "Why wait?" She cocked the hammer back on the pistol, but before she could take the shot, the man who had been standing across the room barreled toward her. Since she knew she didn't have time to get a good shot, she whipped out her knife and made sure the dagger met its mark.

She could feel the flesh slice open, the warmth of his blood spewing onto her hand as she shoved the tip into his exposed neck. With a grunt, he raised his arm, but she'd already withdrawn the weapon as he stumbled back into the bookcase and fell to the floor—where he stilled.

"Ye bitch!" Granelli shouted. "Ye'll pay for tha'!"

Constance faced Granelli as he reached for a pistol and aimed it directly at her. She dove out of the line of fire just as the ball pierced the bookcase and splintered the wood.

She hadn't yet made it back to her feet when a strong arm was around her neck and squeezing. Her air supply was fading, and Constance knew she had to act quickly if she didn't wish to pass out. She whipped her dagger around and aimed the blade backward. She was rewarded with a howl of pain as the blade found its mark in the middle of Granelli's ribs.

However, her victory was short-lived, as he released her only long enough to deliver a strong blow to the jaw that whipped her head to the side. Temporarily dazed, Constance was attempting to fight off the stars that blotted her vision when suddenly, there was a deep growl, one that sent tremors up her spine as a shuffle began to ensue. She heard the sickening crunch of flesh and bone, the cocking of a pistol, and then the thudding of heavy footsteps running—and then, all was quiet.

"Constance? Are you all right?"

A gentle hand brushed her cheek and for a moment, she was confused. She imagined that she saw Devin's face above her, his gentle hand cradling her cheek, but what would he be doing here?

"Devin?" She blinked several times, and his face finally came into full focus. But instead of throwing herself into his arms, she anxiously looked around the room until she spied Mr. Plainview. "Drennan..." She started to crawl over to where he was slumped on the floor, propped up against the wall behind him.

Devin took her face in his, forcing her to look at him. "Easy, there. Luke is going for the doctor."

She swallowed tightly. "Granelli?"

"That coward ran off with his two thugs, but you can be sure I gave him a few mementos to take with him before one of them took out a pistol." He jaw clenched. "Even then, I would have risked another gunshot, as I have a personal score to settle with

Granelli, but I wasn't sure how you were." He gently touched her cheek and she winced. His dark eyes turned even darker. "Devil take it. I should have broken his damned neck."

Constance shook her head. "I'm glad you didn't." She forced a smile, even though it hurt to do so. "I'm not sure I could have dealt with your arrogance should I had to take care of you a second time."

Finally, he grinned, his dark eyes losing some of their malice. "You know you loved every minute of it."

There was a brief pause, and then Constance admitted, "Yes. I actually did."

~

IT WASN'T the declaration of adoration that Devin might have hoped for, but he knew it was a lot for her to even admit that much of her feelings. He stood and offered her a hand. When she joined him, wavering slightly on her feet, he steadied her with an arm wrapped around her waist.

She tested her jaw. "Goodness, who would have thought such an imbecile could actually throw a punch?" Suddenly, she stiffened. "Oh, my God. I nearly forgot about Brutus." She clutched Devin's arm in alarm. "The man downstairs… he said that he was here somewhere."

Devin cupped her cheek. "You stay here. I'll go look for him."

He was glad when she didn't dispute the order but gave in to the command.

As he walked out into the hallway, Luke was coming up the stairs with a man carrying a black bag. Once he had been directed to the office to look after Constance and Mr. Plainview, Luke joined him. "'Ow is she?"

"Resilient." It was the only thing Devin could think of that truly suited the lady. "Come on. We need to find the doorman."

It didn't take long for them to find the bouncer, because even though he was gagged and tied up in a closet near the opposite end of the hallway, he wasn't quiet about the fact as he struggled with his bindings. When they opened the door, he glared at them furiously, until Devin reassured him that they were there to help.

Once the gag was removed, he let loose a curse. "Damned bastards," he muttered. Only when he rose to his feet did Devin realize he could be a formidable ally. In truth, he found it hard to believe that Granelli and his crew had gotten the drop on him. He had to outweigh Granelli by at least two stone.

He held out his hand to the man. "My name is Devin Blackmore and this is Luke House." The latter inclined his head. "We may have a proposition for you in the near future if you're willing to join forces."

Brutus clenched his fists and held up the scarred knuckles that had witnessed many battles over the years. "If it means I get t' use these, then I'm ready when ye are."

Devin smiled. He had always admired brawny comrades. "Good."

As Devin led the way back to the office, he found Constance sitting by Mr. Plainview as the doctor appeared to finish up his examination. However, she excused herself and walked over to them. "Brutus. Thank God." She embraced the former pugilist, and then spoke in a low tone to all of them. "I fear Drennan is in a sorry state. His nose appears to be broken and perhaps a few ribs."

Devin said nothing about the injuries, because he could sympathize. He'd been through the ringer a few times in the past. "Did he say why they were here?"

Constance looked grim. "After they dealt with Brutus, they ordered everyone out. Apparently, Mr. Plainview hasn't been quite as adept at keeping his ledgers as he would have had me believe. He owes Granelli quite a large sum of money. He was here to collect."

While Devin had seen the same thing happen time and time

again, men getting involved with crooks who promised heaven itself for a small barter in return, not knowing that the exchange was more than they would have ever bargained for if they hadn't been so desperate for a change in their circumstances.

"He can't stay here," Constance said. "I'm going to convince him to come back to Marylebone with us."

He agreed that it wouldn't be wise for Mr. Plainview to remain at Montfree's where he could be visited again, this time with more dire consequences, but at the same time Devin didn't particularly care for the idea that one of her admirers would be staying under the same roof.

"'E can share my room," Luke offered.

"Thank you. That's very kind of you." Those green eyes looked at him as if he'd hung the moon, and the effect wasn't lost on the older man, as Devin swore that he stood up a bit taller.

"What about you, Brutus?" She addressed the brawny man. "I fear that Montfree's is going to have to take a brief hiatus, so you won't have any employment for a time."

Bloody hell. Devin didn't like how the house was filling up with former vagrants when all he wanted to do was keep Constance all to himself, but he had to admire her for being so compassionate.

However, Brutus declined the offer. "I 'ave my own lodgin's."

"Do you feel safe there?" she asked.

He grinned broadly and his gap-toothed grin was almost terrifying. "No one dares t' bother me 'n my 'ouse if they want t' live t' see another day."

Instead of appearing shocked, Constance laughed. "Of course. I should have known better than to doubt you."

As the doctor departed, leaving behind some medicine for Mr. Plainview, as well as ensuring that his ribs were properly wrapped, he got to his feet with a grimace. But when his swollen gaze lit on Constance, the one visible eye looked at her in a forlorn manner. Devin recognized that expression all too well. Guilt.

"I'm sorry for lying and for not taking proper care of Montfree's like I'd promised you."

Constance put a hand on his shoulder. "Don't worry about that now. You just focus on getting well and we'll discuss things another time."

He hung his head, out of weariness or shame, Devin wasn't sure which, and gave a slight nod.

"Good." She put an arm around him for support and said gently, "Now let's get out of here."

CHAPTER 18

That night, Constance sat in the parlor holding a tepid cup of tea. She found that as exhausted as she was, sleep had eluded her although the house was quiet proving that everyone else had found the blessed relief of slumber. Mr. Plainview likely had a good dose of laudanum to thank for his peace.

She sighed heavily. She was starting to become worse than an orphanage or a woman's home. But instead of taking in stray children or single mothers she was caring for thieves, gamblers, and criminals.

Ironically enough, she felt safer and more at ease with Luke, Devin, and Drennan than she did with most anyone else from the *ton*. The question that she couldn't seem to answer was—what sort of person did that make her?

For years Madame Corressa had been the largest part of her personality, the inner harlot who had lived for her next protector, thinking that was the only way she could truly succeed. It was why she had been so determined to live life on her own after Alessandro had died, because she wanted to remember who Constance Freewater was, but even then, that wasn't her true surname. It was the one she'd shared with her mother as an honorary title and nothing else. It was something she could tell people without just saying her name was Miss No-Name.

Strangely enough, Constance began to wonder about who her true father was, although she knew she would never know his identity. She doubted that her mother could even tell her. She'd enjoyed countless lovers over the years, and the king himself could be Constance's sire and she would have no clue.

So, who was Constance Freewater, truly?

A frown creased her brow, because she might never have the answer to that question.

"You should be in bed."

Constance wasn't surprised that Devin was up. He seemed to have a remarkable sense of knowing when she was around. "Don't try to boss me around in the home I'm paying for, Mr. Blackmore." She sipped from her cup, although she couldn't quite hide a smile beneath the rim.

Instead of sitting down on the settee next to her, he took the chair across from her. He was in a pair of dark trousers, although his feet were bare. He'd also donned a green, velvet robe, but since it appeared he'd thrown it on haphazardly, it did little to cover his bare chest. Combined with her white nightdress and robe, her long hair in a plait over her shoulder and her own naked feet peeking beneath it all, it seemed quite normal to be chatting with him in such intimate surroundings. The fire had died down to simmering coals and although Constance had lit a candle to light her way down the stairs, it cast little light.

However, it was enough to ascertain that his gaze was steady upon her.

She hoped he couldn't see her heart pounding beneath her breast in return.

"What are you doing up, Constance?" His voice was deep and smooth, like the finest wine.

"I couldn't sleep?" She attempted a jest, but she should have realized that he wouldn't accept such a feeble answer.

"What's troubling you?"

She shrugged. "Well, it was a rather eventful afternoon. Does that count?"

He sighed. "What made you decide to go to Montfree's?"

"The gardener." At his confused expression, she explained. "Call it a sixth sense or a gut feeling, but Lady Blessington had recently taken on a new gardener. I saw him when we took a turn about the grounds, and something didn't settle well with me. I thought perhaps Granelli and his men had returned to London."

"If they had ever left at all."

This time it was Constance who tilted her head curiously. "What makes you say that? Do you think Drennan lied to me?"

"Not by choice. He could have been coerced into doing so in order to throw us off of Granelli's scent."

Constance considered this. "I see your point, and it could very well be. Nevertheless, Granelli is here now and he will be more of a threat than ever before."

Devin remained silent, no doubt because he agreed with her assessment.

"And now you know why I'm awake."

"Granelli is not your concern."

"I would have to dispute that claim," she countered. "I didn't tell you that before you and Luke burst into the room to save the day, Granelli told me that he had been inquiring after our whereabouts and once he was done with me, he intended to finish what he started with you." She took another sip of her tea, but this time it slithered into her stomach like poison. Setting it aside, she said, "So, you see, it appears that we share a mutual villain after all."

"I won't let him hurt you again."

Constance smiled at the determination in Devin's tone, and when she looked up to regard him, his gaze was so fierce that her lungs nearly seized from it. "You won't be there all the time. Besides, I managed just fine on my own."

He moved so quickly that she wasn't quite prepared. One moment he was across from her, and in the next he was kneeling down in front of her, his hands clutching either side of her face. "Why do you have to be so bloody stubborn? I know that you can take care of yourself, but is it so wrong for me to want to do it for you?"

The fervor in his voice matched the sparks swirling in his eyes and she abruptly lost the ability to speak. But it was the yearning she felt inside at his words that made her jerk out of his embrace. "Don't say things like that." Getting up, she put some much needed distance between them. She walked over to the mantel and stood in front of the dying embers and crossed her arms.

For a moment, all was silent and she wondered if he'd left, but then he spoke softly. "Why do you insist on pushing me away, Constance? Or have you done that all of your life? Can't you believe that someone could truly care for you?"

"No!" Constance spun on Devin, her fists clenched. He was standing, regarding her evenly. It angered her that not only could he see through her, but that he actually appeared to *pity* her. "Why must you insist on pushing me at all? What is it that you expect of me? I laid with you. Isn't that what you wanted all along?"

He abruptly stilled, his eyes turning flat. "Is that all you think you mean to me? Someone to fuck?" He shook his head. "Sorry, sweetheart, but if that's all I wanted, I could have found any number of willing women around this city to suck my cock."

"Then why haven't you?" she cried. "Why did you seek me out in the first place?"

His lips quirked and Constance held her breath as he moved toward her. He kept his tone low when he spoke. "Because I thought you were the most beautiful woman I had ever seen. Because I had been a dying man in need of salvation and you were my angel who rescued me from the depths of hell." He stopped before her. "And because I could easily find myself falling in l—"

She placed two fingers over his lips. "Please don't say it. That's a dangerous word and only leads to heartache for those who suffer from it."

He kissed the pads of her fingers and then moved them until they were covering the steady beat of his heart. "Why does it have to be suffering? Have you been conflicted by such strong emotions when you're with me?"

She sighed. "No, but that doesn't mean—"

"You're looking for reasons why something can't build between us." He reached out and ran the backs of his knuckles down the length of her braid, pausing at the tip, directly where it encircled her breast. "We are both broken in our own way. Maybe we were brought together for a reason. To find happiness with one another."

Constance swallowed. "Maybe we don't deserve happiness."

"I disagree." His arm slowly snaked around her waist. Lowering his head, he breathed against her lips, "And you, my dear, deserve so much more."

~

DEVIN DIDN'T INTEND to allow things to get out of hand. He only wanted to tempt and taunt Constance, to show her that there was something worthwhile to be had whenever they were together. He didn't want them to end up in the bedroom, as that was how she evaded breaking down that fortress around her heart, if not her entire soul. She assumed sex was the answer and he yearned to show her that there was more to being with a man. It was about touching and caressing, cherishing each other's bodies. It was about leaning on each other after a difficult day, it was gaining the courage that they required to face another dawn when it appeared that the entire world was crashing down.

He intended to teach her how to let go of her inhibitions and trust in him, because he was quite sure he wasn't falling in love with her, that he had been there from the first moment he'd laid eyes on her in that dark alley. If that made him sound like a poet, or a dandy, then he would wear the title with pride, as long as it meant he could keep her by his side.

"Devin…"

The breathy sigh entered his mind like the sweetest benediction, but he'd made a promise and he intended to keep it. He reluctantly broke the embrace, even if the passion filled look that Constance gave him shot straight to his groin. "We have to stop now."

"Do we?" she murmured huskily, and he had to close his eyes and pray for restraint against this tempting siren.

"Yes." He forced himself to step back. "I'm not here to be just another man who wants to use you for what he can gain. I intend to prove that I'm more than that."

"By *not* making love to me?"

He could tell by her confused expression that it was a foreign concept to her. "There are ways to enjoy each other's company fully clothed."

She rolled her eyes. "I know that, but why should you want to?"

He laughed. "I've told you, Constance. I want to know everything about you and not just where your body is concerned. I don't want us to just be lovers. I want us to be friends."

She eyed him warily. "What do you suggest?"

He pondered the query for a moment and then a smile spread across his face. It was perfect. "You'll find out tomorrow."

Her eyes narrowed with even further distrust. "I'm not sure I like that look, Mr. Blackmore."

"This is the part where you have to trust me." He offered her a teasing wink. "Because I'm going to show you what your life could be like with me."

"Indeed." She sounded unimpressed. "And how long would that be, exactly?"

"That, sweetheart, is up to you to decide."

With that parting remark, he sauntered out the door.

~

CONSTANCE DIDN'T IMMEDIATELY RETIRE, because she knew that sleep would not come after Devin's delicious promise.

'You'll find out tomorrow.'

Instead of tossing and turning all night, she decided that she would check on Drennan again. While it had only been a few hours since she'd left his side, she was concerned for his welfare. He'd told her that there wasn't anyone she needed to contact that might be worried over his absence, and that bothered her.

He had been committed to taking over Montfree's when she'd sold it to him five years ago, but she never imagined that he wouldn't allow for anything else outside of the gaming hell. Just because he owned the establishment, that didn't mean he had to give up his own life to see it succeed. And considering Granelli was demanding payment for an unpaid loan, something had gone terribly awry.

She intended to find out what it was.

Constance didn't knock as she let herself into Drennan's temporary room. It wasn't as grand as some of the other guest chambers, but it was modest and cozy, and most importantly, safe.

A bedside lamp had been kept lit for a modest amount of light and as Constance drew closer to the bed, she thought perhaps Drennan might be asleep. Instead, she was surprised to find he was staring at the ceiling, his mouth turned down grimly.

No doubt he had a lot on his mind.

He didn't look at her, although he spoke quietly. "Are you here to tell me how you wish you would have sold the gaming hell to anyone but me?"

Constance sank down in a chair near the bed. "Not at all," she chided. "I thought you would have known me better than to believe I would kick a man when he's already down."

His lips twitched and he finally turned his brilliant blue gaze on her. Her heart cracked when she saw the sheen of tears there and fought the urge to wince at his bruised face. At least the swelling had gone down. "If it's any consolation, I regret it all." He sighed. "Unfortunately, I suppose there's no turning back now."

"The best thing is to press forward, but first you have to get better," she advised.

"What about Granelli?" He swallowed hard. "He won't leave me in peace until he gets what I owe him."

"Let me worry about him," she returned evenly.

He almost looked pained. "What can you do except become another target?"

She lifted a brow. "You mean, because I'm a woman?" When he adopted a sheepish expression, she sat forward. "You'll find that I don't deal well with bullies, which is all Granelli is. I wouldn't even be surprised if he tricked you into playing his game of greed. I won't be as easily deceived."

He looked at her steadily. "That may have been true at one time, but it has been five years since you traversed the London underground. You don't have the resources you once did and Granelli has become known as a rather lethal adversary."

She smiled. "Oh, I doubt that Madame Corressa's reputation has completely faded with time. While I may not have Bull by my side, rest assured I can still find ways of dealing with problems that might arise."

This time a single drop of moisture trailed down Drennan's cheek. "I'm sorry that I failed you, Constance."

She reached forward and brushed a stray strand of his light-colored hair away from his forehead. "Don't you worry about anything. People like us are resilient. We face the censure of society, and yet, still we rise. Don't ever forget that."

He took a deep breath and swiped a hand across his eyes. Finally, he offered a hint of that charming smile. "If it wasn't for my certain proclivities, I might just be tempted to fall in love with you. As it stands, you are the only woman who shall ever hold my heart."

"So you've told me on countless occasions," she teased. "And I hope it will stay that way."

His eyes twinkled. "On that, my lady, you have my word."

CHAPTER 19

By the time Constance left Drennan's room, she was feeling more determined than ever to see that Granelli's reign came to an abrupt end. She intended to put some ideas into motion very soon, but first, she had to face Devin.

Late the next morning, she was awoken by a brisk knock on her door. She didn't even call out before it was pushed open and Devin strode inside looking as handsome and seductive as he'd been the night before—with one minor change. He was fully dressed in a pair of buff trousers, black boots, a bottle green jacket and matching waistcoat and—dare she even believe it—a cravat?

If that wasn't enough for her to sit up and take notice, he was also carrying a silver tray. "What is this?"

"Why, your luncheon, my lady, since you chose to be a slugabed all morning." He lifted a mocking brow. "I did say you had employed a fabulous cook, so I asked her to make you all of my usual favorites." He set the tray on her lap and whipped off the lid with a flourish.

Instantly the tantalizing scents of ham, eggs, various little pastries, and tea assailed her nostrils. Instantly, her stomach began to rumble. "Mmm. It smells heavenly."

"Indeed. See what you've been missing? Instead of rushing out the door the moment the sun rises like you normally do, perhaps you might take time to enjoy what's right underneath this very roof." He sat down on the edge of the bed as if he did it all the time and was perfectly acceptable to do so. But it was the heat warming his eyes that made her stomach clench.

She took a sip of the tea and tried to banish the swirling sensation spreading throughout her limbs. "If you will recall," she noted firmly. "I told you Lady Blessington agreed to host a metamorphosis ball. I was merely helping her decide on the proper décor."

He lifted a brow. "And that takes weeks of preparation from dawn to dusk?"

No. It was a way to escape you. She swallowed a bite of ham to keep from saying that out loud, and instead answered with something a bit more vague. "There is a lot involved to holding a society ball, yes."

"In that case it's a wonder that anyone wishes to hold such a fete if there is so much extensive arrangement involved."

"Generally, such events are reserved for the upper classes where the servants take care of most of the work we've been doing." She shrugged. "But since I was the one who suggested the idea, I felt compelled to offer what assistance I could."

"How very selfless of you."

Constance frowned, but then she realized he was teasing her, the twinkle in his dark eyes causing her toes to curl beneath the blankets. "So, what is the purpose of all of this?" she asked.

"I believe that we discussed all that last night."

She crossed her arms, her fare temporarily forgotten as she tilted her head to the side. "Don't tell me this is some sort of courting attempt?"

He lifted one shoulder. "Call it what you like, but yes, that does sound appropriate."

Constance couldn't help but laugh. In nearly four decades, she'd never been properly wooed by a potential suitor. Granted, she'd been showered with some of the finest gowns and jewels that money could buy, but only if she offered herself in return. But Devin was only asking for her trust, and eventually her heart.

The problem was that she wasn't even sure if she was in full possession of it to give away.

And for some reason, that made her sad.

Pushing aside her melancholy, Constance concentrated on her meal. As she devoured her last bite, the fork hadn't even fully left her mouth before Devin stood up and announced, "Are you ready for your next surprise?"

She eyed him warily, but he looked so hopeful and excited that she couldn't refuse. "All right." She clasped her hands in her lap as he removed the tray and set it on a nearby table.

As he reached out for her hand, and helped her to stand, she said, "I hope you don't think we're leaving the house." She waved a hand. "As you can see, I'm not properly dressed."

He offered a scandalous wink. "That is about to change."

He walked over to the door to admit her maid, who was conveniently standing on the other side. Constance merely shook her head. She was the one who was paying to let this house and the servants who were in it, and yet, they seemed to be in on Devin's little plan.

"I'll be right back," Devin instructed. He left, only to return a short time later with a box in his grasp.

"You bought me a dress?" She blurted. Constance instantly thought of the day she'd saw him walking along Bond Street. She hadn't imagined at the time that the item had been intended for her.

He rubbed his chin. "In a fashion." He handed it to her. "If you don't like it, you don't have to keep it, of course. But I'd like it if you wore it just this once."

Constance decided right then, that it didn't matter if it was a hideous shade of puce, she would never dispose of it. The idea he had personally chosen something for her was worth more than the finest silks and satins her former paramours had showered upon her, for they had purchased them with no actual thought to her likes or dislikes.

She took the box and headed for the bed where she laid it on top. With a solemn breath, she lifted the lid, gasping when a light blue muslin dress was revealed. She carefully lifted it out and stared at the simple, yet perfect design. There were no adornments, no lace around the cuffs, or pearls sewn into the bodice.

It was just perfectly... perfect.

Tears actually stung her eyes, and she realized it had been years since she'd been so moved when it came to something so material. It was infinitely more special than anything else she'd ever had, because it was a gift given freely without the expectation of anything in return—unless, of course, she wished it.

When she could be assured that her voice wouldn't crack, she said, "It's lovely. Did Madame Elodie design it?"

"No."

When nothing else was forthcoming, Constance frowned. But then, as she glanced at the dress and then back at him, she remembered the day she'd caught him on a ladder repairing the canopy above his bed. But surely... "Don't tell me that *you* made this?"

He gave a mock wince. "I'm quite offended that you didn't think I was that accomplished. I can also play the pianoforte and paint with watercolors if the occasion calls for it." He grinned broadly now. "I know I'm not Madame Elodie, but I didn't think it was too terrible for my first ladies' fashion. It was actually easier than sewing a pair of men's trousers." When she just stared at him, he explained, "Less seams."

As if his ability with a needle and thread was the reason she was speechless. She looked back at the dress and shook her head. While that didn't explain his reason for being on Bond Street, it didn't really matter.

"You're remarkable."

～

DEVIN STILLED. It wasn't so much what Constance said, as the reverent *way* she uttered the word, as if he was the true angel in the room, the heavenly, celestial being that she was finally able to see on her own.

Unfortunately, it couldn't be further from the truth. While Devin had chosen to carve out a better path for himself, leaving the life of thievery and criminal activity behind, if Constance knew everything that he had done in that colony just to survive... she might never look at him without disgust on her face ever again.

But since he didn't want to bring up that old drudgery, intent on having a good day with the woman who held his heart, he said, "Meet me downstairs in the foyer when you're ready."

"We're going somewhere?" she asked hesitantly. "Are you sure that's wise? Especially after what happened last night?"

He winked at her. "Just get dressed."

With a perplexed look on her face, he walked out of her chamber and shut the door behind him.

When he arrived downstairs, Luke was standing in the doorway of the parlor, leaning against the frame. Devin rubbed his hands together in excitement. "Is everything ready?"

"Aye." The older man rubbed the side of his beard. "Th' servants 'ave rearranged th' library t' yer specifications."

"And the entertainment?"

Luke nodded with a roll of his eyes. "Aye. Tha' too."

Relief flooded through Devin. In all of his life he hadn't

wanted anything more than to keep that smile on Constance's face. He could tell that the recent interaction with Granelli had disturbed her more than she wanted to admit. It was his intention to push all of that ugliness aside, if only just for one day.

"Ye really do care about 'er."

Devin turned to his long-time friend. "Haven't I been telling you that all this time?" His mouth kicked up at the corner. "Surely this isn't Luke House admitting that he was *wrong?*"

"Bah!" He waved a hand. "Don't be gettin' used t' it."

Devin laughed as Luke walked off in a huff.

It wasn't until he heard a noise behind him that he turned around.

The moment Devin spied the vision of loveliness gliding down the stairs, he sobered instantly, his lungs ceasing to draw a proper breath. Constance had always had a timeless beauty that had captivating him from the very first moment he'd laid eyes on her, but as she drew closer to him, wearing the gown that he'd specifically designed for her—there were no words to describe the sensation that was growing and expanding throughout his chest. It was warm and exotic and completely... wonderful.

He watched her until she paused directly before him. She raised her arms and did a little pirouette. "Very nicely done, Mr. Blackmore. It fits like a glove." She bestowed a brilliant smile on him.

Devin held out his arm to her, pride filling every part of him to have such a beautiful woman next to him. "Shall we?"

She accepted his offering warily. "That depends on where we're going."

His gaze captured hers. "Don't worry. It's not far."

~

CURIOSITY WAS BURNING through Constance as she laid her hand upon his strong arm. She slid a sideways glance at Devin, and considering the sharp way he was dressed, if he were to mingle with the upper ten thousand, they would have no idea that he wasn't born with blue blood. With his broad shoulders, tall stance, and confident air, he commanded the very atmosphere around him.

As he led her toward the rear of the townhouse, she couldn't imagine why he was going through so much trouble for her on that particular day, but she would be lying if she said she didn't appreciate the gesture. Excitement was rushing through her veins and she realized it had been years since she'd had such a girlish thrill.

They paused before the library door where he gave a light knock. Immediately, the sound of solemn music came through the oak. But Constance didn't have time to question it before Devin gave her a wink and the inside of the room was revealed.

Constance gasped, as candles had been lit and strategically placed along the bookshelves. The furniture and rugs had been removed, leaving behind a shiny, bare wooden floor that had been strewn with velvety, red rose petals. The music was coming from one of the footmen, who stood in a corner playing a violin.

She blinked, more than a little overwhelmed. "What is all this for?" she breathed.

He held out a hand to her, his expression intense. "It's your birthday, Constance. You take such good care of those in need, I thought it was time for you to enjoy a bit of indulgence."

Her jaw went slack for a moment, as it hadn't even occurred to her until then that she had actually *forgotten* about her own birthday. But then, was it any wonder? She'd been so tied up with the planning for the metamorphosis ball, trying to fight her attraction to Devin, and the threat of Granelli striking when they least expected it that everything else had quite slipped her mind.

And yet...

"How did you find out?"

"I have my ways," he returned smoothly. "Now are you going to take my hand or not?"

Constance obediently slipped her hand into his and he pulled her into the elegant formation of a waltz. When he began to lead her in a perfect set, twirling her about the room, she found that she was once again, impressed by his prowess.

"Who taught you to dance?" When his face shuttered slightly, she instantly regretted the query. "I'm sorry. It's none of my business. I shouldn't have pried—"

"Her name was Annalise Coventry, the Countess of Tyne," he interrupted softly. "She was my former mistress."

Constance's stomach clenched at the image of one of Devin's former lovers teaching him such an intimate set that had likely led to something even more sensual in the bedchamber. Her gaze dropped to the floor. "Oh."

There was a moment of silence, and then he added, "She died a few years ago."

She wasn't even sure what to say to that. But when his hand tightened ever so slightly on hers, she couldn't resist looking back at him. "She was a widow who was mourning her husband. We were only together for mutual companionship."

"Did you love her?" Constance cursed her suddenly loose tongue, because she hadn't meant to blurt out such a personal question. It certainly wasn't like her to act so jealous over a past relationship. And it wasn't as if she hadn't had her share.

Although, when Devin nodded his head, her heart sank. "Yes, I did, but not as you might think. It wasn't because of an all-consuming passion. We had a shared respect for each other." His eyes were fixated on her face, holding her captive as he spoke. "I owe my life to her. She saved me from the noose but lost her own life by making a bargain with the devil himself."

It didn't take much for Constance to put the pieces together, especially considering his hatred for the baronet. "Sir Isaacson."

"Yes." His throat worked as he swallowed hard. "He married

Annalise after I was sent to the colonies, and then recently confessed to me that she'd suffered a nasty spill down the stairs. He took particular joy in telling me that she'd been carrying our child when she died, and I can only assume he's been enjoying the wealth he gained from their union."

Constance ceased to breathe as her eyes filled with tears. For a woman she had never met, she felt empathy for her plight. "Oh, my God, Devin... I had no idea he was such a monster." She shook her head as a drop of moisture fell from her lashes. "And here I was taunting you about him—"

He halted their movements and gently lifted her chin. His gaze was fervent as he searched hers. "You did nothing wrong. There was no way you could have known. But I am glad that you stopped entertaining him."

Her jaw hardened. "I should like to give him a piece of my mind."

His face relaxed. "There's no need for that, my angel." He kissed the tip of her nose and drew her back into the dance. "I plan on taking care of Sir Isaacson in my own good time."

She gasped. "You don't mean to—?"

"Trust me, I won't do anything that takes me away from you." He looked away. "I certainly don't want to spend another five years in the colonies."

She recalled the scars on his back. "Did you suffer terribly?"

His focus turned distant. "Worse than you can imagine."

Constance hated to see the pain in his gaze. And although she had never spoken of Sir Timothy to anyone, she wanted to ease the suffering in Devin's eyes now. "I was in love once too." When he glanced back at her questionably, she added, "The squire and I met at a hotel in London. He was a widower and missed his wife terribly. I was there to offer comfort, much like your time with the countess. I was only a vessel for his grief. What we shared was deep and abiding, but more of a friendship and a way to heal his wounds. It was his kindness to me that I shall always remember with the most fondness."

When there was a lull in the music, Devin took her hand. "I want to be alone with you," he said huskily.

Whether it was the mutual pain of the past, or the heady moment of the present, Constance found that she couldn't refuse him. She nodded, her vow broken, but she couldn't find it within her to care. Being with Devin seemed… right and she was tired of fighting her attraction to him any longer.

She wanted to be this marauder's mistress.

It was all the encouragement Devin needed for him to lead her up the stairs to her chamber. The moment they were inside, he shut the door and caught her against the wall, capturing her lips with his own. It was a gentle kiss, but there was enough pressure there to let Constance know he was claiming ownership.

And she wasn't inclined to care.

CHAPTER 20

⨍

*D*evin hadn't meant to allow the ghosts of his past to interfere on his time with Constance, and most especially on her birthday, but for some reason the words just poured forth. For the first time since he'd returned to London, he'd been able to open up without any hesitation. He hadn't even told Luke everything, most notably what the baronet had revealed about Annalise. Instead, he'd chosen to keep it all locked inside, but he'd known from the beginning that Constance had the ability to change him. She'd always been different.

Unique.

His.

Devin slid his hand down her bodice and cupped her breast. Her lungs hitched and he growled. Her response was more heady than the finest brandy, and he wanted it all. "If you don't want this to go any further tell me now."

"I want you, Devin."

He closed his eyes, her words the sweetest music to his ears. He kissed her passionately, toying with her breasts until her legs began to move restlessly beneath her skirts. He knew what she really wanted because he wanted it too.

He gathered a handful of material in his fist and with his other hand, he reached between her thighs and began to caress her. She laid her head back against the wall and moaned lightly. "Faster..." she commanded.

He readily complied, but before he could slide a finger into her passage and bring her to completion, she laid a hand on his arm, ceasing his actions. He blinked, wondering what he'd done wrong, but she merely grabbed his jacket collar and, with eyes that seemed to be illuminated from within, she said, "I don't want this to be one-sided." She urged him backwards until the backs of his knees touched the mattress of her bed. "Lay down."

Devin did as she commanded, her willing servant, and nearly lost his mind when she started to unbutton his trousers. He watched as she freed his aching cock, but when she bent down and took his length into her mouth *completely*, he had to resist the overwhelming urge to come right then. Instead, he gave a low hiss. "Constance..."

She didn't reply but continued to torture him with each suck and lick from that glorious mouth. Just as he was on the brink of release, she sat up. "Not yet." Her green eyes were bright as she straddled him with one leg on either side of him. When she positioned him at her entrance and slowly sank down on him, Devin was lost.

He no longer had any control as she began to move, any hope of holding himself back was useless as the sensation of her wet heat surrounded him. He grasped her hips, his eyes fixated on her face right until the moment her core trembled around his cock. Her head was thrown back in rapture as she cried out his name and it was enough to send him over the edge. With a guttural shout, he emptied everything he had inside of her. Unlike before, this time he held nothing back because he knew that there would never be anyone else for him.

Once Devin caught his breath, he sat up and embraced her. They were no longer joined, but she was still on his lap. As he cradled her within the circle of his arms, he temporarily closed his eyes, just to enjoy the sensation of having her there. Everything that he'd ever suffered before had been worth it for this tender moment.

"I'm forty years of age."

Devin pulled back and looked at her, those shining green eyes still swirling with pleasure and her strawberry-blond hair in slight disarray around her face. "And more beautiful than any woman twenty years younger."

She laughed. "Don't be nonsensical. I'm nearly a decade older than you."

He shrugged. "And?"

She turned serious. "I'm past my childbearing years."

While Devin would have loved to carry a daughter around on his shoulders that had Constance's green eyes, he kissed her lightly on the lips. "All I need is you. Besides, I'm not sure I would be a very good father."

She placed a hand on his chest. "I disagree. And you should have the chance if you want it." She sighed. "I don't want you to have any regrets—"

"Listen to me very closely." He held her face immobile. "The only regret I would ever have is letting you go. And you can rest assured that is not going to happen."

～

Now that her ardor had cooled, the doubts that Constance had held on to so tightly came rushing back with a vengeance. She desperately wanted to believe in Devin, she prayed that he was telling the truth, but so many of her previous lovers had disappointed her in the past. They promised her the moon and the stars—until they tired of her company. And something told her if Devin did the same, she would be devastated.

Destroyed.

But instead of dwelling on an uncertain future with a broken heart, she didn't want anything to mar this moment. She wound her arms around his neck. "Thank you for a wonderful birthday," she said sincerely.

He kissed her softly on the lips. "Now you just have to make it through the metamorphosis ball tomorrow night."

She groaned and then bit her lower lip anxiously. "I nearly forgot about it already. Perhaps Lady Blessington will understand if I cry off..."

"Don't you dare!" She blinked at the vehemence in Devin's tone. "You worked hard to make this event a smashing success. You need to go and enjoy it."

"Aren't you concerned about Granelli? What he might do?"

He rolled his eyes. "Granelli might be the leader of an underground gang, but even he isn't stupid enough to try to invade a society ball and take the risk of insulting a duke. He would be in the noose within a week."

She exhaled heavily. "I suppose you're right. I just don't want to take any unnecessary chances."

He grinned. "Are you that worried about me, sweetheart?"

She smacked him on the arm. "Be serious. Do you *want* another gunshot wound? It might be fatal this time."

Devin's expression sobered. "I won't let him win, Constance. If it takes me the rest of my days, I will end his reign over London."

The image of him leaping over rooftops and dodging chimneys with a cape and mask caused her lips to twitch. "I suppose instead of the Mysterious Marauder, you could become the Masked Avenger."

He lifted a brow. "And will you be my prize at the end of the day?"

She straightened, rubbing the tips of her breasts against his chest. "I might consider it."

His eyes darkened to molten chocolate and Constance wanted nothing more than to lose herself in those depths forever.

As his lips found hers once more, she gave herself over to the wonder of their combined passion.

～

THE NEXT MORNING, Devin slipped out of Constance's bed and donned his trousers. Gathering the rest of his clothes, he looked back at her one last time, resisting the urge to climb back into bed and wake her up with a scorching kiss. His cock was certainly up for the task. It throbbed with eager energy, even though they had come together once more during the night.

Unfortunately, there was work to be done. And while he had done his best to soothe Constance's fears about Granelli, he hadn't told her that the real threat might not even be located in the East End, but at the heart of the ball itself. Sir Isaacson had been known to converse with thieves in the past, including Luke and Devin, and he didn't think much had changed in the past five years. The baronet was certainly cutthroat enough to get what he wanted by any means necessary, and a partnership with Granelli would be ideal.

Besides, how else had Granelli come up with the funds to lend Mr. Plainview when he believed the gaming hell was having financial trouble? Devin would bet his own money that Montfree's wasn't doing as bad as Mr. Plainview might have imagined in the beginning, but when desperation was at stake, it was easy to manipulate someone into believing that an alliance was the answer, however corrupt, when all it might have taken was a bit more planning to correct the error.

Unfortunately, now it was too late and Drennan might lose it all. Nevertheless, it made sense to Devin that Sir Isaacson was behind Mr. Plainview's ruin, as it was the sort of business the baronet enjoyed conducting when it came to the suffering of others. The question that bothered Devin the most was why target Montfree's, and not any of the other hells in London? What made that particular establishment unique?

If he intended to end this charade once and for all, it was one thing he needed to find out.

Donning his shirt but leaving the rest of his formal wear in his room, Devin headed down the hall to pay a visit to Mr. Plainview. It was nearly dawn, so hopefully the man would be awake. If not, he soon would be, because Devin needed answers.

Instead of pushing his way inside the guest room impatiently, Devin forced himself to pause and knock.

"Yes?"

Following the soft command, at least Devin knew the man was awake. He walked inside and the owner of the gaming hell glanced at him warily. "Mr. Blackmore." He cleared his throat and carefully sat up in the bed. "Good morning. I daresay this is an unexpected surprise." As Devin strode over and took a seat next to the bed, he added, "Something tells me you didn't come out of a deep concern for my wellbeing."

Devin had to respect that. "While I do wish you well, I need some answers and I fear you are the only one who can provide them for me. For instance, considering you appear to be a man who is quite astute, it makes me wonder how you became a target for a ne'er-do-well like Granelli."

Even though there was still a shocking amount of bruising on Mr. Plainview's face, Devin didn't miss the flash of apprehension in his eyes. "You don't miss much, do you, Mr. Blackmore?"

"Not usually." Deciding there was no point in concealing his own truth, he admitted, "At one time I was very familiar with these streets. But I made the mistake of trusting the wrong person for the benefit I thought it would bring." He paused. "It appears you've done the same. And my gut tells me that it might very well be the same individual who betrayed me."

Those blue eyes studied him, and then Drennan said, "You would be correct, Mr. Blackmore." His gaze shifted and he glanced down at the coverlet on the bed. "I believed that this... person cared for me, but I was duped into believing a lie. I allowed certain... emotions to cloud my judgement. When Granelli came to me with an offer I couldn't refuse, I accepted because I was desolate. I had allowed the gaming hell that I had been entrusted with to falter because I had been blinded by my own fabrication."

Seeing the battered face in front of him looking so melancholy, Devin had the need to offer some sort of consolation. "You wouldn't be the first person who has been deceived. At least now you will know not to gamble on the devil's bargain."

"Perhaps," Drennan conceded in a quiet manner. "But that doesn't mean the problem doesn't remain. And now I feel I've brought further trouble to my friend's door."

"Don't worry about Constance," Devin said firmly. "I will protect her with my life if needed."

Drennan glanced back at him. "Yes," he smiled faintly. "I believe that you will."

Feeling as though the conversation might slip into more intimate territory where Constance was concerned, he turned it back to the subject at hand. "I know you may not wish to reveal the name of your acquaintance, but I need to know his name to confirm my own suspicions."

Drennan's eyes fluttered for a moment and then he gave a nod. "It was Sir Brooks Isaacson."

The fist in Devin's lap clenched. "Tell me," he said slowly. "When the baronet came to Montfree's, did you notice anything unusual?"

The other man frowned. "What do you mean?"

"Did it appear if he was looking for anyone? Did he come at a certain time?" He tried to keep his impatience from showing. "Even the smallest details can make a big difference."

There was a brief pause as Drennan appeared to consider the query, and then he murmured, "I never thought about it before, but yes, he did appear to take a particular interest in the patrons in attendance."

Devin sat up straighter. "Did he approach anyone in particular? If so, can you describe them?"

After a few more moments of reflection, the other man shook his head. "I'm sorry," he said in defeat. "I can't recall that much, but then, my focus wasn't on the hell as it should have been at that point."

Deciding that there was someone else who might be able to offer assistance, Devin got up. Before he left, he offered Drennan a slight smile. "We all make errors in judgement from time to time. The point is to learn from them."

Mr. Plainview nodded as Devin took his leave.

He was shrugging on his jacket in the foyer when Luke appeared from the direction of the kitchens. Devin rolled his eyes. "I see you've been to visit the cook already. Did you get her out of bed with an entreaty to your growling stomach?"

Luke grinned. "Nope. In fact, she was rather accommodatin' t' this ol' man. Gave me a whole tray o' tarts t' myself." He winked.

Devin stared at him. "You'll pay for that."

He started for the door, but Luke stopped him. "An' where do ye think ye're runnin' off to this early?"

"To see if Brutus can help solve the mystery of Montfree's."

Luke's gaze narrowed. "Wha' do ye got cookin' in tha' 'ead o' yers?"

"Nothing but my instincts which seldom steer me off course."

"Hmm." Luke reached for his jacket and shrugged it on.

"What are you doing?" Devin frowned.

"Goin' wit' ye," Luke returned with that stubborn mien he recognized quite well. "I can't let ye take th' chance o' gettin' caught out in th' open again."

Devin snorted. "Granelli might have gotten lucky the first time, but it won't happen again, I assure you."

"All th' same." Luke clapped him on the shoulder and waited.

With a heavy breath, Devin lead the way outside where he hailed down a hackney to take him to the East End.

CHAPTER 21

*C*onstance rolled over in bed with the early morning sun's rays, expecting to encounter a warm, male body, but instead, her eyes opened when there was nothing but a cold, flat sheet beneath her hand. Disappointed, she decided it was probably for the best, in the off chance her maid might walk in and find them together. She certainly didn't need that sort of scandal right now when Granelli was breathing down their necks and causing trouble of his own.

She rolled over on her back and thought of the night ahead. It was the metamorphosis ball and the last thing Constance wanted to do was rub elbows with the upper echelon. While she didn't have to put on a false mask of her own, since one was being provided, the idea of encountering Sir Isaacson again after what Devin had told her wasn't appealing in the least. From the beginning she hadn't considered him to be trustworthy, and it seems it was for good reason.

Although it cut her to think of Devin with any other woman, sharing the same intimacies they had done just hours ago, she couldn't help but feel a bit of empathy for the Countess of Tyne. After losing the love of her life, and then a steady companion in

Devin, it was likely very difficult to turn to someone as cold as the baronet. Granted, Sir Isaacson had treated Constance gallantly at the beginning, but it hadn't taken much to reveal his true nature. Once she'd spurned him, she realized the sort of monster he was beneath all that gallantry.

She threw back the covers and got out of bed, fully awake now. She had been enjoying pleasant dreams of being with Devin until images of the baronet had intruded to fill her with disgust. It also didn't take long for her to admit that she couldn't allow him to continue moving about society with no repercussions for his actions. Surely there was a way she could trap him into ruining his own reputation...

After a moment, a coy grin spread across Constance's face. She walked over to her writing desk and sat down to pen a quick missive to Lady Blessington. Not only would the metamorphosis ball be a night to remember, but she was quite sure that Sir Isaacson would never forget it.

Sealing the letter, she threw on a robe and headed downstairs to find a footman to post it as soon as possible. Once that was done, she decided that she would check in on Devin. She bit her lower lip in eager, girlish anticipation, finding that it had been years since she'd been so excited to see a certain male face, but when she knocked on his door and received no answer, she dared to peek inside. It was empty.

With a concerned frown, she checked the kitchens, where the cook offered her a warm greeting and attempted to ply her with several fruit tarts. Constance didn't wish to be rude, so she paused in her search and bit into the flaky crust with a murmur of delight. After a compliment that made the buxom woman gleam, Constance continued on, although she told herself that even when her lease was up on the townhouse, she intended to employ the cook at her next residence—wherever that might be. In truth, she hadn't yet decided if she wished to remain in

London, especially if her relationship with Devin began to fall apart.

She hadn't wanted to admit it, had fought against it as long as possible, but there was no denying the yearnings in her heart anymore. After last night when she'd finally allowed herself the freedom to love him with her body, her heart had also been freed. She'd kept her emotions locked tightly inside for years, but Devin had managed to find a way past her defenses, and they had crumbled to dust at his feet. She wasn't quite sure how to tell him, or even if she should, as that was how nightmares became reality. She'd witnessed it time and time again.

Pushing her admission aside for the time being, she stood in the middle of the hall and looked at another empty bedchamber, the one Luke used, and wondered what was going on. Apparently, they had taken it upon themselves to take off to God only knew where, while she was left behind to cool her heels.

With a frustrated huff, Constance tried the last male guest in the house. She was relieved when Drennan looked up at her entrance and offered her a friendly smile. "Finally!" She threw up her arms. "I was starting to wonder if I was here alone."

"Ah." There was a wealth of meaning in that single syllable.

"You know something, don't you?" She walked over and set her hands on her hips. "You better start talking."

In turn, he held up his hands in mock surrender. "I had nothing to do with it. Mr. Blackmore merely paid me a visit this morning. After our discussion, he decided to go speak with Brutus."

"At least he had the sense to take Luke with him." She exhaled heavily and sank down in the chair next to the bed.

There was a pause as Drennan eyed her steadily. "I've never seen you this upset over anyone before. This must be serious."

"You could say that." Constance chose to stare at her intertwined fingers rather than meet his knowing gaze. Being so unsure of herself was another sensation she wasn't quite familiar with. Madame Corressa had always known the right things to say and do, her flirtatious nature swooping in to assume control when Constance faltered. But it appeared that the lady was finally sitting back and letting her take over. Unfortunately, that was where she began to allow those terrible insecurities of the past to slide in.

"It's all right to let yourself love, Constance."

She glanced up at the softy spoken assurance. "Is it?" she asked just as quietly.

"It's a risk we must all take if we truly wish to experience life." His smile was melancholy. "It might be sad or disappointing, but if it wasn't for the regrettable occurrences we face, the good days wouldn't be worth celebrating as much."

Her lips twitched. It was either laugh or cry and she had never been a watering pot. "Since when did you become so philosophical?" she teased.

His blue eyes were steady on her face. "I suppose it was when my own heart was broken."

She sighed. "I suppose men and women aren't so different after all, are we?"

He grinned. "Not at all."

※

THE HACKNEY DEPOSITED Devin and Luke at the address Brutus had given him at Montfree's. However, the moment they stepped to the ground and the carriage rolled away, Devin's instincts went on high alert. He scanned the area around them, but there didn't appear to be anyone lurking in the corners. However, it was the silence around them that was the most concerning. "Something's not right."

"Aye." Luke lifted his face, as if scenting something in the air. He reached behind him and pulled a pistol out of the waistband of his trousers. "It's a good thin' I came prepared. An' tha' I came wit' ye," he added pointedly.

Devin reached into his boot and withdrew a dagger with a shiny, steel blade. "Aye. Me too. On both counts." Clutching the weapon tightly in his grasp, he led the way into the row of lodgings. Brutus had told him that his residence was on the upper floors and something told him that he would need the protection the entire way.

Starting the slow, but steady ascent up the rickety staircase that had seen better days, he kept the knife at his side, while carefully observing the closed doors that he passed. Every nerve ending was on alert should someone rush at him with lethal intent, because he was faced with that same, unnerving silence he'd been faced with outside.

Thankfully, they reached the top landing without incident, but Devin wasn't breathing a sigh of relief just yet. When he reached Brutus's apartments, he glanced behind him to see Luke in position. It wasn't the first time that they had faced possible adversity, but he prayed it would be the last. He was weary of a life where he had to continually look over his shoulder. He just wanted to spend a quiet life in country solitude, perhaps even look into becoming a farmer, with Constance and their family by his side. If there was a merciful God, that day would come to pass.

Luke stayed out of sight of the door as Devin gestured to the doorframe. It was broken, splinters hanging from the area of the knob, as if someone had entered by force.

Grimly, he realized that wasn't a good sign. It would be a miracle if Brutus was even alive.

He carefully pushed the door open and found the initial room to be empty. He hesitated, searching for signs of a struggle—or blood—but there was nothing.

When he prepared to take another step, a boot suddenly shot out in front of him. He stumbled over it, but recovered quickly, turning his fall into a flip that had him jerking upward in a crouched position and ready to do battle.

However, when recognition struck him, Devin lowered his weapon and put his hands on his knees. "Thank God."

Luke had been ready to rush at the assailant, but when he entered the room and saw Brutus, he shut the door behind him and holstered his pistol once again. "I'm surprised t' see that yer still standin'."

The former boxer offered a tight smile. Blood trickled from his temple, but otherwise, he didn't appear to have any other injuries. "They tried t' get me down, but I reminded them who I was right quick."

"Was it Granelli's men?" Devin had no doubt that the bouncer of Montfree's was familiar with all sorts of unsavory visitors to the gaming hell, as well as the ones who prowled about the city in search of prey.

"Aye," Brutus confirmed.

Now that the excitement had settled down, Devin wasted no time in asking what he had come there to find out. "I believe that Granelli isn't working alone. That he's attempting to ruin Mr. Plainview by some means of treachery, but I have yet to discern the reasons why. I came here hoping you might shed a bit of light on my current theory."

Brutus crossed his arms with a frown. "What's that?"

"Drennan told me that he was…involved in certain dealings with Sir Isaacson. It sounded as though the baronet was particularly interested in the patrons that frequented Montfree's." He paused. "Do you have any idea if he showed any interest in someone particular?"

Brutus nodded his head. "Oh, aye, that he did."

Devin's brows raised with interest. "Do you know his name? Or what he looked like?"

"*Her* name is Gwen Hollowell," Brutus corrected.

Devin blinked. "He was after a woman?" He hadn't considered

that possibility, but he should have known it wouldn't just be a man who had the wherewithal to spurn a man like Sir Isaacson into action. Nor that a female mind couldn't be just as conniving. Constance had been firm proof of that.

"She was a former housemaid to the Countess of Tyne and she told me she has the proof to send Sir Isaacson to the gallows for the murder of her mistress."

Devin's ears instantly started ringing. Finally, he might have the means necessary to enact his revenge on the baronet while gaining justice for Annalise. His fists clenched in anticipation of that moment. "Where is she?"

Brutus shook his head. "I told her that I wouldn't give away her location to anyone and I mean to keep that vow, even when it comes to you, Blackmore." He lifted his chin, as if daring him to challenge his honor. "She was a good friend to my mother before she died and used to live in this very building, but when Granelli and his men started to come after her she had to flee. She spent a lot of time at Montfree's where she knew I could watch over her, but she did ask me to convey a message to Madame Corressa."

He stilled. "And what's that?"

"She will be at the metamorphosis ball tonight and intends to seek her out."

～

CONSTANCE STARED at her reflection in the mirror and resisted the urge to tug at her starched, white cravat. While she admitted that the freedom of the black trousers, white silk stockings, and buckle shoes were much better without the confines of a corset and the layers of petticoats she had to don normally, she didn't care that everything was bunched up around her neck. And the silver waistcoat and black jacket made her feel as though she couldn't properly move her arms. Her hair was pulled back into a tight bun and a powdered wig sat upon her head and she resisted the urge to yank it off and scratch her irritated scalp. With a sigh, she supposed that gentlemen had discomforts for the sake of fashion, just as their counterparts did.

However, the reason for most of her irritation likely rested in the fact that it was late afternoon and Devin and Luke had yet to return from their visit with Brutus. She was starting to grow extremely concerned that something terrible had happened, but since she was obligated to attend the ball, not to mention terribly disappoint Lady Blessington if she decided to cry off, her hands were tied. At least the countess had replied to her message with the understanding of her plight and that she was willing to help in any way she could when it came to Sir Isaacson. The count had also offered his assistance, so Constance didn't feel quite alone as she set out that evening.

As the front door closed downstairs, Constance stopped pacing and rushed down the stairs. The moment she spied Devin, with Luke at his side, relief poured through her until her knees were weak, but her frustration was enough for her to snap, "I've been worried sick about the two of you!"

Luke had the grace to adopt a chagrined expression. "I do apologize for tha'. We lost track o' time."

She crossed her arms. "That's the only excuse you can give me?"

"It's the truth," Devin returned firmly.

She slid her gaze to him while Luke slowly slunk off, but when her eyes clashed with Devin's, it wasn't sparks of anger that shot through her body. His dark gaze was smoky with desire as it traveled over her form. "I could get used to you in men's clothing."

Her body flushed, but she tamped her own arousal down. "Don't change the subject," she returned, annoyed that her voice sounded so breathless. "You could have sent a message—"

He walked toward her and anything else she might have said was broke off by a smoldering kiss that made her stomach clench and a soft sigh escape her lips. When Devin pulled away, he said, "I'm here now, and there's something I need you to do for me."

She frowned at the seriousness in his tone. "What?"

"Brutus told me that you will be approached by a lady this evening." He hesitated. "She was a housemaid to Annalise and claims she has the necessary information to prove that Sir Isaacson murdered her." His Adam's apple bobbed slightly. "If this is true, I can finally give her the peace that she deserves."

Constance's heart was moved. She reached up and touched his cheek, relishing the feeling of the stubble beneath her hand. "You are good man, Devin Blackmore. Much more than I probably deserve to have in my life."

He grabbed her hand and brought it to his chest. He placed her palm directly over his heart, which pounded strong and steady. "Annalise was my salvation for a time, but this will always be yours." His eyes burned bright. "Constance, I—"

"Stop." She shook her head. "Please, don't say it. Not now. Not until after this night is over."

He adopted a curious expression. "Why?"

"Because we don't know what might happen tonight. Madame Corressa is about to embark on her grand finale, and I can't allow her to be distracted by what you might reveal to me."

The sincerity must have shown through her eyes, because he stepped back out of her embrace. "In that case, I wish you a successful performance."

Constance's lips curved at the corners. "Oh, rest assured, Madame Corressa never disappoints an audience."

CHAPTER 22

Constance adjusted her cuffs and walked down into the heart of the ballroom with her black domino on her face. Madame Corressa had taken over completely, had erased the nerves that Constance might have suffered from, and moved among the assemblage with a coy expression. She bowed to the "ladies" in their colorful silks and satins, while their lustful glances glittered beneath their lavish masks, as they followed the backsides of the "men."

It was a night garnered for mischief and deviltry, for sensual promise and teasing encouragement. The air was filled with an edge, a release tottering on the brink, and Constance knew that more than one affair would be conducted this evening. While masquerades were daring enough, when the gender roles were reversed, the field of warfare became entirely different. The women could take the control that was often denied them and make their own rules. And the men were more than happy to oblige.

Lady Blessington, of course, had greeted Constance with a broad smile upon her arrival, attired in a royal blue jacket and matching waistcoat. She'd bent down to whisper in her ear, "You are marvelous, Mrs. Hartford. While I dared to send an invitation to the king, he declined, but sent along the most amazing center-piece for my refreshment table. A pineapple, dear Constance! Can you imagine the length of his generosity? It just proves that tonight is a smashing crush. I am forever indebted to you, my precious girl."

Constance was pleased for her hostess and realized that if she wished for a similar recognition in society, she would have it with the backing of Lady Blessington. But while that had once been her aim, to garner the respect she had always been denied as a courtesan, a woman who flitted about society but was never truly part of it, now her wish was to leave it all behind.

The only thing she wanted was to enjoy a quiet life with Devin for the rest of her days.

A rush of longing poured through her, because she regretted that he wasn't there to share this moment. She thought of her vow to lift his skirts and have her wicked way with him, but unfortunately, it was not meant to be.

Constance was on the alert for Miss Hollowell, the maid Devin had told her would be approaching her, but at the same time, she did her best to appear as though she was there solely for the entertainment. She even asked a "lady" or two to dance and had to laugh when the role reversal caused a rather unruly set to take place.

When Constance finally paused to take a break, her intention to quench her thirst, she accepted a glass of Madeira. However, when she lifted the flute to her lips, it froze halfway to her mouth. Her attention was ensnared by a "lady" who had just arrived. She wore a remarkable white gown with silver thread sewn throughout, and even a few seed pearls along the bows of her bodice. The sleeves were lined with lace which flowed about the collar. Not only was it one of the most breathtaking gowns she had ever seen, but it was the individual wearing it that made Constance feel hot and cold at the same time. But then, she would have recognized Devin, no matter if he wore a wig and costume or not, because his air of command was unmistakable.

She glanced around and saw that she wasn't the only "gentleman" in attendance who had taken note of the new arrival.

Constance quickly downed her wine and set it aside.

She moved forward, likely elbowing a few guests out of her way as she went, but she didn't care. Her focus was solely on the "lady" in white.

She arrived at his side at the same moment another rival interceded. "My lady, might I have the pleasure of—"

Constance smoothly threaded her arm through Devin's. "I fear this dance is already promised to me." She gave her competition a look that dared to defy her, but after a brief grumble of annoyance, they spun and headed in the other direction.

Constance led Devin to the dancefloor where the musicians were tuning their instruments for a new set. And by the sound of it, a waltz was about to take place.

Perfect.

She looked up into those familiar, dark, piercing eyes, visible beneath a silver mask with white ostrich feathers and whispered, "What are you doing here?"

He sniffed and withdrew a fan from his reticule. "As if I would allow any other lady to capture your attention this evening."

Her lips twitched. "You're doing it a bit brown, aren't you?"

He winked. "I should hate to disappoint you when you've worked so hard to make this fete such a success."

As the first strains of the violin reached Constance's ears, she bowed and then pulled him into her arms. Even though he was wearing a dress, he was the furthest thing from being feminine that she could ever imagine.

"We're a bit close to be proper, aren't we?" he teased huskily.

The sensation of that deep voice washed over her and made her skin break out in gooseflesh. "I intend to be much closer than this before the night is over," she whispered back.

His stance stiffened beneath her hands and she could only hope that other parts of his body were just as excited as she was.

"Have you seen Sir Isaacson or the maid yet?"

The dose of reality was exactly what Constance needed to cool her ardor. "Neither. But I've been on the lookout."

"Perhaps my presence will shake one of them loose," he noted. "It should certainly bring about the baronet. He still thinks he can manage to steal you from me."

She cocked her head at this revelation. "Indeed? Well, then, perhaps I should let him believe it."

His eyes flashed as they narrowed. "What are you planning?"

She shrugged. "Nothing." She prayed she sounded convincing.

~

DEVIN WAS QUITE sure that Constance was lying, but then, that was why he was there, to make sure nothing happened to her. If she didn't want to tell him the truth, that was fine, but that didn't mean he intended to ignore what she was doing.

Unfortunately, the only thing that might distract him from Constance—was the lady herself. Or more particularly, the saucy way she moved in those infernal trousers. That enticing backside was driving him mad. He might decide that a brief interlude was in order before they continued the search for their quarry, and by the high color on her cheeks, he was confident that she was feeling the same.

Lowering his head to her ear, he said, "I'm feeling a bit light-headed. Is there somewhere we can be... alone?"

He hoped that his request was received properly, but by the way her hands tightened on him, it was. "Yes." It was more of a moan than a reply, but enough for him to stop in the middle of the set.

While she was supposed to be in control, he was the one who led her away from the other dancers. "Where to?" he asked, since she knew the countess's townhouse better than he did, considering he'd never stepped foot inside before tonight.

"This way." He smiled, as the roles had abruptly reversed as she tugged him along behind her. She chose the second door on the left of the hall to reveal a music room. "We won't be disturbed here," she said as she shut the door behind him—and locked it.

After that, wigs were tossed aside and masks ripped off and added to the pile as they came together in a blazing inferno of desire. "I've been dreaming of this moment for weeks," she admitted, her breath coming in deep pants as she began to lift up Devin's skirts.

When she dropped to her knees and disappeared beneath the layers of material, followed by the sensation of her hot mouth encircling his engorged manhood, Devin saw stars in his vision. His hips bucked as she sucked him until he was close to release, almost painfully so. As good as it felt, he wanted to be inside of her.

"Stop." It was all he could do to utter the word, but she obeyed, standing up to look at him with eyes so beautiful and bright that they shook him to his core.

With a growl, he reached out and kissed her deeply as he reached for the buttons of her trousers. They were soon sagging down around her ankles and he took advantage of her inability to move to lift her into his arms. He carried her over to the wooden pianoforte and set her down on top, and then discarded her trousers. Her feet landed on the ivory keys and filled the air with a discordant music, but neither of them cared.

He gathered her naked thighs in his grasp and opened her to him. Her glistening core beckoned for him to taste the delights she offered and he was happy to comply. He lowered his head and began to worship her with his tongue. She clutched at his shoulders and cried out his name on a plea.

He forced himself to stop just before she found her release. "Not yet," he said with deep breaths. He straddled the piano bench and pulled her down to sit on his lap, one leg on either side of his hips. Moving the mountain of dress and undergarments out of the way, he impaled her on his cock. He hissed when she took him fully, and when she began to move, they were both lost to the sensation of their joining. Devin truly was feeling faint as his body tightened in anticipation of the pleasure that was so close. He clenched his jaw and held himself back, because he knew Constance was on the verge of her own climax.

He grasped her hips and increased his pace, watching through hooded lids as she bit her lip. Their eyes met for a brief moment, and then her green eyes closed and her entire body trembled as she reached her pinnacle. His cock thrummed with his need, and when he was sure he had every last bit of her pleasure, he finally allowed the pressure to release. He groaned deeply as he poured everything that he had into her.

When it was over, he opened his eyes and looked at her. Her expression was dazed, as if she'd been to another universe, and he felt the same. Each time they were together it was more spectacular than the last. And he realized that he couldn't hold back his feelings for her any longer.

"I love you, Constance. I think I have from the first moment I laid eyes on you." Her breathing halted, but he didn't pause. "I'm sorry if this isn't what you wanted to hear right now, perhaps ever, but I can't keep silent any longer. I want you in my life from now until the end of our days, until eternity dares to try to part us."

~

TEARS STUNG CONSTANCE'S EYES. Her heart was shattering, but for the first time in her life, it wasn't from pain or anguish, but pure, unadulterated… joy. She never imagined that she would be lucky enough to find someone who would dare to love Constance Freewater, the woman beneath the shell of the courtesan, but with Devin she had found, not only love, but everything she'd ever wanted.

"Devin, I—"

There was a brisk knock at the door and she cursed whoever dared to intrude on this intimate moment.

Devin, on the other hand, instantly sobered. "It could be the maid."

He carefully lifted her and stood. He shook his skirts back into place and walked over to don his wig and mask once more. He glanced back at her and now that her trousers were set back to rights, she joined him and put the rest of her costume back in place. He nodded at her and she called out, "Yes?"

No answer.

She cleared her throat and said a bit more loudly, "Is anyone there?"

Nothing.

Devin moved over to take his place behind the door, as Constance moved forward. She unlatched the door and pulled it open. She glanced out into the hall, but after checking both ways, it was empty. "It must have been someone playing a prank," she muttered. She glanced at Devin, where he had moved to stand beside her, but by the muscle ticking in his jaw, she didn't think he felt the same.

"Do you want me to head back to the ballroom first?"

He seemed to be arguing with himself, as he finally gave a heavy sigh and shook his head. "No, I'll go." He glanced at her. "But if you don't arrive in ten minutes, I'm coming back."

"Yes, ma'am."

He snorted in reply and headed toward the direction they had come from. Constance waited until his gown was out of sight, and then began to follow suit.

As she passed a shadowed alcove, prickles of warning crawled up her spine—just before she was attacked from behind.

A sharp pain split through her head as she crumpled.

~

Devin tapped his foot and glanced anxiously at the ormolu clock on the mantel. Several "gentleman" had already approached him with girlish giggles as they eyed him, but he had spurned their hopeful advances with a curt wave of his hand. The disappointment on their faces didn't even register. The only thing he had on his mind was that it had already been ten minutes and Constance had yet to reappear in the ballroom.

He was about to head down the hall and drag her back by her ever loving cravat when a movement near the terrace caught his gaze. A lone figure wearing simple black and white men's clothing with a white domino was staring in his direction. However, when he made eye contact, the "man" quickly slipped outside.

Uttering a curse, he would bet everything he had this was the maid who wished to meet with Madame Corressa. Debating whether he should give chase to her or check on Constance, he regrettably chose the latter. He didn't feel as though anything could befall Constance with so many people about, and although he wouldn't put a single bad deed past Sir Isaacson, he had yet to see him make an appearance.

He strode onto the terrace and scanned the dimly lit area. It was empty. Exhaling heavily, he heard the snap of a twig below him. He quickly descended the steps and turned—at the exact same moment he stared down the barrel of a pistol.

Devin held up his palms to show that he wasn't a threat as he faced his opponent. But even in the dark he could see the slight tremble of the feminine hand as she held the gun in her grasp. "I know that you don't trust me," he began slowly. "But I can assure you I'm not here to hurt you. In fact, we have a mutual enemy in the baronet."

She didn't reply for a moment, but after a time, she said shakily, "Y…you're Blackmore?"

"I am," he returned gently, as if soothing a spooked horse. "Did Brutus tell you about me?"

She hesitated, but then nodded. Then, as if the weight of the world was finally too much for her, her grip on the gun wavered. "I'm tired of hiding," she whispered brokenly.

"I can protect you, but you have to trust me. I intend to deal with Sir Isaacson, as he killed a very dear friend of mine, but I need your help to do that." He paused to allow his words to sink in. "If you will only lower your weapon and talk to me, reveal the information that you have, I promise that you will be free."

He waited several minutes for her to make a decision, each moment chipping away at his patience and his concern for Constance, wondering if she had yet returned to the ballroom.

Finally, the gun was lowered, although Devin noted the maid didn't tuck it away. "I saw you sneak away with Madame Corressa earlier, so I know you two are close."

"Yes." He wasn't about to deny the truth. He even took it one step further and revealed his feelings. "I love her."

Her mouth twisted and her tone held a touch of melancholy. "I wish that I could have found the same."

"You're young," he returned. "There's still time."

She shook her head. "No, there's not. I'm dying, and the last thing I want for my last days is to keep running. I just want some... peace." She uttered the last as if it was a dream she was unable to attain.

Devin dared to take a single step closer. "Tell me what you know and I will ensure you have your last wish."

He waited, until finally, she nodded.

≈

CONSTANCE WOKE up with a pounding head and a foul mood. "Bloody bastard," she snarled. She touched the back of her head, where the wig no longer rested, and winced at the tenderness there. When she looked at her hand, it was free of blood, so she supposed that was a good sign. Either way, she wasn't pleased.

"Someone isn't a morning person," came a mocking, male drawl.

She snorted. "Something told me you were behind this." She slit open an eye and even though her head throbbed in protest at the light, she was relieved to see that her surroundings still looked familiar, so she was still in Lady Blessington's townhouse. Although now she glared at Granelli. "Two-tooth. That's your moniker, isn't it? How *did* you come by such a worthless title? You do have more than two teeth in that miserable head, don't you?"

He chuckled with more than a hint of malice. "Keep on laughing, because it won't be for much longer." He bent down to her eye level and grinned broadly, showing off a mouthful of more than just two teeth. "I got that alias because I ensured one of my enemies left this world with only two teeth in his miserable head, just before I dumped his body in the Thames."

She rolled her eyes. "That wasn't very sporting of you."

"But it made the other gangs in London take notice of me after that," he pointed out smugly.

"Good for you." She feigned a yawn.

He grabbed hold of her hair, and she gritted her teeth against the discomfort. "I'll be glad to deal with you once Brooks has his fill." He released her abruptly and Constance started to rise to retaliate, but the bounds around her ankles, tying her to a chair, kept her immobile.

"We didn't need you running off just yet," Granelli said. "Not until you agree to our terms."

She crossed her arms and leaned back in a bored manner. "And what is that?"

"We understand you're going to be visited by a certain lady this evening. I want to know what she tells you."

"And if I don't?" she challenged.

Another masculine voice answered from behind her. "Then I'll be glad to run your lover through with his own blade."

She waited for Sir Isaacson to come into her line of vision. He was dressed as he normally was. "And here I thought for sure you'd be wearing a pink gown for this evening's festivities," she said sweetly.

He smiled slowly. "Someday, someone is going to remove that razor sharp tongue, and I do believe it may be me."

Granelli chuckled at that, but she ignored him. "What are you hoping to find out from this woman?" She addressed the baronet and pretended ignorance about the maid's identity.

He sat across from her and casually crossed one leg over the other. "She has some pertinent information about my past. I want it back."

"Like what?" she prodded. "Some sort of family heirloom? More than likely the gems have been sold and replaced with paste by now."

"Not exactly," he returned patiently. "It's more of a false accusation."

She tilted her head to the side. "Oh, dear. What did you do, Sir Isaacson? Was it something terrible? Did you spill punch down the front of your latest mistress's dress?"

His eyes flashed dangerously, and Constance knew she had nearly pushed him past his limits. But it was the only way she would have any hope of a confession from him regarding Lady Tyne's murder.

"You are very trying, Madame Corressa." He withdrew a dagger and balanced the blade before him. "I'm honestly trying to decide if you're worth the trouble."

She shrugged. It was better not to show fear when faced with such a cretin. A lesson she'd learned long ago. Most men enjoyed the power they believe they wielded over a helpless female. "Do what you think is necessary. It will honestly spare me any more time with that imbecile, Blackmore."

He laughed. "Oh, come now, my lovely courtesan. You can't expect me to believe that there isn't something deeper between the two of you. I watched you dance tonight and there didn't appear to be anything fabricated when you were together."

"Didn't it?" She appeared to mull this over. "Then it appears my acting skills have only improved with time." She reached up and slowly began to untie her cravat. "Why don't you send your dense accomplice on his merry way so we can discuss matters in a more... intimate setting?"

She allowed her legs to relax as she slipped the knot of silk free. She held it out beside her where it fluttered to the ground in a sensual manner that was not lost on the baronet. "Leave us," he ordered Granelli.

The other man looked affronted for a moment, but other than a malicious glare toward Constance, he flounced off behind her, his shuffles quickly disappearing. She grinned, as it was much easier to manipulate one man at a time.

Brooks removed his cravat and wound it around both of his wrists, where he pulled it tight together. "Are you sure you can handle what I enjoy?" he asked.

"Oh, you would be surprised," she returned airily. She slipped off her jacket and then started on the buttons of her waistcoat. When it parted, she slipped her hand beneath the fabric and cupped her own breast through her shirt. "Do you like to watch as a woman pleasures herself?" She started to slide her hand down toward the apex of her thighs. "Or do you want to punish me for being so naughty?"

His breath was heavy, the color high on his cheeks and while she hated what she was doing, she allowed Madame Corressa to take control, because Constance couldn't stomach the thought of entertaining a man like Brooks, even if it was only to catch him in a trap of his own making.

He tugged both ends of his cravat and slowly rose to his feet. "I prefer to watch you reach your pinnacle on the brink of death."

Some of Madame Corressa's courage faltered at that, because while she had heard of men enjoying certain proclivities, she had been spared those horrors. "Indeed? And is that how your wife died? Did you take her last breath a bit too far?"

The pupils of his eyes grew and nearly eclipsed all of the blue. "She couldn't please me properly, and with that bastard in her womb, I couldn't allow her treachery to stand. She had to be dealt with." He walked around behind her. "I made it look like an accident, that she fell down the stairs and broke her neck, but she had been dead before that."

Constance saw the strip of cloth in her line of vision and her heart skipped a fearful beat.

"This was this same strip of cloth that saw her end," he whispered in her ear, making chills crawl up her spine. "It's only fitting that it shall also see yours."

Constance didn't have time to raise her hand to her throat before the silk was choking off her air.

CHAPTER 23

*D*evin headed back down the hall when a quick scan proved that Constance hadn't returned to the ball. While his conversation with the maid had been necessary, it seemed that too much time had passed, even though it had been less than a half hour. Nevertheless, his gut was warning him that something was terribly wrong.

He checked the last place he had seen her, the music room, but it was empty. He clenched his fists, as while Constance could have made a trip to the ladies' retiring room, he doubted that was the case.

Withdrawing the knife from his boot, as ladies' slippers hadn't been part of his costume, Devin started checking doors as he made his way down the hall, careful to keep his weapon out of sight if he encountered anyone. He didn't want to draw any undue attention to himself or sound the alarm just yet. When a crowd this size panicked, it could be worse than the initial danger—and just as easy for the culprit to slip out undetected.

When the downstairs search proved fruitless, he inspected the basement with the excuse that the countess wished for him to check the wine supply in the cellar. Thankfully, the butler wasn't present to assure him that all was satisfactory, thus giving him the freedom to slip past the servants who were busy going back and forth tending to the party upstairs.

Again, Constance was nowhere to be found, so that just left the upper floors, which consisted mainly of bedchambers and the attic.

If she wasn't there...

But no, he had to believe that Granelli's pride would allow him to believe that he'd outmaneuvered Devin.

Making his way to the second floor landing, the first thing Devin noticed was something lying near a console table in the hall. At first, he couldn't make it out, but when he drew closer, his stomach clenched, as when he picked it up, he recognized it as the wig Constance had been wearing. He clenched the false hair in his fist and tossed it on the table, along with his mask, as he strode past, even more determined to find her.

His focus was keen for any sign of a struggle, his ears open to any sort of noise, but when he turned a corner, he stopped briefly, as there was no need to check any further. Granelli was limping in a pace outside of a closed door, which told Devin exactly where he would find Constance.

His nemesis spied Devin, as well as the two men on either side of him. "Ah, Blackmore. You found us." He grinned broadly. "I'm afraid you'll have to wait your turn. The lady is occupied with Sir Isaacson at the moment."

Devin sauntered forward slowly, but no less threatening. "Not for long."

As Granelli gave the signal for his companions to head for Devin, he brought forth his knife, making sure the gaslight in the nearby sconces hit the light and offered a menacing gleam. It was enough to make them hesitate.

"What are you waiting for?" Granelli snarled. "Get him!"

This time it was Devin's turn to smile as he lifted a brow and blew them a kiss. It was enough of a motivation for them to rush forward.

~

Constance heard the shuffle outside, even though black spots were starting to dance in front of her line of vision. She had considered slumping over and acting as though the baronet had won, and then playing her hand when he relinquished his hold, but her heart told her who was outside, so it gave her a renewed sense of purpose.

Gritting her teeth, she used all the strength she had to throw her head back against Sir Isaacson's midsection. He gave a slight grunt and it was enough for him to release his hold so Constance could take a fortifying breath. Although her bound ankles kept her from becoming too mobile, her arms were free to do as she pleased. Grabbing Brooks around the neck, she used her momentum and his weight to pull him off balance and flip over her back. He landed on the floor in front of her with a mighty thud.

While he was working to recover and catch his breath, she started on the ties of the rope binding her to the chair. She was able to get one foot free before he rose on his hands and knees. With a well-placed kick with her buckled shoe, she caught him on the jaw and he fell back down. It gave her enough time to free her other leg. Once that was done, she grabbed the heavy wooden chair and slammed it down on his back. He screamed in agony as more than one of his ribs likely broke from the impact, but she didn't stop to inquire after his health.

Instead, she set her heel against the back of his neck and pressed down firmly. There were more anguished howls as he flopped underneath her, whether from pain or frustration, she couldn't say which, nor did she care.

As she ground her shoe against the tender part of his spine

she said, "Now that the tables have turned, you are going to write a confession, in your own hand, about how you murdered your wife, the Countess of Tyne, and all of the other dastardly deeds that you have done through the years, including the false accusation of thievery against Devin Blackmore."

"I won't do it!" he snapped, spittle flying from his mouth where his face was crushed against the hard wood beneath him.

In turn, she stomped down even more firmly. "I don't believe that you are in any position to argue about my terms." He made a noise between a grimace and a growl, but she kept her foot firmly in place.

In the next instant, the door slammed open, splintered on its hinges as a harried, handsome looking man in a lovely dress, wig askew, pushed his way through. He took one look at Constance and reached up to toss aside the rest of his ruined headpiece.

He was the most magnificent man she'd ever seen as he stalked toward her purposefully. But then, she realized he wasn't focused on her, but rather on the man beneath her hold.

Devin stopped before them and glared at his nemesis with bright, murderous eyes, although he demanded of Constance, "Did he hurt you? If so, I would be glad to deal with him right now."

She reached out and gently touched his arm. "There's no need for violence. I think there's been enough of that tonight."

He glanced at her, and she swallowed the emotion that wanted to leap out of her chest. However, she knew now wasn't the appropriate time to spill out the yearnings of her heart. Unfortunately, he must have caught the slight wince she made, as his focus dropped to her neck, which was still pulsing with the remnants of her nearly fatal attack.

Devin's expression hardened to granite as he bent down to stare at the baronet. "I should kill you for what you've done to her. To Annalise. And to me. But if I've learned anything, it's that there are actually things more important than revenge."

"What's that? Forgiveness?" Sir Isaacson taunted.

"No." Devin shook his head and looked at Constance. "Love."

~

DEVIN SAW the tears shining in Constance's eyes and wanted nothing more than to take her courageous, lovely body into his arms and show her with actions, not just words, how much she meant to him.

But first, they needed to take care of a few problems. While Granelli and his comrades had been subdued outside, thanks to the assistance of Count d'Orsay who had arrived at the precise moment to lend a hand, the countess chose that moment to sweep into the room. With a commanding air, she led the charge as a handful of men entered to trail behind her. They were dressed in uniform and each carried a truncheon at their side. What's more, every single one of their expressions were hard and unforgiving.

It nearly made Devin smile. He had no idea how they had managed to arrive so quickly, but something told him this little episode had been prearranged.

"Take this man into custody at once!" Lady Blessington said, hands on her hips and appearing to wear her men's clothing with pride. "He has disrupted my household entertainment this evening, and I *will* be pressing charges against him!"

Constance stepped back from her captive, but the baronet's relief didn't last long, for the police walked forward and dragged him to his feet none too gently. Sir Isaacson turned his head to glare at Constance, one of his eyes already swelling shut, but she merely blew him a kiss and said, "Remember our bargain. If you choose not to comply, I'm sure allowances can be made for a transfer to a far less welcoming accommodation within the penal system. Perhaps the colonies in Australia?"

He instantly blanched at this suggestion and clamped his mouth together tightly.

Once the police had departed the room, the countess walked over to Constance. She must have spied the injury around her neck as well, because she winced. "Oh, my dear, girl! I'm so sorry it took me longer than necessary to arrive. Are you well?"

"I'm fine," Constance assured her.

Her shoulders slumped slightly in relief. "I daresay you are a genius to have contrived such a fitting end for that cad! Rest assured I will do what I can to ensure he does not leave police custody a free man." She sniffed. "I honestly think the noose is a fitting end for someone of his abominable character and now that I shall have the ear of the king, I will make sure he is aware of all of the man's misdeeds." She looked at Devin. "Granelli will also not be a problem any longer. I instructed the police to see to him as well before they headed out, and I made particular note to tell them that he is just as guilty as Sir Isaacson when it comes to threatening members of the peerage."

Constance reached out and hugged her. "Thank you for all your help."

"As if I would ever say no to you." She winked as they parted. "As for you, Mr. Blackmore, I see you went with my suggestion of silver thread for your costume. It's nice to see a man will actually take a lady's advice."

With a saucy glance to Constance, the countess left the room. When she was gone, Constance turned to Devin and crossed her arms. "You never said you had *planned* to come to the ball." Her lips twitched. "Although, I suppose that explains why I saw you with a box on Bond Street. I shall have to speak with Luke about keeping such secrets from me."

Devin gathered her against him. "I didn't want to spoil the surprise, because what fun would that have been?" he murmured.

She sighed dramatically. "I suppose it was worth it to see you attired thus." She slowly looked him up and down and he could feel his cock rise to attention beneath all the layers of fabric. Even dressed as a woman, he didn't appear feminine in the slightest.

"Does that mean you approve?" he teased.

"Very much so." She reached up and threaded her arms around his neck, her nails scraping lightly along the length of his neck. "Although I'm relieved that you got rid of that horrible wig."

"Indeed," he returned softly. "It was a travesty to cover up those luscious locks of yours." He lifted a brow. "But I'm definitely keen on those trousers and how you fill them out quite deliciously."

"Hmm." She rose on tiptoe and pressed her lips to his. "Let's say we get out of here and into something a bit more... comfortable?"

He grinned slowly. "I like the way you think."

CHAPTER 24

*C*onstance headed downstairs the next morning with a certain lightness to her step. But then, with Sir Isaacson and Granelli no longer a problem, there was little that could mar her buoyed spirits after a blissful night spent in Devin's arms.

After returning home from the ball, they had taken their time in her bedchamber, savoring every inch of each other, and finally coming together in an explosion of passion.

She smiled, picturing his handsome profile as she'd slipped out of bed that morning. She yearned to remain, but her stomach was protesting her lack of nourishment, so she'd been forced to leave his side, but only temporarily. While she was still uncertain of her future, she knew Devin would be a part of it. She didn't need a marriage contract to tell her that. He'd whispered how he'd felt to her more than once during the night. She had nearly done the same, had opened her mouth countless times to utter the words, but he would always find a way to distract her.

But today was full of hope and new promises yet to be discovered. In all of her forty years she'd never felt this way before and there was no doubt in her mind it was love. Just the thought of being reunited with Devin, even though she'd just left his side moments before, was enough to make her giddy with excitement.

Oddly enough, while she was still just a tenant in this house, it was already starting to feel like a home, because of him. She'd certainly never felt that way about any of her previous relationships. She's always known her place as her protector's mistress. Even if she might have had her own residence, it was due to their generosity, so nothing had ever truly been *hers*. But with the funds Alessandro had left her, she intended for that to change. She would purchase a house that she could finally call her own and invite Devin to share it with her.

"Someone's 'appy this mornin'."

Constance merely grinned at Luke's dry tone. He was already seated at the dining table and she walked over to him and gave him a sound kiss on the cheek. "Good morning, Mr. House," she said in a singsong tone.

His eyebrows instantly lifted to his forehead, his beard twitching with surprise.

She laughed as she filled her plate from the selection of delights on the sideboard. She took a moment to enjoy the mouthwatering scents and told herself that she intended to spend many more days just like this one.

She sat down across from Luke and laid her cloth serviette in her lap. She poured herself a cup of tea from the pot on the table and added sugar and cream. Next, she picked up her toasted bread and slathered it generally with butter and orange marmalade. When she took a bite, she couldn't help but murmur her appreciation. "Isn't this the most delicious thing you've ever eaten?" she asked Luke.

He didn't reply, so she glanced up to see him eyeing her strangely.

"What?" she wondered innocently.

"Goodness me. It's worse tha' I thought," he grumbled with a shake of his head, and then tossed down his napkin as he left the table, muttering something about lovesick fools as he departed.

Constance shrugged her shoulders, as she didn't mind being alone, although it wasn't for long. When she heard a shuffle near the door, she looked up, imagining that Devin had arrived, but it was Drennan instead. His ribs were free of their bindings and he was dressed casually in a shirt and trousers. While his face was still healing from the bruising he'd suffered, it was improving greatly and there was no more swelling.

She tried not to let her disappointment show, but she must have failed, as he teased, "I'm sorry if I'm not who you were hoping for."

She sighed but offered a polite smile. "Please don't think my reticence is anything personal against you. I'm very glad to see you moving about at long last."

"I know," he returned evenly, his blue eyes steady upon her. "And it would be impossible not to believe you weren't in love with Blackmore."

She paused with a forkful of eggs halfway to her mouth. "Is it that obvious?"

"Only to someone who knows what it's like."

Constance set down her fork at the hint of melancholy in his tone. "It will happen for you too, Drennan. I promise. And for someone who appreciates all of your good qualities."

"And what would those be, exactly? How I managed to run a perfectly good gaming hell into the ground?"

"I'm not so sure about that," Constance returned. "Count d'Orsay was going to pay a visit to the baronet today to pick up his confession and is to report back to me about a few other things as well."

Drennan nodded, and then walked over to the sideboard. While he was gathering his breakfast, one of the footmen appeared in the doorway. "A messenger just brought this." He held out a card on a silver salver.

Constance eagerly got up and accepted the sealed wax message. "This should be the update from Alfred." She winked coyly at Drennan and broke the seal. However, after reading the contents, she gritted her teeth. It was the update she'd been waiting for, just not the one she'd been hoping to hear.

"What is it?" Drennan asked hesitantly.

She quickly folded the letter. "Nothing. Although it does seem that my presence is required at Lady Blessington's townhouse. If you'll excuse me?"

She rushed out of the room before Drennan could question her further and see the lie for what it was.

Constance reached her bedchamber and found Devin had just finished tucking his shirt into his trousers. The intimate sight nearly sidetracked her from what she was doing, especially since she knew what lay beneath that outward façade, but she reminded herself that time was of the essence.

Devin, of course, instantly picked up on the fact something was amiss. "What happened?"

She spoke as she rummaged around in her wardrobe for a day dress with the best ease of movement. After a night wearing trousers, she realized how much she detested women's attire. "Apparently, Sir Isaacson has a few contacts in the Metropolitan Police Department, as he was released early this morning."

Devin uttered a curse. "What about Granelli?" he asked grimly.

"Not to worry," she assured him. "The baronet left him to his fate." She held up the letter that the count had sent, before tossing it on her dressing table. "Alfred tells me that he actually wrote a confession, but it wasn't the one we were expecting. It was against Granelli, placing the blame for all of his wrongdoings at his feet."

Devin snorted. "I'm not surprised. He's deceitful enough to do anything."

"The question now is, what can we do to stop him?" She

turned back to the wardrobe where she continued rummaging inside. "I, for one, intend to gather a posse and—"

"A what?"

She glanced over her shoulder and waved a hand. "You know, rally a group of people to apprehend a criminal."

"I know what it is," he returned dryly. "But we don't have to go to such extremes in this case. We'll leave that to the Americans kicking up dirt in the west."

She paused and set her hands on her hips. "And what is it that you suggest?"

"We just find what he wants before he does."

She narrowed her eyes. "And what is that?"

He mirrored her stance. "While you were entertaining the baronet last night—" She pursed her lips at that. "I had a conversation with the maid we had been waiting for."

Her mouth went lax at this. "Why didn't you tell me?" she demanded.

He scratched the slight bit of stubble along his jaw. "Well, it wasn't as if we were doing much *talking* when we got back from the ball."

She could feel her cheeks warming at the memory, and with the bed standing as a firm reminder so close... She released a slow breath. "What did she say?"

He gestured to her wardrobe. "How about you get dressed and I'll go one step further and show you."

~

DEVIN SAT in the hackney beside Constance, while Luke sat across from them. When he found out what was going on, he insisted on going with them. They all sat in silence as they waited for the carriage to deposit them at the door of Montfree's. Devin hadn't wanted Constance to go with them, since he knew it was likely going to be dangerous, but he would have been hard pressed to make her cool her heels. She was one of them, after all, a woman who had lived a harsh life and learned the lessons that went along with it.

But there was one person who wouldn't win in this particular game.

With the weight of the pistol in his grasp, he realized that it all came down to this. The moment of truth with Sir Isaacson was about to culminate.

It was the final act, and he had saved one last trick up his sleeve until the end.

When the carriage shuddered to a halt, they all regarded the other, as if conveying a silent message. Devin was the first to step to the ground, where he held out a hand for Constance. Luke jumped down on his own and the hackney drove away.

For a moment, Devin just stared at the front door of the gaming hell. He didn't know what awaited him on the other side. All he knew was that he had to find the evidence Miss Hollowell had promised him was still there—a letter written in Annalise's own hand detailing all of her husband's illicit business dealings, which sounded rather plentiful, along with the suspicions that her life would be in danger if she revealed her secret.

His throat tightened at the memory of what that "secret" was, but then he turned that unfortunate circumstance into determination. With his gaze sharp, his mind clear, and his weapon in his grasp, he started forward.

There was no one at the front door when he pushed it open, which surprised him. But then, perhaps the baronet believed that reinforcements weren't necessary. His arrogance was likely enlarged due to his cunning thus far.

Devin held a finger to his lips as he moved forward. He watched the shadows where the light from the windows didn't quite reach, alert to any sort of movement.

The evidence that the maid had told him he would find was

upstairs was in Constance's former quarters, hidden behind a loose stone in the wall.

He stealthily headed to the second level, his footsteps never making a sound. Constance and Luke moved just as lightly, the only noise coming from the slight rustle of her skirts. In another life, he imagined she would have made a rather competent thief.

There was nobody around when they reached the top of the stairs, but Devin wasn't letting down his guard. That was how mistakes were made and people were killed. A harsh lesson he'd learned through the years, before he'd been sent to the colonies— and again after he'd arrived.

It wasn't until they began to draw closer to the slightly ajar door that Devin heard the commotion coming from inside the room. He exhaled heavily, because it was as he thought. The baronet was alone.

There was a curse followed by a muttered insult. "Where did she *hide* it?"

Devin steadied his aim and pushed open the door. "I might be able to help with that, but then I'd have to kill you."

～

CONSTANCE WAS ready with her own weapon, and when Sir Isaacson spun around upon their entry, she dared to wink at him. "Did you miss me, darling?" she cooed sweetly.

The baronet's fists clenched and his face turned a mottled red. "You good for nothing wh—"

"If you finish that sentence, I can't account for the conse-quences." Devin gestured to the pistol in his grip. "My trigger finger tends to get a bit twitchy when the woman I love is slandered."

The baronet dared to laugh. "You're a fool if you think she's ever going to return your affection. She doesn't know the true meaning of the word."

"Don't I?" Constance dared to step out from behind Devin. "I beg to differ." She tilted her head to the side. "You seem to be the only man in this room who doesn't know what it is to truly care for someone."

"Why should I waste my time with those who are beneath me?" he sneered. "I'm a baronet!"

He nearly screeched the title and Constance realized how unhinged he was. His madness had gone on so long that he imagined he spoke the truth. If she didn't detest him so, she might actually feel sorry for him. His view of the world would never change and he would die a pitiful, lonely man who had never known love.

"Yes, you are," Devin spoke up. "And one that is about to go back into custody. And *stay* there this time, because I know where to find the proof that will ensure your permanent tenure. At least, until your sentence is declared, and I am finally free of the sight of you."

The baronet's lip curved back from his teeth. "I won't be defeated."

"You already are," Constance returned evenly.

Without warning, Brooks dove for a pistol that had been lying nearby, unnoticed until that point. However, when he brought it up and pointed it directly at Devin, he growled, "Then I might as well finish what Granelli started?"

He didn't hesitate but pulled the trigger.

"Nooooo!" Constance screamed and dove in front of Devin, intending to shield him with her body, but right before Brooks discharged his weapon, a knife came sailing through the air and struck the butt of the gun, causing the single bullet in the barrel to go astray. It struck the plaster ceiling and rained down bits of debris on top of them, the only extent of the damage. After that, everything was still.

Devin held Constance tightly against his chest as he returned fire on Sir Isaacson. His aim was steady and true, the silver ball landing exactly where he wanted it to—in the center of his enemy's chest. The force, along with the shock of the wound, sent the baronet pinwheeling backward toward a window. His momentum sent him against the glass, shattering it as he fell.

There was the sound of a distant woman's scream as the baronet's body fell to the ground outside, followed shortly thereafter by the sound of a whistle as the alarm was sounded.

Constance finally turned toward the door where she expected to see Luke standing there with a pleased look on his face for offering his assistance with the knife that made the bullet go astray, but it was Brutus there in the opening. He didn't pause to say anything, but merely nodded at Devin as he turned and walked away. Seeing that the danger had passed, Luke followed suit.

For the first time in years, the damp moisture of tears began sliding down Constance's cheeks. She had never allowed herself to give in to the emotion, believing that it was a weakness she couldn't afford. But knowing that Devin was safe and the nightmare that had surrounded them both for so long was finally over, filled her with so many feelings that she couldn't contain them all.

Not only that, but the last turn of the key inside of her heart finally unlocked, freeing Madame Corressa for good. The lady sauntered off with a saucy wave and a sway of her hips before dissolving into the mist.

"I love you."

Devin grabbed her shoulders and set her back from him. His throat worked for several moments. "What did you say?" he breathed.

The droplets were falling completely unchecked now. "I said, I love you." She smiled broadly and exclaimed, "I love you! I love you! *I love you!*"

Devin's eyes softened to the color of molten chocolate. "Since you already know that I love you too, I suppose there's only one thing left for us to do."

"What's that?"

"Marry me, of course." He lifted a brow. "Unless you don't like the idea of being wed to a former thief who—"

She tackled him with a kiss that left them both breathless. "How's that for an answer?"

He nodded his head. "Perfect."

CHAPTER 25

onstance read the paper two days later and exhaled with relief.

The *Times* had printed an article about the death of Sir Isaacson and the upcoming execution of Granelli, and with the evidence they had recovered from Montfree's, Devin's name was cleared. It turned out that Annalise had blamed all of Devin's prior thievery on Granelli, so it hadn't taken long for a jury to decide his fate, and with the rest of the criminal activity exposed from the baronet, he would no longer be a concern.

She noticed that Devin had been oddly quiet when he'd uncovered the Countess of Tyne's confession exactly where the maid had said it would be. Constance knew that even though Devin had dealt with her murderer, he would always be troubled by her death and the sense of guilt that went along with it. But Constance intended to ensure that she was there to comfort him when those melancholy days crept up on him.

For now, all she could offer him was a bit of closure, something she had uncovered along the way.

She slowly folded the newsprint and set it aside. They had been at the breakfast table enjoying a quiet meal. Luke had gone out with Drennan to pay a visit to the bank to see what could be done about Montfree's.

"Devin?"

He glanced up expectantly, his mouth full of ham.

She wasn't sure how to say it, so she just blurted it out. "I know where Annalise was laid to rest."

He instantly paused in chewing, and then swallowed hard, his Adam's apple bobbing distinctly. He said nothing for a moment, and she wondered what he was thinking. Perhaps he was angry, or that he thought she was interfering where she didn't need to be.

"I would be willing to go with you, if you like, but if not…" She started to get up, just so that she would quit rambling. "I can easily write down the location for you, or—"

"Constance."

His voice was firm, but gentle as he said her name, enough to get her attention, but not enough to believe he was upset. Slowly, she met his gaze and her heart flipped in her chest when she saw his soft, dark eyes on her face. "I would like for you to be there." He smiled slightly. "I've honestly known her burial place for some time, but I just haven't brought myself to go there."

She sat back down and reached across the table, where he took her hand and threaded her fingers through his. "We'll do it together."

~

As the hackney deposited them at a Westminster Abbey later that morning, Devin exited the carriage and looked upward at the tall, Gothic spires of the church. He'd never actually been inside the chapel, feeling that he wasn't worthy to pass through such consecrated doors, but if it would give him the chance to pay his final respects to Annalise, then he would brave the fires of hell to do so. She had taught him what really mattered in life.

Combined with the deep admiration he'd felt for her, and the love for Constance, he was able to breathe properly for the first time in his life. It was as if a heavy weight had been lifted from his chest that he hadn't even known had been present.

"Are you ready?"

He glanced at Constance and reached down to clasp her hand. Her courage is what would get him through the Chapel of St. Nicholas.

They walked up the steps and passed through the large, double doors. When the interior was revealed, Devin squeezed Constance's hand, although he wasn't truly aware of doing so. It was just so... magnificent and solemn, and oddly humbling for a former thief.

She waited until he was prepared to move forward, but said nothing, for which he was grateful. The silence is what allowed him to continue.

Hand in hand, they walked through the hollowed interior until they reached the Chapel of St. Nicholas. It was a modest area, but quiet and reverent, and Devin couldn't help but smile, because he knew that Annalise would have liked it here. He was glad that Sir Isaacson hadn't been petty and kept her from a proper burial in a church, knowing that she was carrying Devin's child, but considering Brooks was the cause of her death, he likely didn't care where she was laid to rest, so long as she was gone.

He wasn't sure how he would feel when he finally saw her stone, but when he walked upon her marker, the name carved into the marble, something told him that she was at peace. Perhaps it was the fact a calmness had fallen over him for the first time in the past five years that told him it was true, or maybe it was because he had the sensation that Annalise was giving him her blessing with Constance.

Either way, when they finally left the Abbey, it was with a positive outlook toward the future.

When they returned home, they found that Luke and Drennan had returned. They were in the parlor, but considering the forlorn expression on their faces, he knew the meeting hadn't gone well.

"I'm ruined." The gaming hell owner held his head in his hands and spoke like a man who had truly reached the end.

"No, you're not," Constance said firmly, as she walked over and sat beside him on the settee. Luke was leaning by the fireplace mantel. "We'll figure something out, even if I have to give you the necessary funds to—"

He shook his head adamantly. "I won't accept charity, and especially from you. It's my fault that I acted so rashly and believed such lies." He put his hands on his knees. "I shall just accept my fate, and if it lands me in debtor's prison, then I can only blame myself."

Constance stood and held out her hand to him. "Come on. What you need is a nice cup of hot tea. Perhaps then you'll think a bit more clearly."

Reluctantly, Drennan allowed himself to be led away.

Once Devin was left alone with Luke, he made an announcement. "I'm going to clear Drennan's debts, by an anonymous donation, of course."

If Devin wasn't so serious, he would have laughed aloud at the expression on Luke's face. As it was, his companion's eyes nearly bulged out of his head. "Are ye daft? Tha' money was supposed t' be for yer retirement!"

Devin shrugged. "That may have been true at one time, but where did all that money truly come from? I didn't earn it. It was stolen from others just like Drennan's money was stolen from him. At least this way, it will keep an innocent man's reputation from being destroyed."

"But..." Luke sputtered. "Ye 'ave nearly fifteen thousand pounds!"

"And Mr. Plainview is worthy of it. If anyone deserves

redemption, a second chance to make things right, don't you think it's him?"

Luke grunted. "Aye. I take yer point. But wha' about Constance? Are ye plannin' on livin' off o' 'er former paramour's trust?"

Devin eyed him steadily. "No. That money was intended for her. I intend to find proper employment and earn her respect."

For a moment, Luke just regarded him with narrowed eyes. "Ye've definitely changed since ye came back from tha' island. I can only imagine 'ow 'ard it was for ye. I never did say 'ow sorry I was tha' I couldn't free ye."

Devin walked over and put a hand on the older man's shoulder. "You had nothing to do with it. Like Mr. Plainview, I made a mistake and had to pay for the consequences of my ignorance." He clenched his jaw. "I wouldn't wish the same fate on any man, so if I can spare him the same horrors, I will."

"Will ye ever tell me wha' 'appened to ye?" Luke asked quietly.

"And what purpose would that serve but upset both of us?" Devin returned softly. "That part of my life is over, and I will be glad not to ever revisit it ever again."

Luke finally shook his head. "I still think ye're mad, but I'll make th' necessary arrangements."

"Thank you, old friend. I'm not sure I ever told you how much I love you."

Devin saw the glimmer of tears in Luke's eyes before he straightened. "Bah! Don't be gettin' all mushy o' me. Ye know I can't abide a waterin' pot!"

He stalked out of the room, but Devin knew that was his way of saying I love you too.

～

"ARE you sure this is what you want to do?"

Constance hesitated for only a moment when Lady Blessington made her inquiry in her personal parlor that afternoon, before she nodded her head. "Yes. I'm canceling the lease early and going back to Paris. France was where I was the happiest and after dealing with the latest turmoil in London, I realized that my time here has run its course."

The countess sighed heavily. "I will miss you dreadfully, of course, as will Alfred, but I wish you well. My only stipulation is that you write often and tell me of your adventures. Or, at least, the lastest fashions!"

"You can be assured that is an easy promise to keep." Constance smiled as she took a sip of her tea.

"What of your special friend? You have failed to mention his part in all of this. Is he eager to leave his country since he's only recently returned?"

Constance set aside her plate and clasped her hands together in her lap. "I have yet to say anything to Devin about my plans." In truth, because she had been concerned about that very thing. She wasn't sure how he would react and the thought of leaving without him caused a gaping hole to form in her chest, but she couldn't stay in London anymore. Her mental state wouldn't allow it.

"Are you sure that's wise?" the countess murmured. "After all the trouble I went through to see that he had the most enchanting dress at the metamorphosis ball, you would simply turn your back on your love for him?"

Her mouth fell agape. "*You* bought him that gown?"

"Well, of course." The lady rolled her eyes. "I thought it was obvious that I approved of his suit, even though he employed a rather shady past, but then, haven't we all at some point or another?"

Constance certainly couldn't argue with that. "I know you're right, but I just don't know how to tell him I want to leave when he has everything here, like Luke..."

"But not you, dear. You told me that he asked to marry you.

So why are you hesitating? I should be halfway to Gretna Green by now," she sniffed. "And don't try to tell me that you are still reticent about matrimony. I've never seen a woman with stars dancing in her eyes more than yours. They practically light up the night sky when you see Mr. Blackmore."

Constance couldn't contain the heat from rising into her cheeks, although it had been years since she'd dared to allow herself to give in to the urge to blush. But then, Devin had freed many things inside of her, including her inhibitions. "It's true. I love him more than anything else in this world."

The countess crossed her arms. "Then why are you still sitting here with me?" She waved a hand. "Go back to that townhouse and carry *him* off over the border to Scotland. There's no rule that says ladies always have to be the ones who are swept off of their feet. Sometimes, certain gentleman are actually worthy of a grand gesture too."

Constance laughed, feeling the giddiness of her younger days rising up within her. She got to her feet and embraced the other woman. "I will always cherish our time together and I expect you to visit me often in Paris."

The countess winked. "My dear, you may count upon it."

∼

THE ANTICIPATION BUILDING in Constance's veins yearned to burst forth as the hackney drove her back to Marylebone. The eagerness to see Devin and fling herself into his arms was almost overwhelming. She imagined what his reaction would be when she told him what she intended and prayed that he was just as excited about the prospect of France as she was.

And not only that, but she had another surprise she'd been keeping, one that she hadn't thought was possible. But she was starting to learn that love was able to conquer many obstacles that seemed unsurmountable.

However, when the hackney came to a stop in front of the townhouse, she frowned, as there was another carriage on the street. As she stepped to the ground, a smartly dressed gentleman was shutting the front door and heading down the steps. He was tall and middle-aged and had a large moustache. The instant he glanced up, she recognized him as the investigator she had contacted about her mother.

Her stomach did a nervous flip, but she forced herself to remain calm as she greeted him. "Mr. Lionel. What an unexpected surprise."

He doffed his hat. "Mrs. Hartford." His tone was professional, but polite. "I left my card, but I'm glad we were able to connect in person."

"Indeed." Her head started to spin. "Does this mean you found out something about my mother?"

His face was grim and even though she knew what was coming, she wasn't quite prepared to hear it aloud. "I'm afraid she passed on several years ago. I would direct you to a gravesite, but I fear it is unmarked somewhere in Bunhill Fields."

"Yes, I imagine that would be the case," Constance murmured. She tried to appear unaffected by this news, as she hadn't parted from her mother on good terms all those years ago, but she had always dogged her steps wherever she went, her final threat ringing in her ears whenever she least expected it. It was the last part of Madame Corressa's life and she'd hoped to put an end to it, but it appeared the past would never fully depart.

"I regret that I don't have better news for you," Mr. Lionel said empathetically. "Oft times this happens with unfortunate relation in London."

"No, it's all right," Constance returned, some of her shock starting to fade. "I was expecting this, but even so, it still doesn't fully prepare you for the result."

He inclined his head and replaced his hat. "On that, you would be correct." He touched the brim and walked away.

Constance stood where she was for a time, trying to gather herself, when Devin said her name. "Yes?" she attempted to smile, but it felt brittle.

He instantly frowned. "Are you unwell?" He glanced in the direction Mr. Lionel had gone. "Who was that man?"

He acted as though he would pursue him if needed, but Constance laid a gentle hand on his arm. "He's an investigator. I hired him to inquire after my... mother." She still found it difficult to refer to the woman who had given birth with such an intimate title.

He instantly stilled. "I assume that the news wasn't positive?"

"Not really, but I expected as much." She took a deep breath when her throat wanted to close up. "I just don't understand why I feel so... upset. I hadn't seen her for years, ever since I was fifteen, so there is no love lost between us."

He reached out and pulled her against his strong, warm chest. She closed her eyes and relished the comfort he offered. When he spoke, his voice rumbled against her ear with a delightful sound. "Sometimes it's what we didn't have that we miss most. I'm sure you are mourning, not the woman herself, but what she could have been to you."

Constance sighed, as it made sense. She lifted her head. "Would you mind coming somewhere with me?"

"Of course." He reached out and tucked a strand of her hair behind her ear. "You should know by now that I'll go anywhere with you."

Thinking of her plans for France, Constance prayed that was so.

But for now, there was another destination she had in mind.

CHAPTER 26

*S*ome of the breath left Constance's lungs when she stared at the only true home she'd ever truly had. Anywhere she'd resided through the years had been at the generosity of her current protector. Even so, this ramshackle building in Spitalfields had never possessed the warm atmosphere that she'd always yearned for.

Although she had started from such humble beginnings, over the years she had rubbed elbows with the ranks of the aristocracy, but then, she had never fit in to that glittering world either. It was all a façade, because while she had used her body to change her situation, she could never rid herself of the memory of this place.

She hugged herself and stared at the pitiful structure in front of her. It looked just as it had the day she'd left and never looked back, when her mother had threatened to sell her to a local brothel now that she was no longer a virgin. At first, she'd been horrified, as the idea that she might end up like her mother was not something she had ever wanted. But sometimes, you make mistakes in life and you might never get a second chance.

Devin was fortunate enough to do so, and now, so was she.

At least, she hoped so.

"I want to move back to France. To Paris." She didn't look over at Devin, but kept her eyes on the dilapidated building, but she could feel his eyes upon her skin as surely as if he'd reached out and touched her. "I was happy there, whereas London has only brought me misery and pain. I realize that you just returned to London and I know you may not want to leave—"

She was cut off by a kiss that made her heart flutter.

When Devin pulled back, there was such a fierce intensity in his gaze that her breath seized in her lungs. "My home is wherever you are, my love. It doesn't matter what country it is, just so long as you are by my side."

Her eyes instantly stung with tears. "Are you sure? Because I don't want my happiness to come at the expense of yours. If you have any doubts at all—"

"I don't," he interrupted again. Abruptly, his gaze faltered. "But I do agree that we need to discuss some important matters."

Her gaze searched his face. "What is it?"

He took a deep breath. "I won't be someone beholden to you. I know that your last protector made sure that you were properly settled. I won't take money from you like some sort of cadge." His focus returned to her. "I intend to gain your respect by earning an honest wage. I had a cache upon my return, but those funds were donated to a better cause."

"Oh, Devin." She reached up and put her hand along the side of his cheek, where stubble teased her palm. "I have a confession to make to you. I have nothing." She smiled, as it was freeing to be able to tell him another secret that had been brewing ever since she'd overheard him and Luke in the parlor.

He stilled. "What are you talking about?"

She shrugged. "I gave my fortune as an anonymous donation for Drennan so that Montfree's could be saved. I decided that it should be me since it was originally my gaming hell. And to be able to do something so freeing was worth every shilling."

Devin looked confused. "But I told Luke to do that with mine. I said I didn't want it because it wasn't really mine to begin with."

"Wasn't it?" Constance asked, which appeared to puzzle him even further. "Alessandro gifted me that money, but you took a talent, however sordid it might have been, and gained your own fortune."

He laughed, although it didn't hold any humor. "Surely you aren't calling thieving an acceptable *trade?*"

"No, but neither am I saying you have to continue paying the price for your misdeeds. You already did that when you were sent to the colonies." She shook her head. "I know you suffered terribly and I won't ask you to tell me what happened. In truth, I'm not sure either of us could withstand the torment, but neither should you continue punishing yourself."

"So, I should just turn away from the fact the money we could live off of for the rest of our days isn't ours?" he scoffed.

"But it's not *ours,*" she corrected.

Again, he appeared at sea. "What do you mean?"

"You told Luke to give it to Drennan to pay off his debts and save Montfree's, but since I already did that, Luke decided to take your advice and dispose of it in another fashion."

He blinked. "I can't believe the old codger actually did something worthy for a change."

"Indeed. He was quite generous." She laid a hand on his chest, directly over his heart. "He took your funds, but replaced it with his own, into a trust so that we might raise our child properly, that our son or daughter could be taught the mistakes of their parents and ensure that history doesn't repeat itself." She lifted a brow. "If that isn't a worthy cause, then I don't know what is."

He shoved a hand through his hair. "It still isn't right. I—" It appeared to take a moment for her words to fully sink in, but when they did, he stopped midsentence, his eyes growing wide with a mixture of disbelief and... hope. "Did you say...?"

He couldn't even seem to finish the sentence, so she did it for him. "Yes. I've had my suspicions for a while now, and while it isn't fully confirmed, I know that it's true. We're going to have a baby."

~

DEVIN WASN'T sure what to do. It was as if his emotions wanted to pull him in several different directions at once. He wanted to shout and cry and laugh, all at the same time. In the end, he did the most appropriate thing and hauled Constance against his chest and kissed her soundly. He released her, but kept her face clenched in his grasp. "Dear God, tell me you aren't just saying this so I won't refuse Luke's offering."

She laughed. "I promise." She ran a gentle hand over his hair. "Just accept this blessing we've both been offered and hold on to it tightly. We can't change the past, but we can embrace the future as a true family."

Devin closed his eyes and dropped to his knees in the middle of the dirty and crowded cobblestone street. He didn't care who might be watching as he held on to Constance's waist and laid his head against her lower abdomen—and wept.

A child. He could hardly dare to imagine that after a lifetime of deviltry and coarse beginnings, he would be given such a wondrous gift. With Constance at his side and their child in his arms, his life truly was complete. All the horrors of the past didn't matter anymore, because he'd finally gained the only thing that he'd ever wanted.

"Devin?"

His angel's softly spoken voice called out to him and he got back to his feet. "Let's get out of here and find us a true home. In

France. Right on the Seine in Paris, so that every morning when we get out of bed, I can see the sunlight shining off of the water and admire the way it illuminates that red-gold hair, and those expressive, green eyes."

She nodded. "It sounds perfect."

EPILOGUE

*P*aris, France
One Year Later

"WHAT IS your father up to now, little Patricia?" Constance cooed to her four-month-old daughter.

In reply, she scrunched up her tiny, chubby face and opened her mouth, but the only thing that came out was a bunch of gibberish.

"Oh, surely you can say, Papa? That would make him so proud."

Again, the baby merely made a few adoring sounds, and Constance could only smile. She had never thought her life would ever be this fulfilling, or this satisfying, but becoming a wife and a mother had made her eager to wake up to the dawn of each new day. Granted, she knew women who were perfectly content to be independent, to not have children, and at one time, Constance imagined herself to be the same. She certainly hadn't expected to feel this deep, abiding love each and every day toward her husband.

As if he knew she was thinking of him, Devin walked back in from the terrace of their apartments overlooking the Seine, just as he'd promised they would be, and the sight of him nearly took her breath away. So many times, she watched him when he wasn't looking and imagined the hair around his temples beginning to turn gray and his waistline starting to grow a bit thicker. Her body had certainly changed with the arrival of her daughter, but Devin had never told her she looked anything other than beautiful.

Attired in a pair of simple, black trousers and a white shirt rolled up to the elbows, the summer sun was starting to bronze his skin. If it were possible, he was even more handsome than before, but while some of the ladies on the street passed by and admired him with a lingering glance when they were together, Devin's focus was wholly on his family.

"You're doing it again."

Constance snapped out of her reverie and smiled at Devin who had been talking to their daughter. "What are you talking about?"

He rose to his full height and lifted a dark brow. "Looking at me when you think I'm not aware of it."

Her jaw slackened. "How—?"

He bent down and kissed her softly. "Because I know my wife and when her gaze is upon me." He glanced down at Patricia and returned his eyes to her, where they heated considerably. "How about you lay the baby down for a nap and let me take advantage of you?"

She laughed. "I would like nothing more." Her body was already heating in response. "But you know our company is due to arrive at any time. It would be rude to keep them waiting."

Devin snorted. "Your former gaming hell partner and his wife have had three children in the past few years. They obviously know how important time alone is. I'm sure he wouldn't mind sparing us a few moments."

Constance bit her lip, considering the enticing prospect, but a knock at the door made the decision before her. "They're here." She tried to sound excited, but instead it almost came out as disappointment. She handed Patricia to him and poked him in the chest with her forefinger. "Do try to be on your best behavior. I shouldn't like for you and Logan to be at odds with one another."

Devin rolled his eyes. "You're absolutely no fun."

She ignored him and walked over to open the door. It had been nearly six years since she had lain eyes on the Duke of Fenton. They had parted ways when she had been planning a trip to the continent and he had gone back to his dilapidated estate, Montague Manor, to live a pathetic, lonely life. However, his American wife, Korina, had managed to change all that, as Constance had read about their marriage in the society papers in Italy with a smile.

She had considered reaching out to them over the years, but decided it was best to leave the past where it belonged. In truth, she was afraid that Logan wouldn't want to see her and drudge up old memories of his own tumultuous past, which she had witnessed. Not only that, but she was a commoner and her former partner was a peer of the realm. She didn't want to feel as though she was dragging him down to associate with someone of her ilk now that their situations were decidedly different.

However, it was because of her happiness with Devin that had made her write an impromptu letter in congratulating them on their family and telling them the news of her own good fortune. A few days later, she had received a reply from the duchess and said that they were coming to Paris for a visit.

For the next month, Constance had been anxiously awaiting this reunion.

But the moment she opened the door, Korina squealed with delight and embraced her in a decidedly American fashion. She was relieved to see that some things didn't change.

"Constance!" She pulled back to look at her, the duchess' hazel eyes shining brightly with unshed tears of delight. "I daresay you could have knocked me over with a feather when I received your letter! We've been fretting about you for years, wondering how you have been faring. I was relieved to find out that you were happily settled with a family of your own. Our children are with their nanny, but I hope you will find the time to meet them." She clutched her hand and gave it a warm squeeze. "I have told them all about their reticent aunt over the years."

"Aunt?" Constance managed to choke out, her own emotion clogging her throat.

"Of course!" Korina grinned mischievously, her blond curls dancing with merriment. "I told them you were the one responsible for our marriage, because truly, if it hadn't been for your urging, I might have been just as stubborn as he was."

She rolled her eyes and Constance's gaze shifted to the tall, black-haired gentleman standing proud and tall, his familiar ice blue eyes regarding her evenly. Logan had always been a difficult man to read.

As if sensing the need for privacy, Korina offered Constance a wink. "I'll leave the two of you to get reacquainted. I'm anxious to meet this paragon you've married and meet darling Patricia!"

Korina left in a flurry of mauve skirts, while Constance clasped her hands before her and looked at Logan. "Hallo." It sounded so distant and absurd after everything they had been through over the years, but it was all she could manage to think of to say.

He shoved his hands in his pockets and snorted. "Mrs. Blackmore."

Constance swallowed. She waved a hand toward the door. "Would you care for a cup of tea, or perhaps—?"

"No." He interrupted firmly. He crossed his arms. "What I want is to know why you never contacted us all these years. Why you never told me when Bull died. Why you never sought out my assistance when Sir Brooks Isaacson was giving you trouble." He narrowed his eyes. "You do recall that I'm a *duke*. I could have disposed of him—and Two-Tooth Granelli—long ago and saved you the trouble of sending both of them to the gallows."

Constance shrugged. She should have remembered that Logan wasn't the sort of man who minced his words. "Yes, I could have. But I didn't want to involve you in my sordid life any more than you had to be. We had a business partnership, and while we might have been friends at one time—"

"You don't stop becoming friends with someone just because they decide to make a life for themselves." He took a step toward her and now she could clearly see the turmoil wrestling on his face. "If nothing else, that is when you rely on their council even more. Do you realize how much Korina worried herself over you? How much *I* did?"

Constance took a deep breath. "I assure you, that wasn't my intention. I just didn't want you to feel as though you had to… associate with someone like me."

"And who is that exactly?" he countered. "A kind, smart, independent woman who saved me from drinking myself to oblivion on more than one occasion? A woman who finally got me to see what a stubborn ass I was being when it mattered the most? Who knew what I needed when I didn't even see it standing right in front of me?" He shook his head. "You have got it all wrong. I am the lucky one to have you in my life, not the other way around."

She couldn't hold back anymore. She burst into tears. "Oh, Logan. I'm so sorry. I thought I was doing the right thing. I never considered…"

He reached out and held her against his chest. While it wasn't the same sort of comfort that she received from Devin, it was the same as if she was embracing a close friend or a family member, and she supposed that was what Logan had been for her. She just hadn't realized how much she'd missed him until now.

She sniffed back the rest of her tears and they parted when a masculine voice spoke up behind her, "You're not even here for five minutes and my wife is crying. Duke or no, if you've hurt her in any way—"

Logan stepped forward and shocked both Constance and Devin when he clapped him on the shoulder. "I approve." With that, he disappeared inside.

Devin looked at Constance in such a puzzled manner that she had to laugh. "The nobility are a mad lot," he muttered. "I'm not sure we're going to get Patricia back from his American wife." He lifted a brow. "I'm starting to wonder if this was a good idea."

Constance threaded her arm through his. "Let's gain you a proper introduction, shall we?"

She shut the door.

AFTERWORD

.

I'd like to thank you for purchasing this book. I know you could have chosen any number of stories to read, but you picked this one and for that I am humbled and grateful! I hope that the romance captured your heart and added a smile to your day. If so, it would be awesome if you could share this book with your friends and family and post a review! Your feedback and support will help improve my writing and help me to continue growing as an author.

Tabetha Waite began her writing journey at a young age. At nine years old, she was crafting stories of all kinds on an old Underwood typewriter. She started reading romance in high school and immediately fell in love with the genre. She gained her first publishing contract with Etopia Press/Wolf Hill Publishing and released her debut novel in July of 2016 - "Why the Earl is After the Girl," the first book in her Ways of Love historical romance series. Since then, she has become a hybrid author, published with both Soul Mate and Radish Fiction, as well as transitioning into Indie publishing. She has won several awards for her books.

She is a small town, Missouri girl who continues to make her home in the Midwest with her husband and two wonderful daughters. When she's not writing novels filled with adventure and heart, she is either reading, or searching the local antique mall or flea market for the latest interesting find. You can find her on most any social media site, and she encourages fans of her work to join her mailing list for updates.

https://authortabethawaite.wix.com/romance

Made in the USA
Las Vegas, NV
14 February 2022

43901560R00163